PATRICIA \
DOWN UNDER

PATRICIA WENTWORTH was born Dora Amy Elles in India in 1877 (not 1878 as has sometimes been stated). She was first educated privately in India, and later at Blackheath School for Girls. Her first husband was George Dillon, with whom she had her only child, a daughter. She also had two stepsons from her first marriage, one of whom died in the Somme during World War I.

Her first novel was published in 1910, but it wasn't until the 1920's that she embarked on her long career as a writer of mysteries. Her most famous creation was Miss Maud Silver, who appeared in 32 novels, though there were a further 33 full-length mysteries not featuring Miss Silver—the entire run of these is now reissued by Dean Street Press.

Patricia Wentworth died in 1961. She is recognized today as one of the pre-eminent exponents of the classic British golden age mystery novel.

By Patricia Wentworth

PATRICIA WENTWORTH

DOWN UNDER

With an introduction by
Curtis Evans

DEAN STREET PRESS

Introduction

BRITISH AUTHOR Patricia Wentworth published her first novel, a gripping tale of desperate love during the French Revolution entitled *A Marriage under the Terror*, a little over a century ago, in 1910. The book won first prize in the Melrose Novel Competition and was a popular success in both the United States and the United Kingdom. Over the next five years Wentworth published five additional novels, the majority of them historical fiction, the best-known of which today is *The Devil's Wind* (1912), another sweeping period romance, this one set during the Sepoy Mutiny (1857-58) in India, a region with which the author, as we shall see, had extensive familiarity. Like *A Marriage under the Terror*, *The Devil's Wind* received much praise from reviewers for its sheer storytelling élan. One notice, for example, pronounced the novel "an achievement of some magnitude" on account of "the extraordinary vividness...the reality of the atmosphere...the scenes that shift and move with the swiftness of a moving picture...." (*The Bookman*, August 1912) With her knack for spinning a yarn, it perhaps should come as no surprise that Patricia Wentworth during the early years of the Golden Age of mystery fiction (roughly from 1920 into the 1940s) launched upon her own mystery-writing career, a course charted most successfully for nearly four decades by the prolific author, right up to the year of her death in 1961.

Considering that Patricia Wentworth belongs to the select company of Golden Age mystery writers with books which have remained in print in every decade for nearly a century now (the centenary of Agatha Christie's first mystery, *The Mysterious Affair at Styles*, is in 2020; the centenary of Wentworth's first mystery, *The Astonishing Adventure of Jane Smith*, follows merely three years later, in 2023), relatively little is known about the author herself. It appears, for example, that even the widely given year of Wentworth's birth, 1878, is incorrect. Yet it is sufficiently clear that Wentworth lived a varied and intriguing life that provided her ample inspiration for a writing career devoted to imaginative fiction.

It is usually stated that Patricia Wentworth was born Dora Amy Elles on 10 November 1878 in Mussoorie, India, during the heyday of the British Raj; however, her Indian birth and baptismal record states that she in fact was born on 15 October 1877 and was baptized on 26 November of that same year in Gwalior. Whatever doubts surround her actual birth year, however, unquestionably the future author came from a prominent Anglo-Indian military family. Her father, Edmond Roche Elles, a son of Malcolm Jamieson Elles, a Porto, Portugal wine merchant originally from Ardrossan, Scotland, entered the British Royal Artillery in 1867, a decade before Wentworth's birth, and first saw service in India during the Lushai Expedition of 1871-72. The next year Elles in India wed Clara Gertrude Rothney, daughter of Brigadier-General Octavius Edward Rothney, commander of the Gwalior District, and Maria (Dempster) Rothney, daughter of a surgeon in the Bengal Medical Service. Four children were born of the union of Edmond and Clara Elles, Wentworth being the only daughter.

Before his retirement from the army in 1908, Edmond Elles rose to the rank of lieutenant-general and was awarded the KCB (Knight Commander of the Order of Bath), as was the case with his elder brother, Wentworth's uncle, Lieutenant-General Sir William Kidston Elles, of the Bengal Command. Edmond Elles also served as Military Member to the Council of the Governor-General of India from 1901 to 1905. Two of Wentworth's brothers, Malcolm Rothney Elles and Edmond Claude Elles, served in the Indian Army as well, though both of them died young (Malcolm in 1906 drowned in the Ganges Canal while attempting to rescue his orderly, who had fallen into the water), while her youngest brother, Hugh Jamieson Elles, achieved great distinction in the British Army. During the First World War he catapulted, at the relatively youthful age of 37, to the rank of brigadier-general and the command of the British Tank Corps, at the Battle of Cambrai personally leading the advance of more than 350 tanks against the German line. Years later Hugh Elles also played a major role in British civil defense during the Second World War. In the event of a German invasion of Great Britain, something which seemed all too possible in 1940, he was tasked with leading the defense of southwestern England.

Like Sir Edmond and Sir William, Hugh Elles attained the rank of lieutenant-general and was awarded the KCB.

Although she was born in India, Patricia Wentworth spent much of her childhood in England. In 1881 she with her mother and two younger brothers was at Tunbridge Wells, Kent, on what appears to have been a rather extended visit in her ancestral country; while a decade later the same family group resided at Blackheath, London at Lennox House, domicile of Wentworth's widowed maternal grandmother, Maria Rothney. (Her eldest brother, Malcolm, was in Bristol attending Clifton College.) During her years at Lennox House, Wentworth attended Blackheath High School for Girls, then only recently founded as "one of the first schools in the country to give girls a proper education" (*The London Encyclopaedia*, 3rd ed., p. 74). Lennox House was an ample Victorian villa with a great glassed-in conservatory running all along the back and a substantial garden--most happily, one presumes, for Wentworth, who resided there not only with her grandmother, mother and two brothers, but also five aunts (Maria Rothney's unmarried daughters, aged 26 to 42), one adult first cousin once removed and nine first cousins, adolescents like Wentworth herself, from no less than three different families (one Barrow, three Masons and five Dempsters); their parents, like Wentworth's father, presumably were living many miles away in various far-flung British dominions. Three servants--a cook, parlourmaid and housemaid--were tasked with serving this full score of individuals.

Sometime after graduating from Blackheath High School in the mid-1890s, Wentworth returned to India, where in a local British newspaper she is said to have published her first fiction. In 1901 the 23-year-old Wentworth married widower George Fredrick Horace Dillon, a 41-year-old lieutenant-colonel in the Indian Army with three sons from his prior marriage. Two years later Wentworth gave birth to her only child, a daughter named Clare Roche Dillon. (In some sources it is erroneously stated that Clare was the offspring of Wentworth's second marriage.) However in 1906, after just five years of marriage, George Dillon died suddenly on a sea voyage, leaving Wentworth with sole responsibly for her three teenaged stepsons and baby daughter. A very short span of years,

1904 to 1907, saw the deaths of Wentworth's husband, mother, grandmother and brothers Malcolm and Edmond, removing much of her support network. In 1908, however, her father, who was now sixty years old, retired from the army and returned to England, settling at Guildford, Surrey with an older unmarried sister named Dora (for whom his daughter presumably had been named). Wentworth joined this household as well, along with her daughter and her youngest stepson. Here in Surrey Wentworth, presumably with the goal of making herself financially independent for the first time in her life (she was now in her early thirties), wrote the novel that changed the course of her life, *A Marriage under the Terror*, for the first time we know of utilizing her famous *nom de plume*.

The burst of creative energy that resulted in Wentworth's publication of six novels in six years suddenly halted after the appearance of *Queen Anne Is Dead* in 1915. It seems not unlikely that the Great War impinged in various ways on her writing. One tragic episode was the death on the western front of one of her stepsons, George Charles Tracey Dillon. Mining in Colorado when war was declared, young Dillon worked his passage from Galveston, Texas to Bristol, England as a shipboard muleteer (mule-tender) and joined the Gloucestershire Regiment. In 1916 he died at the Somme at the age of 29 (about the age of Wentworth's two brothers when they had passed away in India).

A couple of years after the conflict's cessation in 1918, a happy event occurred in Wentworth's life when at Frimley, Surrey she wed George Oliver Turnbull, up to this time a lifelong bachelor who like the author's first husband was a lieutenant-colonel in the Indian Army. Like his bride now forty-two years old, George Turnbull as a younger man had distinguished himself for his athletic prowess, playing forward for eight years for the Scottish rugby team and while a student at the Royal Military Academy winning the medal awarded the best athlete of his term. It seems not unlikely that Turnbull played a role in his wife's turn toward writing mystery fiction, for he is said to have strongly supported Wentworth's career, even assisting her in preparing manuscripts for publication. In 1936 the couple in Camberley, Surrey built Heatherglade House, a large two-story structure on substantial grounds, where they resided until

Wentworth's death a quarter of a century later. (George Turnbull survived his wife by nearly a decade, passing away in 1970 at the age of 92.) This highly successful middle-aged companionate marriage contrasts sharply with the more youthful yet rocky union of Agatha and Archie Christie, which was three years away from sundering when Wentworth published *The Astonishing Adventure of Jane Smith* (1923), the first of her sixty-five mystery novels.

Although Patricia Wentworth became best-known for her cozy tales of the criminal investigations of consulting detective Miss Maud Silver, one of the mystery genre's most prominent spinster sleuths, in truth the Miss Silver tales account for just under half of Wentworth's 65 mystery novels. Miss Silver did not make her debut until 1928 and she did not come to predominate in Wentworth's fictional criminous output until the 1940s. Between 1923 and 1945 Wentworth published 33 mystery novels without Miss Silver, a handsome and substantial legacy in and of itself to vintage crime fiction fans. Many of these books are standalone tales of mystery, but nine of them have series characters. Debuting in the novel *Fool Errant* in 1929, a year after Miss Silver first appeared in print, was the enigmatic, nautically-named *eminence grise* Benbow Collingwood Horatio Smith, owner of a most expressively opinionated parrot named Ananias (and quite a colorful character in his own right). Benbow Smith went on to appear in three additional Wentworth mysteries: *Danger Calling* (1931), *Walk with Care* (1933) and *Down Under* (1937). Working in tandem with Smith in the investigation of sinister affairs threatening the security of Great Britain in *Danger Calling* and *Walk with Care* is Frank Garrett, Head of Intelligence for the Foreign Office, who also appears solo in *Dead or Alive* (1936) and *Rolling Stone* (1940) and collaborates with additional series characters, Scotland Yard's Inspector Ernest Lamb and Sergeant Frank Abbott, in *Pursuit of a Parcel* (1942). Inspector Lamb and Sergeant Abbott headlined a further pair of mysteries, *The Blind Side* (1939) and *Who Pays the Piper?* (1940), before they became absorbed, beginning with *Miss Silver Deals with Death* (1943), into the burgeoning Miss Silver canon. Lamb would make his farewell appearance in 1955 in *The Listening Eye*, while Abbott would take his final bow in mystery fiction with Wentworth's last published novel, *The Girl in the Cellar* (1961), which went into print the year of the author's death at the age of 83.

The remaining two dozen Wentworth mysteries, from the fantastical *The Astonishing Adventure of Jane Smith* in 1923 to the intense legal drama *Silence in Court* in 1945, are, like the author's series novels, highly imaginative and entertaining tales of mystery and adventure, told by a writer gifted with a consummate flair for storytelling. As one confirmed Patricia Wentworth mystery fiction addict, American Golden Age mystery writer Todd Downing, admiringly declared in the 1930s, "There's something about Miss Wentworth's yarns that is contagious." This attractive new series of Patricia Wentworth reissues by Dean Street Press provides modern fans of vintage mystery a splendid opportunity to catch the Wentworth fever.

Curtis Evans

Chapter One

ELFREDA MOORE turned round from the telephone with a despairing gesture.

"Aunt Hortensia, she says she sent them off yesterday morning—she *swears* she did."

"Then she's not speaking the truth," said Miss Hortensia Carew. "Any time before one o'clock, and they would have been here by the first post."

She spoke in her most decided manner, and she could be very decided. She was small, pretty, with fluffy white hair, eyes of the brightest china blue, and a complexion which was still admired, especially by Miss Hortensia Carew. She had managed her brother and her brother's house for twenty-two years, and now that Rose Anne was to be married, there would never be any question of the reins being taken from her hands. From this point of view the marriage had her approval. But why make such a fuss about it? Girls were married every day, weren't they? One could have been married oneself several times over if one had wanted to.

She put her gold-rimmed pince-nez straight, and frowned at Elfreda, who continued to bleat.

"She swears she sent them. She says they were posted before ten. Isn't it grim?"

The Reverend James Carew looked suddenly over the top of the *Times* and enquired in an irritated voice,

"What's the matter now? What hasn't been posted? What hasn't arrived? There isn't a minute's peace! I am reading an article about the stratosphere. Remarkably interesting—if I could get a minute's peace!"

"Oh, Uncle James—the bridesmaids' wreaths. The dresses came yesterday—from Madame Frederica's, you know—and she hadn't put in the wreaths, and we rang up at once, and she swore she'd send them by the very next post, and they haven't come."

"Your uncle is not interested in wreaths," said Miss Hortensia acidly.

Elfreda couldn't believe it. You might be old, and an uncle, and a person who read articles on the stratosphere, but it wasn't possible that you should take no interest in the wreaths for your own daughter's bridesmaids. She said protestingly,

"Isn't it *grim*, Uncle James?"

Mr Carew got to his feet and began to drift towards the door, paper in hand. He had the same regular features as his sister. All the Carews had regular features—it annoyed Elfreda dreadfully that she should have taken after her father's family—but James Carew's eyes were hazy instead of sharp, and his fair skin had gone tired and grey. His sister managed him because he had stopped taking much interest in his own life when Rose Anne's mother died. He had a vague fondness for Elfreda though he considered her noisy. He said quite kindly,

"The wreaths will probably come."

"But the last post's in."

He paused at the door.

"There will be one tomorrow."

"But the wedding's tomorrow—Rose Anne's wedding."

She spoke to an empty doorway. Mr Carew had disappeared.

"Aunt Hortensia—what are we to do?"

Miss Carew was engaged in ticking off names on a long, neat list. Every time she had to look up she lost her place and was obliged to go back to the beginning again. As the list had already been checked at least a dozen times, this did not really matter, but every time it happened she became a little crosser. Weddings always made her cross, and Rose Anne's wedding had already filled the house with people, upset its well ordered routine, and turned two capable, well trained maids into giggling chatter-boxes. Goodness knew how long it would take to get settled down again, and she couldn't go away and shut herself up in the study with the *Times* like James. She looked up with a frown and a jerk of the head.

"Go and tell Rose Anne. It's her business, I suppose."

Elfreda hesitated.

"Oliver's only just come. They're in the garden."

Miss Hortensia coloured sharply.

"Good gracious—isn't he going to have her for the rest of his life? Go and tell her at once! And she must make her own arrangements. I can't do everything."

Elfreda ran out of the room—quickly, because she didn't want to have a row right in the middle of Rose Anne's wedding and she felt one coming on. How Rose Anne had contrived to live all those years with Aunt Hortensia she simply couldn't imagine. Uncle James wasn't too bad, but Aunt Hortensia was a menace.

She opened the garden door and stepped out. It was going to be fine for the wedding all right—bright sun, cold air, a nip of frost tonight perhaps, and a lovely October day tomorrow for Oliver and Rose Anne.

She stood looking down the garden, a plump girl with a lot of fair hair. She had good grey eyes but rather light lashes. Her thick fair eyebrows rose to a peak in the middle and gave her rather a surprised look. She would have been prettier if she had weighed less. She had a soft heart and a sweet tooth. She adored Rose Anne, who was twenty-two to her nineteen. She didn't want to break in on her and Oliver. She stood there hesitating and thinking about the wedding. Mary Leigh, the other bridesmaid, was dark, and they were going to wear stiff dresses of lilac and white shot taffeta with flat wreaths of pink and mauve flowers like highly sophisticated daisies, and they were to carry sprays of Michaelmas daisies and pink chrysanthemums. The wreaths were very becoming. Frederica was a beast. If they didn't come, they might use some of the biggest Michaelmas daisies—pink and mauve ones, just single flowers nipped off and sewn on a narrow strip of net. They must be looked over for earwigs though. Grim to have an earwig in your hair at Rose Anne's wedding.

She went down the narrow path between the apple trees. She knew just where they would be, in the sheltered sunny corner where a bit of old brick wall kept the wind off and you could look across at the dahlias, and the daisies, and the orange heleniums.

But Rose Anne and Oliver Loddon were looking at each other. Rose Anne saw a fair young man with lines of humour about his mouth and a little frown between his eyes, a quick frown which came, and went, and came again. The eyes told very little as a rule.

Just now they were telling Rose Anne that he loved her. They were no-coloured eyes and could be secret. She saw this. She saw Oliver who had made love to her the third time they spoke together. And tomorrow he would be her husband.

Oliver saw Rose Anne, lovely and beloved, most gentle, most gracious—a loving heart, a gentle mind, a sweet intelligence—the turn of her head sheer grace, the texture of her skin fine as the rose petal just drifted from the wall. He would have liked to set it against her cheek, rose against rose, but he refrained, because any movement, any word, must break the enchantment of the hour. He looked at her, and wondered whether he could love her more, whether the years which steadied and deepened love would rob him of this quivering delight in her beauty, her perfection—the sun on her chestnut hair and the lovely shades in it, grey-blue eyes, very dark, very deep, the same thick lashes that Elfreda had, but dark instead of light, and in place of surprised fair brows a delicate arch much darker than her hair. He saw these things, and the way she had of smiling without seeming to move her lips, and the little ripple which saved her nose from being merely straight.

Elfreda came round the last apple tree, and thought, "She's lovely. He's awfully in love with her. Lucky them!"

They both moved. Oliver frowned, and then smiled quickly, because he was in a smiling mood, and life was good and he liked Elfreda. "Rose Anne—" Elfreda thought—"she was in a dream—I've waked her—I wish I hadn't. Why couldn't Aunt Hortensia leave them alone?" She said in her pretty, fresh voice,

"I didn't want to come—Aunt Hortensia made me. I do hate her, don't you? But the wreaths haven't come, and she said I was to tell you. And Frederica swears she sent them off before ten yesterday, and of course she couldn't have, or else they've got lost on the way. And don't you think we could do something with Michaelmas daisies instead?"

"I expect we could," said Rose Anne. Her voice was gentle and a little aloof.

Oliver laughed.

"What do you want to do with them?"

He was the first person who had taken the least interest. Elfreda's heart warmed to him.

"Well, I thought we might take some of the big ones, just the single flowers—October Dawn, and Lil Fardell, and Queen Mary— and put them on a strip of net and wind them in and out of our hair, only the snag is that Mary simply can't wear real flowers. She says they just look at her once and die. That's why we were having the wreaths from Frederica."

"Flowers die on flirts, don't they?" said Oliver. "I shall look forward to Mary."

Elfreda giggled.

"Oh, but she isn't. That's the comic part—she couldn't flirt to save her life—doesn't know how to. Do you like flirts?"

"In reason," said Oliver Loddon.

"Rose Anne can't flirt," said Elfreda in a teasing voice.

"She doesn't want you to marry me under false pretences," said Rose Anne.

"Rose Anne doesn't need to flirt," said Oliver. "She just looks, and we fall down flat—at least that's what happened to me."

Rose Anne got up. She was smiling. She didn't say anything. Her lashes came down and hid her eyes. She moved away from them, going down the border, not picking among the flowers, but looking at them and touching one here and there. All at once she looked back over her shoulder and spoke.

"Did anyone ring up—for me?"

Chapter Two

ELFREDA SAID, "No."

Rose Anne went on down the border as far as the tall pink dahlias. She stood looking at them for a moment, or looking past them, and then turned and came back again walking slowly, her eyes downcast and just the hint of a smile about her lips. Afterwards, when every word and look were being gathered up and put under the microscope, Elfreda was questioned and cross-questioned as to just what Rose Anne had said, and just how Rose Anne had looked.

"But what did she say, Elfreda? Tell us exactly what she said."

And Elfreda in tears: "She said, 'Was there a call for me?'"

"That is not what you said before." This was Miss Hortensia.

"Well, that's what she meant. She said, 'Did anyone ring up for me?'"

"You should be accurate. It might be very important. Are you sure that that is what she said?"

In the midst of her misery Elfreda was heartened by a flare of rage. She stamped an angry foot.

"Yes, I am sure! She just looked over her shoulder and she said, 'Did anyone ring up for me?'"

"And how did she look?" said Miss Hortensia.

Elfreda choked. They might badger, and harry, and confuse her until she didn't know what anyone had said, but she would never forget how Rose Anne had looked, with the pale bright sun shining on her, and the pink, and lilac, and blue of the Michaelmas daisies, and the very bright pink of the dahlias. She choked and ran out of the room, and presently they brought her back and asked her the same questions all over again, and a lot more besides.

But all this was not yet. This was the moment when Rose Anne was coming towards them and the sun was bright on her, and Oliver's love was bright on her. She walked in this double brightness, and it dazzled Elfreda a little and made her want to cry. She ran back to the house, and was scolded because, after all, nothing had been settled about the wreaths. The scolding took place in the dining-room where Miss Hortensia was putting out the best glass. Right in the middle of it the telephone bell rang. The telephone lived in the schoolroom, which had once been Rose Anne's nursery.

The sound of the bell was most welcome. Elfreda had just been going to lose her temper, and it's no good losing your temper—not with aunts anyway. Thank goodness no one could expect you to stay and be scolded with the telephone ringing its head off. She bounded joyfully out of the room, slammed the schoolroom door behind her, and took up the receiver. It might be news of the wreaths—

A man's voice said, "Is that Miss Carew?"

There were endless questions afterwards as to his voice. Elfreda could only say and stick to it that it was a man's voice. It made no more impression on her than that, because her mind was full of Rose Anne, and the wreaths, and Aunt Hortensia being so disagreeable. The voice might have been young or it might have been middle-aged, it might have been rich or it might have been poor, it might have had ginger eyelashes or a bald patch on the top of its head, or it might have been like Gary Cooper. As far as she was concerned it was just a man's voice, and it said, "Is that Miss Carew?"

"Miss Hortensia Carew, or Miss Rose Anne Carew?" said Elfreda briskly. She wasn't going to drag Rose Anne in from the garden if she could help it.

"Miss Rose Carew—"

Elfreda was quite sure he said Rose and not Rose Anne, because that was how she knew that he couldn't be a friend. Rose Anne always had her two names from everyone who knew her, so a person who said Miss Rose Carew must be a stranger. And that was the first hint of the strangeness that was going to break in upon them— just a man's voice on the telephone asking for Miss Rose Carew.

Elfreda dealt firmly with him.

"She's engaged. What is it? I can take a message."

The voice said, "I'm afraid you can't." And then, "It doesn't matter—I can ring again," and right on the top of that the click of the receiver.

Elfreda hung up at her end. She meant to tell Rose Anne at tea, but there was an influx of cousins up from Devonshire for the wedding, Carews and Leighs—Madeline and Robert Carew, and Mary Leigh, who was the other bridesmaid and Madeline's sister, and Hugo Ross, who wasn't a cousin but was married to Loveday Leigh, who was somewhere between a fourth and fifth cousin of Rose Anne's and a second cousin twice removed of Madeline's and Mary's. They were all staying at the Angel. So was Oliver Loddon, and there was a great deal of talk about how they had all been fitted in, and how pleased and excited the Garstnets were, and how comfortable Mrs Garstnet made you, and how absolutely thrilled she was about the wedding.

"She's a Devonshire woman, you know, and she was Rose Anne's nurse. She married Mr Garstnet when his first wife died about ten years ago." This was Elfreda explaining to Hugo Ross, who said, "It all sounds very j-jolly."

Miss Hortensia stopped in the middle of pouring out a cup of tea for Loveday.

"I was thankful when she left. She had no sense of discipline whatever. She allowed Rose Anne to do anything she liked."

"Now I thought her a very comfortable woman," said James Carew. "I don't think you've given me any sugar, Hortensia."

"It's extremely bad for you, James—Elfreda, pass your uncle the sugar—Mrs Garstnet may have been what you call comfortable, but I can only repeat that I was thankful when she left."

"I cried myself sick though she was only going as far as the Angel," said Rose Anne.

"It's a pity the child is so delicate," said James Carew, stirring his tea. "Poor little Florrie."

Miss Hortensia sniffed.

"Ruined by indulgence! Just exactly what I always complained of here. Florrie wants treating with firmness. She's a naughty spoilt child, and those crying fits of hers are nothing but temper. She should be whipped for them instead of being cossetted and encouraged. No, James, I know you don't agree with me, but that is my opinion, and as for allowing Rose Anne to be at the Garstnets' beck and call every time Florrie has a tantrum, I consider it the height of folly. Anyhow they'll have to do without her after tomorrow, so perhaps they'll try a little discipline for a change."

Rose Anne coloured up. She was very fond of Florrie Garstnet, and it troubled her to think of the little creature crying for her when she was far away. She said in a low voice to Madeline,

"She had some sort of fright. No one knows quite what it was, but it started these crying fits. They send for me because she seems to think she's safe when I'm there—I don't know why. It's dreadful to see a child so frightened, but they hope she'll grow out of it. She is much better."

"She wants a good sound whipping," said Miss Hortensia in her small acid voice. "And as for those two step-sisters of hers, if they had been properly corrected when they were children they wouldn't have grown up the way they have."

Mr Carew looked up with a frown.

"Really, Hortensia—that's a little drastic. Fanny and Mabel—"

Miss Hortensia broke in scornfully.

"Fanny and Mabel can always get round a man—you don't have to tell me that, James! Red-haired flirts both of them! I'm sure I was thankful when Fanny married, though I was sorry for the young man. And if there wasn't something odd about the whole thing, why wasn't she married here, and why haven't they been back to stay?"

"Beast!" said Elfreda to herself. "She's just doing it out of spite because she knows Rose Anne is fond of Fanny, and that Fanny simply adores Rose Anne. She can't bear people who adore Rose Anne."

Rose Anne had coloured deeply. She said,

"It's not very long, Aunt Hortensia—it's only a year."

Miss Hortensia laughed tartly.

"You see what you have to expect, James. Rose Anne will be letting a year or two go by before she thinks of paying you a visit."

Elfreda forgot all about the telephone call. There was going to be a big family dinner—not only the cousins who had dropped in to tea but an uncle who had gone for a walk, two aunts who were resting, and a grandmother, Mary and Madeline's, who had absolutely refused to stay quietly at home in Torquay though everyone except herself was quite sure that the wedding festivities would be too much for her. She replied to all and sundry that she had been at dear Rosabel's wedding, and that she meant to be at Rose Anne's if she had to walk every step of the way, and she meant to be at the dinner too in her new black velvet and her best old lace, and the diamonds which she had left to Madeline and Mary in her will but had no intention of parting with as long as she could wear them herself. And for the wedding she had a puce taffeta, and a sealskin cape, and a most fashionable hat with a purple ostrich feather shading into one of the discreeter pinks. Old Mrs Leigh had been a beauty, and she could still carry fine clothes with an air. She too was resting at the Angel.

Presently the cousins melted away. Oliver got out his car and went off to Malling to meet his best man. Rose Anne went up to her room. Elfreda ran Aunt Hortensia's errands, thought for the hundredth time how much she disliked her, and was finally told to go away and make herself tidy, a most irritating injunction.

The Vicarage was a long, straggling house with a good deal of passage on either side of which rooms seemed to occur more or less fortuitously. The schoolroom was on the left just before you came to the back stair. The door was not quite shut, and there was a light in the room and someone talking. Elfreda pushed the door a little wider and looked round it.

It was Rose Anne who was talking. She had her back to Elfreda, and she was speaking into the telephone. She said, "I don't see how I can—it's too late." And then she looked round and saw Elfreda.

"Oh, Rose Anne—I thought you were resting."

Rose Anne put her hand over the mouthpiece of the receiver.

"I won't be a moment. Shut the door like an angel."

Elfreda stepped back into the passage and shut the door, but before she could move away she heard Rose Anne say, "I oughtn't to." And then she thought she heard a "but." She wasn't sure. She never could be sure.

There were two strokes from the hall clock as she ran upstairs. That was half past six. Dinner was at half past seven. A whole hour to dress in, a whole hour away from Aunt Hortensia. She had a very pretty new frock, pale blue but so beautifully cut that it made her look quite slim, and she was going to do her hair the new way with curls all round the front. It took simply ages, and when it was done she wasn't quite sure whether she liked it. She went along to show it to Rose Anne, but Rose Anne wasn't in her room. Glory—it must be later than she thought, and brides may be late, but bridesmaids definitely not. She heard the bustle and flutter of arriving aunts, and ran down all in a hurry, because old Aunt Marian Leigh would be most frightfully insulted if everyone wasn't there to meet her.

She was only just in time. The black velvet and point lace were emerging from a tremendous fur coat. Aunt Marian was declining to be led upstairs to a bedroom. She kissed Elfreda, made her usual remark about its being a pity she took after the Moores, and then turned to snub Miss Hortensia, who was urging her to come into the drawing-room out of this terrible draught.

"My dear Hortensia, if I thought as much about draughts as you do, I should probably be an invalid by now. Fresh air never hurt anyone, and I am thankful to say—"

She passed into the drawing-room, and Elfreda greeted her daughters—Aunt Agnes, weather-beaten and mannish, with a stiff crop of iron-grey hair and a black satin dress which had cost a good deal some years ago when she was slimmer; and Aunt Maud, very thin and droopy in pale blue lace, with the sort of hair that will neither stay up nor lie down. They were both kind and full of interest in the wedding, Aunt Agnes practical and hearty, Aunt Maud rather sentimental.

Uncle Frank was hearty too. He still alluded to his sisters as "the girls." He made jokes, and laughed at them with gusto.

Oliver and his best man came in—Captain Russell, a gunner like Oliver and really quite frightfully good-looking. Hugo and Loveday Ross arrived, Loveday in pink, looking a dream. And then Robert, and Madeline and Mary. Trust Mary to be last. And what could possibly have induced her to go and wear black for a wedding party like this? Why did Madeline let her? She was gay enough herself, in a very bright royal blue, and there was Mary, a bridesmaid, as dowdy as a hen, in a dress which was at least two years old and hadn't ever been anything to write home about. "Grim" was Elfreda's verdict.

They all trooped into the drawing-room, everybody talking and laughing. Elfreda found herself next to Captain Russell. She began to feel quite reassured about her hair. He had that sort of way of looking at you. Of course it didn't mean anything, but it was very agreeable and made you feel right on the top of your form.

It was Oliver who said, "Where's Rose Anne?" He said it quite quietly, so that only Elfreda heard.

Elfreda felt a little shock of surprise, because she had taken it for granted that Rose Anne was here, somewhere among the cousins. There were so many of them, and they had all been so busy saying how-do-you-do, that she hadn't had a minute to think about Rose Anne. She said, "Isn't she here?" and Oliver shook his head.

Chapter Three

ELFREDA LOOKED down the long, bright room. Aunt Marian lecturing Aunt Hortensia—what fun. Aunt Agnes talking about horses to Hugo, whilst Uncle Frank chaffed Loveday. Madeline and Mary were talking to Aunt Maud, and Robert was describing his last round of golf to Uncle James. She caught the words "I was dormy two," and made a face.

Rose Anne certainly wasn't here, and in about half a minute Aunt Hortensia would tumble to it, and then there would be trouble. She and Oliver and the nice Russell man were quite close to the door. She said,

"I'll go and get her," and slipped out of the room. Awfully silly of Rose Anne to be late, but even Aunt Hortensia couldn't be very hard on the bride. All the same, the sooner Rose Anne got down the better, because there went the three strokes which made it a quarter to eight, and if the soup was cold, even Uncle James wouldn't be pleased.

She burst into Rose Anne's room, and found it empty. Appalling to think that she mightn't be out of her bath. But the bathroom was empty too. She made a rapid tour of all the other rooms in case Rose Anne should have felt an urge to admire herself in Aunt Hortensia's mirror or to powder her nose at Uncle James's shaving-glass. But all the rooms were empty.

Elfreda wasn't frightened yet. She was puzzled, and a little bit cross, because dinner was going to be absolutely grim if Aunt Hortensia lost her temper.

She came back to Rose Anne's room, and the first faint feeling of fear came knocking at the door of her mind, because Rose Anne hadn't changed. She hadn't even begun to change. She had been going to wear one of her new dresses, a blue and silver brocade, high in the neck and long in the sleeve, in which she looked like one of the lovelier Italian angels, but the dress was on its hanger, and the silver shoes and pale grey stockings were there on the bed, just where Elfreda herself had laid them out before tea. The hot water was still in its can.

Elfreda opened her door, and the fear came in. It was past a quarter to eight, and Rose Anne hadn't come up to dress. She looked into cupboard and wardrobe. There was no sign of the clothes which Rose Anne had been wearing—blue jumper, blue tweed skirt. There was no sign either of something else, the warm tweed coat which belonged to the suit. Rose Anne hadn't been wearing the coat, but she must be wearing it now, because it was nowhere to be found, and that meant that Rose Anne had gone out.

Elfreda got as far as that, and remembered Rose Anne at the telephone saying, "I don't see how I can—it's too late," and then, "I oughtn't to." And had she said "but" after that—or hadn't she?

She pushed the fear out of her mind and slammed the door on it, because there was only one thing that would have made Rose Anne run out like that. Florrie Garstnet must have had one of those crying fits they had been talking about at tea, and Mrs Garstnet had had the nerve to send for Rose Anne.

Elfreda went down to the schoolroom in a boiling rage. It really was outrageous, and for the first time in her life she felt in sympathetic agreement with Aunt Hortensia. Florrie wanted slapping, and Mrs Garstnet wanted to be told where she got off. She was going to be told too—by Elfreda Moore, and no later than this very minute. She jerked the receiver from its hook, asked briskly for the Angel, and waited, spoiling for a row.

And after all there wasn't one, only Mrs Garstnet's comfortable voice saying,

"Miss Rose Anne? Oh, no, she's not here, Miss Elfreda."

Fear tried the latch again. Anger took wing and was gone.

"You haven't seen her?"

"Oh, yes, my dear—she came down. Florrie had one of her fits, and Matthew said, 'We can't trouble Miss Rose Anne for her, not tonight we can't.' And I said, 'Don't you be a fool, Matthew. She'd never forgive us if Florrie was to cry herself sick and not able to come to the wedding.' So I rang up, and she said she'd come over just for a minute like, and so she did."

"You shouldn't have asked her," said Elfreda—"you really shouldn't. There's a drawing-room full of relations all waiting for their dinner, and Sarah probably throwing fits in the kitchen, and what Aunt Hortensia's going to say, I don't know. When did she start back?"

"Now, my dear, don't you go upsetting yourself. And it's all very well to say 'You shouldn't,' but we couldn't do nothing with Florrie, and the minute she see Miss Rose Anne she quietened down."

"When did Rose Anne leave?" said Elfreda in her most determined voice.

Mrs Garstnet was one of those slow, diffuse talkers who can't tell you anything unless they tell you everything. If you put her out, she just went back to the beginning and started all over again. Elfreda ought to have known this.

"Now, Miss Elfreda, don't you upset yourself. I'm sure it was heart-aching to see her. We couldn't do nothing with her—nothing at all. Matthew as good as promised her a pony. There's one he could get cheap that'd be the very thing for her—been ridden regular by Mr Jackson's little girl that's gone to boarding-school—but he couldn't get Florrie to take no manner of notice. 'Well, Florrie,' I said, 'if that isn't ungrateful! I'm sure either of your step-sisters 'ud have jumped out of their skins for the chance'—that's Matthew's two by his first—Fanny's married since you was here last year, but we've still got Mabel at home."

"Mrs Garstnet, when did Rose Anne leave you?"

"Why, my dear, we didn't keep her no time. Florrie come round beautiful, and—"

"When did she leave you? Mrs Garstnet, *please.*"

"Now, now, Miss Elfreda—you don't give me time to tell you nothing. When did she leave? Now let me see—just after the half hour it was when she come in, because the bar clock was striking, and it's a minute or two slow."

"Half past six?" It was half past six when she had seen Rose Anne at the telephone. She must have run across the road to the Angel straight away.

"Yes, half past six," said Mrs Garstnet in her comfortable voice. "And she wasn't above ten minutes with Florrie, and then Matthew and me we arst her into the parlour for a minute just to wish her happy and to drink her health. And she wouldn't touch nothing but just my ginger wine that she always had such a fancy for, so we drank it in that, and she must have been out of the house by ten minutes to seven."

More than an hour ago—more than an hour ago—and the Angel just across the road from the Vicarage...

Elfreda said in a slow, cold voice, "Then where is she?"

"Oh, my dear soul—hasn't she come home?"

"No, she hasn't."

"She must have done."

"I've looked everywhere. They're all in the drawing-room waiting for dinner, and Rose Anne isn't anywhere at all."

"Oh, my dear soul!" said Mrs Garstnet. She must have dropped the receiver at her end. There was a thud and a bang. Elfreda could hear her calling, "Matthew—Matthew!"

Then the schoolroom door opened and Oliver Loddon came in.

"Where's Rose Anne? They're getting a bit restive in the drawing-room. She isn't—ill?"

Elfreda turned round with the receiver in her hand. She knew that her knees were shaking, but she didn't know how pale she was. Oliver's heart stood still. Without the least warning his happiness had crashed. Like a flash of light—no, like a flash of darkness—there came the conviction that it was all over. He had lost Rose Anne. He said very quietly,

"What is it?"

"She went over to the Angel. She hasn't come back."

A wave of relief surged up. It broke against that unreasoning conviction and fell back again. The conviction held.

"When did she go?"

"Half past six," said Elfreda with a frightened catch in her voice. "And she hasn't come back. They sent for her because Florrie was bad, but Mrs Garstnet swears she left at ten minutes to seven."

"She couldn't have—or if she did she's in the house. Where have you looked?"

"Everywhere." This time the catch had become a sob.

"Ten minutes to seven—" said Oliver, still in that quiet voice.

The clock in the hall outside struck eight.

Chapter Four

No one at the Vicarage went to bed that night. Rose Anne had walked out of it at half past six on her wedding eve to go and see her old nurse's sick child. At that moment the Vicarage lost her. Twenty minutes later she left the Angel—Mrs Garstnet was very positive about this—and Hillick St Agnes lost her too.

It is not at all a large village. You could not lose yourself in it if you tried. Rose Anne had lived there all her life. The church, the Angel, and the Vicarage are clustered together at one end of the green. There are a number of cottages, two or three better houses, and, on the far side of the village, the entrance gates of the Hall, which has stood empty ever since old Lady Fountain died. There is a pond in the middle of the green. Hillick is the Hill Wick—the hill village. It lies in a fold of the hills, and a steepish road runs down from it to Malling. A little way off this road, and only just clear of the village, are some old lead workings, but the entrance was filled in thirty years ago after a child had strayed there and been lost for a day and a night.

Oliver drove the three miles to Malling, and got there in time to miss the 8.37. The red tail-light was all that could be seen of it as he came upon the platform. No one had got in at Malling except Dr Thorpe from Grangecot, who had been in visiting his married daughter and her new baby.

"No young lady got in?"

"Oh, no, sir. Only Dr Thorpe—and a young chap that's working for Mr Penfold."

"No lady?"

"No, sir—only Mrs Thorpe that was with the doctor."

In the end it did seem certain that Rose Anne had not boarded the 8.37. Oliver's heart contracted. Rose Anne running away from him—Rose Anne catching a train to escape him... In what unimaginable nightmare had he to act as if such a thing were possible? Yet as an alternative there were worse nightmares still. If she had not gone of her own free will, how had she gone, and to what? The Angel and the Vicarage lay a bare two hundred yards apart. Within the space of those two hundred yards Rose Anne had disappeared. By mischance?... What mischance? By foul play? He shrank appalled... Of her own free will?... It was the least dreadful possibility of the three.

If she was not on the 8.37, what other train could she have caught? Mrs Garstnet said she was out of the Angel by ten to seven. She might have reached Malling station by five-and-twenty to eight if she hurried—if she hurried to get away from him.

He asked, "When was the last train?"

"Eight thirty-seven, sir—just gone."

"No, no, not the eight thirty-seven. What other trains have there been since half past seven?"

"Up or down, sir?" The porter was a little rosy man, most anxious to help.

"Either—it doesn't matter—anything that stops."

"Well, there's the seven-fifteen."

Oliver shook his head. She couldn't have walked it in the time. But she might have got a lift, and if they had to take lifts into consideration, they must go right back to seven o'clock, because Mrs Garstnet's "ten to seven" was nothing to rely on.

There had been five trains since seven o'clock—the 7.15 down, the 7.17 up, and the 7.22, also an up train but slow and stopping at every station. After that nothing till the 8.10 down, and then another gap until the 8.37. The 7.15 had put down a lot of passengers and taken none up. The porter was quite sure about this. The 7.17 hadn't taken up anyone either, but half a dozen passengers had boarded the slow local train at 7.22. Five of them were men, but the sixth was a lady. The porter hadn't seen her face, but she had on a bright green hat.

"I couldn't say nothing about the rest of her clothes, sir, and I never saw her face. The light's terrible in the booking-hall, but she went right under a lamp going out on to the platform and I took particular notice of her hat—very bright green, sir."

Rose Anne hadn't a green hat. At least he had never seen her in one. Elfreda said there was no hat missing. Rose Anne wouldn't have worn a hat just to run over to the Angel. She might have worn one if she had meant to run away.

"She took a ticket for London," said the porter, friendly and helpful.

No, it couldn't have been Rose Anne.

There was one more train, the 8.10 down... The 8.10 was a complete wash-out. Nobody had got out, and nobody had got in.

Oliver tipped the porter and drove back to Hillick St Agnes. At intervals of a few hundred yards he stopped the car to stand by the side of the road, to call Rose Anne's name, to listen for some possible faint response.

Until you listen in the night for a sound that does not come, you do not know how many sounds there are. There seems to be no wind, but when you listen like that you hear the breath that moves a leaf, and the breath that stirs the grass—dry leaf, dry grass, dry whispering breath. Oliver's own throat was dry as he called, "Rose Anne!"—and his tongue dry in his mouth—and his heart dry in his body. The whisper went in the grass. Something moved, scuttering on the hill above. Something went by on an almost noiseless wing. But Rose Anne did not answer.

He came back to the Vicarage, and went out again, walking the paths, walking the road, walking the hills till the dawn. Then back to the Vicarage.

The house was full of red-eyed women. There might have been a death. Perhaps there had been a death. Perhaps Rose Anne was dead... Something in him said "No" very insistently. Then she had left him... Either way he had lost her...

It was his wedding day. He ate and drank, and went down to the Angel with James Carew.

"You are sure she left you before seven, Mrs Garstnet?"

They were in the parlour of the Angel. Mrs Garstnet, dissolved in tears, sobbed out her answer.

"Oh, indeed yes, sir."

"Please, please, Mrs Garstnet, you must control yourself," said Mr Carew impatiently.

Oliver said nothing. He stood by the window, his clenched right hand hidden in a pocket. It was all over. He had lost her. All this was mere torture, but it must be gone through.

"She's that upset, sir," said Matthew Garstnet in a deprecating tone. A bluff, good-natured man, Matthew, to match his comfortable wife. Ruddy of face and stout of build, with red hair turning grey, he stood with his back to the fire in frowning embarrassment. He liked jollity and good fellowship. In the presence of grief he very heartily wished himself elsewhere.

"Oh, Mr Carew, I can't say no different!" sobbed Mrs Garstnet.

Mr Carew sat up stiffly in the parlour's best plush chair. His face was grey, and a muscle in his cheek twitched perpetually. He tapped on his knee and said sharply.

"Stop crying! You've got to help us. We shall have to go to the police. You were the last person who saw her. What was she wearing?"

Mrs Garstnet dabbed at her eyes with a soaking handkerchief.

"Her blue jumper and skirt, sir—and the coat that goes with them."

"Miss Elfreda said there was a coat. She was wearing it?"

"Oh, yes, sir."

"I don't notice clothes. What sort of coat would it be? I mean—" He stopped, steadied his voice, and went on again. "Would it be the sort of coat she would wear if she meant—to take a journey?"

Oliver stood still by the window. The world stood still about him. That would be said, that would be thought—that Rose Anne had run away rather than marry him. There would be headlines in the press. What did it matter as long as she was safe? He would give his soul to know that she was safe.

Mrs Garstnet was babbling about the coat.

"A beautiful coat, sir, and such a lovely fur collar—one of the things she'd got for her trousseau. And I told her she didn't rightly ought to wear it, not till she was married."

"What did she say when you said that?" said Oliver. His voice was better under control than James Carew's.

Mrs Garstnet looked at him with her face working.

"She said, 'It's warm, Nannie. I had to have something warm.'"

"You're sure she said that?"

"Oh, yes, sir."

"And it was the sort of coat she would wear for a journey?"

"Oh, yes, sir—lovely and warm."

"Was she wearing a hat?" said Oliver. He forced himself to the question.

Elfreda had said no. She said there was no hat missing. She said anyhow Rose Anne wouldn't put on a hat to run over to the Angel. But if Elfreda was wrong, if Rose Anne had been wearing a hat, then it would mean that she had meant to go farther than the Angel. How far, no one but herself could say. The question came hardly to his lips.

And Mrs Garstnet hesitated. She looked at Oliver with brimming eyes and said with a catch in her breath,

"Not when she come, sir."

Mr Carew drummed on his knee.

"Good gracious! What do you mean by that?"

"She didn't have anything on her head when she come," said Mrs Garstnet dabbing hard. "She borrowed Florrie's hat to go back with."

"Florrie's hat? Good gracious, Mrs Garstnet, why on earth did she borrow Florrie's hat?"

Mrs Garstnet gulped.

"It was one she give Florrie only a couple of days ago. As good as new it was, only she didn't fancy herself in it so she give it to Florrie, and Florrie looked a treat in it, green being her colour as you might say."

Oliver broke in harshly.

"It was a green hat?"

"As green as grass, and Florrie was that pleased with it."

"And Rose Anne took it back after giving it away?" This was James Carew with a faint note of surprise in his voice.

"We didn't take it that way, not at the time, sir. The hat was hanging on a peg, and Miss Rose Anne she said, 'Will you give me the loan of it, just to go back across the road? There was a drop or two of rain as I come along,' she said, 'and I don't want to get my hair wet,' she said. So I told her she was welcome, and she put on the hat and come along down for us to drink her health. And that's the last we saw of her."

"I'd like to see Florrie," said Oliver.

Matthew Garstnet made an awkward movement of protest.

"We don't want Florrie drawn in. She's not fit," he said.

"You won't be able to keep her out, Garstnet," said Mr Carew. "The police will want to see her. There's no reason why she should be frightened. Good gracious me, I christened her! I suppose she can answer a question or two?"

"She's so easy upset," said Mrs Garstnet with a sob. "I'm sure I don't know—"

"Will you fetch her, please," said Oliver.

Mrs Garstnet looked at her husband. And then, before she could speak, the door was opened and a child looked round it. She had a little peaked face and a cloud of copper hair—wonderful hair, with all the glow and colour which were lacking in the small white face. James Carew said, "Come in, Florrie," and she slipped into the room and stood just inside the door looking from one to the other out of greenish hazel eyes.

"Come here, my dear," said James Carew.

She came and stood at his knee, not shy, just waiting to know what was wanted of her.

"So Miss Rose Anne gave you a green hat, Florrie?"

James Carew was at his best with children. He spoke kindly and simply.

"Yes, sir, she did."

"And then she borrowed it again yesterday?"

Florrie looked at her mother.

"She'd just quieted down and wasn't taking much notice," said Mrs Garstnet. "And I'm sure she'd not grudge anything, not to Miss Rose Anne—would you, Florrie?"

Florrie had no answer.

"And you'd be pleased for Miss Rose Anne to have your hat—"

"I'd rather have it myself," said Florrie.

"Now, Florrie—I'm sure you'd not grudge anything to Miss Rose Anne that's always been so good to you!"

"I'd like my green hat back," said Florrie in a little obstinate voice.

They made no more of her. She was neither shy nor distressed. She wanted her green hat. Rose Anne had given it to her, and she wanted it. From Florrie's view point it was the green hat that had disappeared, not Rose Anne. Children want one thing at a time, and want that one thing passionately. Florrie wanted her green hat. She was to have worn it for the wedding. Since it was not there to be worn, the wedding ceased to be of any interest. She looked Oliver straight in the face and said,

"I want my hat. Why did she take it away?"

Chapter Five

ROSE ANNE had gone bare-headed to the Angel at half past six. She had come away twenty minutes later having borrowed the green hat to run across the street. She had told Mrs Garstnet that it was raining and she didn't want to get her hair wet just before the family dinner-party—quite a plausible reason if it had really been raining. But it had not rained, neither between half past six and seven o'clock that evening, nor at any time in the whole twenty-four hours.

Hesitatingly, deprecatingly, James Carew put these points forward as he and Oliver walked away from the Angel. They went past the Vicarage gate and on round the green. It was easier to keep moving, easier to be out of the house, where the women sniffed and whispered, and the telephone bell kept ringing. Guests had to be put off and arrangements cancelled, enquiries answered, the press staved off. It was women's business, so let them get on with it.

"I'm afraid," said James Carew—"I'm afraid she meant to go. She wouldn't have borrowed that hat if she hadn't meant to go. There—there wasn't any rain, Oliver."

"No," said Oliver. He had been driving back from Malling with Russell, and there hadn't been any rain. They had actually reached the Angel at a quarter to seven. Five minutes later and they would have met Rose Anne on her way. He said this in a hard, forced voice.

"Well? What did you do when you got in?" said James Carew.

"I was putting the car away. Russell came round to the garage with me. I had one or two things to see to. It must have been just on seven before we got in."

"I see."

They walked on in silence for perhaps twenty yards. Then James Carew said,

"I suppose—you must forgive me, Oliver—I suppose you can't in any way account for this?"

"No."

"I mean there hasn't been any—any quarrel—any difference of opinion between you?"

"No."

"Girls are impulsive," said James Carew. He was remembering that he and Rosabel had quarrelled quite bitterly on their honeymoon. He remembered the quarrel, but he couldn't remember what it was about. It seemed quite probable now that it wasn't about anything at all. Rosabel had walked out of the hotel and stayed away for hours. He had been off his head with anger, anxiety, remorse. And it was all about nothing at all. They had laughed about it happily that very night, and she had been so sweet, so sweet.

"Have you found Rose Anne impulsive?" said Oliver.

James Carew came back with a start. He had forgotten Rose Anne. He said vaguely,

"Girls do things like that. I thought there might have been something—some quarrel—not serious—"

"There was no quarrel," said Oliver.

The day dragged. The police Inspector came over from Malling. He asked a great many questions, wrote the answers down in a note book, and had some information to give in return. The police had been making their own enquiries.

The lady in the green hat who had boarded the 7.22 had got out two stations farther up the line at Claypole. The green hat had impressed itself upon the ticket collector. The lady was young—oh yes, quite a young lady, but he couldn't describe her at all. She kept her head down a bit, and she just pushed the ticket at him and went by. He thought she was in a hurry. She got into a car that was waiting and went off. In a considerable hurry she seemed to be, but he noticed her hat because it was just about the greenest thing he had ever seen—kind of hit you in the eye and made you stare. No, he hadn't noticed the car at all, only just that it was there and that she got into it. And he couldn't say which way it went, because there was a bit of a drive up from the station yard, and by the time a car got out on to the London road there'd be too much passing for anyone to tell which way it turned.

"And that's all he knows," said the Inspector. "We've pumped him dry—there isn't any more to be got from him. He didn't see her face, and he didn't notice the car, so there's only the green hat to go on."

It wasn't much. Green was the fashionable autumn colour, and there was a spate of green hats. Every shop window was full of them, every second girl was wearing one, from rifle green to viridian and jade.

"Rose Anne got hers by artificial light," Elfreda told Oliver. "You know how dark Jackson's is in Malling. And when she got it home it just shrieked. Too ghastly. And she couldn't change it, because she'd worn it that first day in a fog, so she gave it to Florrie. And I don't believe she'd have borrowed it if she'd meant to go away, because she wouldn't take back a present like that—she *wouldn't*. And she would never, never, never have gone away anywhere in a blue coat and skirt and that flaring green hat. It must have been someone else."

"It might have been hundreds of people," said Loveday Ross. "Oliver, I don't believe she meant to go away. Why should she? She was happy—unless you quarrelled. Did you quarrel?"

Oliver shook his head. Everyone asked him that. He said wearily, "No, we didn't quarrel."

"Then she didn't go away of herself. She wouldn't go like that—without a reason. And there simply isn't any reason."

They were in the garden, the same garden in which Oliver and Rose Anne had sat and talked on their wedding eve, with the sun shining on them. And now it was the wedding day, and Rose Anne was gone, no one knew where, and there was no more sunshine. The clouds hung low and promised rain, and the air was soft and mild, and there was a smell of autumn in it, the smell of damp leaves, and wet earth, and burning weeds. Giles Halliday had a bonfire, and the wind was setting from it.

They were in the garden because, in spite of her name, Aunt Hortensia disliked gardens. She considered them damp, and associated them with rheumatism. And all three of them had had as much of Aunt Hortensia as they could bear. Aunts Agnes and Maud were with her now, and Hugo had taken Uncle Frank for a walk.

"If I were you," said Elfreda, "I should go and see that porter yourself—the one at Claypole. You've only got what the Inspector says about what he said, and you know people don't talk to the police—not like they would to you and me. They're either nervous or—or official. They don't just run on. I know because of living in a village. If you want to find something out, it's no use asking them to make a statement, you want to get them all chatty. Then it's surprising what they'll tell you."

One of the maids came hurrying down the path.

"You're wanted on the telephone, Miss Elfreda."

Elfreda ran.

Oliver said, "That's quite a good idea—I'll go to Claypole. It will be something to do anyhow."

Loveday nodded. She could guess what it must be like for Oliver hanging round the house, waiting for the telephone bell to ring, waiting for news of Rose Anne. She opened her mouth to speak, and shut it again. It was too soon—perhaps it was too soon. Or were they wasting time—very, very precious time which would never come their way again? She stood irresolute, a pretty, friendly creature, young and eager to help.

Something about her youth and that eager kindness stirred Oliver. He said quickly.

"You were going to say something. What was it?"

Loveday rushed into speech.

"I was going to say I don't, don't, *don't* believe she went away because she wanted to. Someone told her lies, or someone made her go. She would never have gone like this and made us so unhappy unless she was so dreadfully unhappy herself that she didn't know what she was doing—or unless someone—made her go." She said the last words in a whisper.

Oliver said roughly, "I've thought of that. I suppose you mean by lies that she might have heard something about me—something that made her feel she couldn't marry me. If that's what happened, she must have had a telephone message or a note, or someone must have spoken to her. Well, there wasn't a telephone call except the one from Mrs Garstnet asking her to go and see Florrie, and nobody took in a note, and if someone spoke to her, it must have been after she left the Vicarage. The Garstnets couldn't possibly have any interest in telling lies about me, so we come back to the time after she left the Angel. Whoever persuaded her to go away must have been waiting for her outside the Angel."

"I don't believe she was persuaded," said Loveday. "I don't indeed. Rose Anne wouldn't. If someone had told her lies, she would have come to you about it. She would have wanted to hear your side. She isn't an impulsive person, and she's very unselfish. She would have thought about her father and all of us. She would never have gone away and left us without a word."

Oliver turned a haggard face on her.

"Yes—I say so too."

"Then—she was made to go. We don't know how, and we've got to find out, and every single minute is as precious as diamonds. And oh, Oliver, won't you *please* go and see Uncle Ben at once?"

"Uncle Ben?" said Oliver. Weren't there enough relations mixed up in this already?

"Not really," said Loveday, flushed and earnest. "I mean he isn't really an uncle—at least not mine or Rose Anne's—but Hugo's sister Susan married his nephew, and he's a Pet Lamb. No, Oliver, please listen. He's a really frightfully important person, and he got Hugo and me out of the sort of jam that it gives you nightmares to remember for the rest of your life. I can't tell you about it—at least I can't without asking Hugo, because it was all very hush-hush, and if it hadn't been for Uncle Ben—"

"Who is he?" said Oliver, frowning.

"He is Mr Benbow Collingwood Horatio Smith, and he is a—a sort of—well, honestly, Oliver, I don't know what he is, but the Foreign Office ask his advice, and Colonel Garratt who is the head of the Foreign Office Intelligence goes and sits at his feet." She gave a faint giggle. "At least I believe what really happens is that Colonel Garratt snaps and growls exactly like a quarrelsome terrier, only rather a pet too, and Uncle Ben just drifts about the room and talks to Ananias. He's got a parrot called Ananias, and they are devoted to each other, and if you listen carefully you come away with something worth having."

"I don't think—" said Oliver in a voice which he tried to make polite.

Loveday coloured high.

"I haven't explained a bit properly—it's so difficult. But he really is the most marvellous person—Uncle Ben, I mean. There's a picture that's like him—an old Doge or something by Titian. I mean he's *immensely* impressive—he really is. He knows *everything* and everyone. I mean he can get things done—he really can. And, Oliver, if you won't go now, do just keep on thinking about it. And—and I've put his name and address on the back of one of my cards, and a message, and if you do go and see him, send it in, because he really is very fond of Susan and Hugo and me."

Oliver took the proffered card and put it away in his pocket-book. And then Elfreda came running down the path again.

"That was Cousin Catherine, and why she didn't get herself called to the Bar instead of marrying a parson in Peckham, I can't think. She's been cross-examining my head off and not believing a single word I said, and when she'd finished, Aunt Hortensia wanted to know who was calling up, and we had it all over again. I do wish all our relations were *dead*!"

Chapter Six

CLAYPOLE is quite a small village. There is a church, an inn called the Hand and Glove, and a couple of rows of cottages. There are two or three fair sized farms in the offing, and Mr Burdock at Little Clay breeds pigs, and takes prizes with them at the County shows.

Everybody in the village knew that Miss Rose Anne Carew had run away from Hillick St Agnes on the night before her wedding. Every woman knew that she had run away in a blue coat and skirt and a bright green hat, and that Inspector Robins had been over to ask George Abbott about the young lady in the green hat who had got off the 7.48 from Malling. And of course George didn't know nothing. George wouldn't—too much taken up with Ellen Wilks to so much as see what any other girl looked like, and goodness knew why, because though it was plain enough that Ellen thought the world of herself, Claypole—feminine Claypole at any rate—didn't consider her anything to write home about—"Lipstick and rouge, and heels as high as stilts! Well, the sooner she gets herself another place the better for her pore old father, and the better for Claypole, and much the better for George Abbott."

Peter Wilks was Mr Burdock's head pig-keeper and a highly respected citizen. Pigs had no secrets from him, but he couldn't manage his daughter Ellen. It was whispered in the village that she now spelled her name Elayne, and required George to pronounce it in that manner.

Oliver found George Abbott digging pig-manure into the garden which he fondly hoped he would one day persuade Ellen to share with him. The trouble was that he had his mother to keep and he was a good son, and Ellen was set against sharing a house with any mother-in-law in the world. Quite enough matter here to make a young man inattentive to passing females whose tickets it was his duty to collect. He had his troubles had George, what with his mother bursting into tears two or three times a day, and offering to go to the institute, and Ellen stamping her foot at him no longer ago than teatime yesterday and saying if he didn't care for her enough to say her name the way she liked it said, she'd take the morning bus into Malling and put down her name at the registry office and go for a lady's maid—"And if it's foreign parts, so much the better, George Abbott, for I'm sick sore and weary of living in a village and hearing about nothing but pigs."

George spread manure gloomily. If Ellen went off to foreign parts, he shouldn't wonder if he never saw her again. This stuff ought to do the ground good. What call had Ellen got to go off foreign when all was said and done? His mother had lived with her mother-in-law, and as happy as happy—or so she said now. What was the matter with women that two of 'em couldn't live happily in a house? And plenty of room too—three as good bedrooms as anyone could wish for. "Why, she ought to be glad of the company when he was out. As for the new-fangled way of saying her name, he was hanged if he could remember it from one time to the next, for all he'd got it written down. He looked up with a jerk of his head when Oliver spoke his name.

"Good afternoon. Are you George Abbott?"

George admitted it. He was a pleasant-faced, rosy young man with big shoulders and big hands. He wanted to get on with his digging.

Oliver came through the gate and shut it after him. He had left his car some twenty yards up the street outside the Hand and Glove. He said,

"My name is Loddon—Captain Loddon. You won't know it of course."

On the contrary, every soul in Claypole knew all about Captain Oliver Loddon whose young lady had run away from him. George Abbott looked at him with a kind of gloomy sympathy, because if Ellen went off foreign, he'd be in Captain Loddon's shoes himself, or as good as.

He said, "Yes, sir," and then had the feeling that he hadn't said the right thing. That was Ellen, that was—always keeping on about the way he spoke, as if plain words weren't good enough for anyone. He had missed something because Captain Loddon was saying,

"I think you took her ticket."

George got hot behind the ears. He must have missed quite a piece. Right down absent-minded that was what he was, and it was all Ellen's fault. He said in an abashed voice,

"I beg your pardon, sir—"

"I think you told the Inspector—"

George recovered himself. The young lady with the green hat— that was what he was after. Everyone was making sure now that she must have been Miss Carew.

"Oh, yes, sir—I took her ticket."

Oliver produced a ten shilling note.

"Look here, I'm taking up your time—"

George said, "Oh no, sir," and, "Thank you very, I'm sure." The ten shilling note went into his trouser pocket.

Oliver watched his rather deliberate movements withan intolerable sense of strain. Since Rose Anne disappeared he had the feeling that everything had slowed down. It was like being part of a slow motion picture—thought, speech, action, all dragging intolerably—moments lengthened into hours—time stretching, sagging—

He said, "Will you tell me exactly what happened—anything you saw—anything you noticed—every single thing you can remember."

George scratched his head, and then remembered that this was one of the things which offended Ellen. He said hastily,

"Well, sir, I didn't notice much, that's the truth."

"She got out of the train?"

"Well, I didn't see her get out, but she must ha' done, because she come along the platform."

"Where were you standing?"

"By the booking-office door."

"You mean the door between the platform and the booking office?"

"Yes, sir."

"So you could see along the platform?"

"Yes, sir."

"How far away was she when you saw her?"

George put up his hand to scratch again, but desisted in time.

"Well, sir, I couldn't say. I wasn't taking notice, and that's the truth."

"Was she the only passenger who got off?"

"Yes, sir."

"Well, when did you notice her?" said Oliver. "You told the Inspector you noticed the green hat."

George leaned on his fork.

"Well, sir, it was this way. First of all I didn't think there was anyone getting off, and I began thinking about something else. And then there was the young lady as if she was going to push past without giving up her ticket, so I said, 'Ticket please,' and she turned round to get the light and started rummaging in her bag."

"Wait a minute," said Oliver. "You say she turned round to get the light. What light was that, and where was it?"

"The lamp out on the platform, sir."

"Show me how you were standing, and where the lamp would be."

George showed him, sticking his fork upright in the ground and retreating half a dozen yards.

"That'd be the lamp, and this 'ud be me, and she turned around like that." He described a curve with his arm.

"So when she turned round she would be between you and the lamp? Is that it?"

"That's right, sir. It's not a very strong light, sir—lots of complaints about it one way and another."

"So you didn't see her face?"

"No, sir—I told the Inspector I didn't."

"Did you see the colour of her hair?"

George took time to think about that. Then he said,

"I didn't notice it, sir."

"You say she was rummaging in her bag. What happened then?"

"She found her ticket, and pushed it at me, and went on quick."

"Where did she go?"

"Right across and out at the other door, and got into the car that was waiting there and drove off."

"Do you mean she drove the car herself?"

"Oh, no, sir—there was a gentleman in the car."

"Did you see him?"

"Oh, no, sir."

"Then how—?"

"I didn't see him no more than just to know there was someone opened the door of the car, and the young lady got in and slammed it and they went off. That's all I saw."

"Then what's all this about a green hat? Where did you see it?"

George was on perfectly firm ground. The hat had struck him all of a heap. He liked a good bright bit of colour. Perhaps that was why he liked Ellen.

"Oh, that was when she was going out, sir—the brightest green hat I ever seen—right under the booking-office light and no mistake about it. I didn't see her face, because she was going away from me, but I see her hat all right."

There was a pause. George's hand went down into his trouser pocket. The ten shilling note felt pleasantly crisp. His fingers slid past it, touched a piece of paper folded over on itself. Ellen—

Elayne—E-l-a-y-n-e. A lot of damned tomfoolery, but if she fancied her name that way, he supposed he'd got to humour her—E-l-a... He pulled out the piece of paper all ready to take a look at it when Captain Loddon should be gone. And Captain Loddon was saying,

"Isn't there anything else at all, Abbott?"

George turned the paper in his hand, and suddenly there it was, staring up at him, a name on a piece of paper—a name on a torn envelope. Not "Ellen," nor "Elayne," but "Miss Rose Anne Carew." He held it out to Oliver, and said in a dazed voice,

"She dropped it, sir."

Oliver said, "*What?*"

"She dropped it when she was looking for her ticket."

Oliver stared at the name. The writing was his own—"Miss Rose Anne Carew." There was just the name, on a torn piece of an envelope. The address was gone and the flaps. There was just a straight torn piece with Rose Anne's name on it. He turned it over mechanically, and saw on the back what George Abbott had written there laboriously with a smudgy pencil—"E-l-a-y-n-e."

"But, Abbott—"

George was all hot and bothered.

"I didn't know there was any writing on it. I wanted a bit of paper and I picked it up. My young lady's got a fancy to spell her name different, and I can't get used to it, not anyhow."

Oliver said nothing. He turned the paper again and stood looking down at the name he had written three days ago—Or was it four... Time had stopped. He had written the name, and thought when he wrote it that it was the last time. "Next time I write I shall be writing to my wife." It was the last time, there wasn't going to be any next time. He stared at the torn envelope, and at the name on it:

"Miss Rose Anne Carew."

Chapter Seven

Mr Smith was in his library. He was, in fact, searching the top shelf for an interesting pamphlet on the *Art of Malediction as Practised in the Near East.* The pamphlet was fifty years old and extremely rare, and as Mr Benbow Collingwood Horatio Smith never mislaid anything, he was beginning to entertain a regretful suspicion about the learned Roumanian professor to whom he had shown it some six months previously. He turned, looked over his shoulder, and addressed the grey and rose coloured parrot who occupied a handsome perch at the far end of the room.

"Not always a very honest world, Ananias?"

Ananias blinked morosely. Of all things in the world, he disliked seeing his master climb the book-ladder and stand there taking out one book after another. He opened his beak and emitted a slight hiss of protest.

"All right, Ananias, I am coming down. I am afraid—I am very much afraid—that our pamphlet has returned to the Near East."

Ananias said "Awk," and the front door bell rang.

Mr Smith came down from the ladder and drifted over to the hearth. There was a pleasant glow from the fire. A dark afternoon—a very dark afternoon. It would really be more cheerful with the curtains drawn. Ananias liked plenty of light. He put out his hand to a switch, and the bowl in the ceiling sprang into brilliance. Miller came into the room carrying a salver with a card upon it and an envelope. Mr Smith picked up the card and read:

CAPTAIN OLIVER LODDEN, R.A.
JUNIOR NAVAL AND MILITARY CLUB.

The name was quite unknown to him. He lifted the envelope, which was addressed to himself, and said vaguely,

"Er—the curtains, Miller—I think Ananias would prefer them drawn."

The envelope was addressed in a strange hand. Good writing— yes, quite good writing. Inside the envelope one of Loveday Ross's cards—Mrs Hugo Ross—and, written all across it in pencil, "Darling Uncle Ben, please, *please* do everything you can."

He gazed abstractedly at the words.

Miller finished drawing the curtains and came back. Ananias, gratified, stretched a wing and, rising upon his toes, began to chant a forbidden ditty of the sea.

"No, Ananias—certainly not!"

"The gentleman is waiting, sir," said Miller.

There came into the room Oliver Loddon who had not slept for a week. That was actually the first thing Mr Smith perceived. His absent-minded gaze, which appeared to go past a guest, informed him that here was a man who had come to the end of his tether.

Oliver himself received a most curious impression. He had come here because it was a week since Rose Anne had disappeared and there was still no news—because he had done everything else that he could think of—because it was easier to do something than to do nothing. The impression he received was one which he could not have put into words—a handsome, dignified room, an almost incredibly distinguished looking old gentleman with an absent, courteous manner. All this was on the surface, and touched only the surface of his mind, but there was something else, something undefined and indefinable, which entered his mood and changed it. He had forced himself to come, but he did not have to force himself to stay. He got no nearer to it than that. The grey parrot on the perch by the window looked over its shoulder and fixed him with a long, unwinking stare.

"If you will sit down, Captain Loddon, and tell me—er—what I can do for you—"

Oliver sat down on the edge of a deep leather arm-chair. He would have preferred to stand.

Mr Smith sank into the companion chair.

"Loveday Ross," he said—"you come from Loveday Ross?"

Ananias lost interest in his toilet at the sound of Loveday's name. He turned quite round and began to execute a kind of solemn dance, two steps this way and two steps that, with an arching claw and wings half spread. He said, "Loveday—Loveday—Loveday!" on a loud squawking note.

"*No*, Ananias!"

Ananias dropped to a crooning whisper. An attentive listener might still have caught Loveday's name.

Oliver Loddon had no attention to spare. For a whole week now, night and day, his thoughts had turned and swung, now slow, now fast, about the central fact of Rose Anne's disappearance, the same thoughts going round and round like some infernal gramophone record which he had no power to check or change. He said in a hard, strained voice,

"I'm taking up your time. I came because of Loveday, but I've no right to be troubling you, sir."

Mr Smith was leaning back. The long fingers of his right hand lay pale upon the arm of the chair. The hand lifted for a moment and fell again.

"If you would—er—tell me why Loveday sent you to me—"

"It's no use," said Oliver. "I don't see what you can do—what anyone can do."

Mr Smith began to remember a headline in one of the papers which he did not read. Garratt had brought it in and dropped it—and there had been a headline... "Vanishing Bride"—yes, that was it—and a photograph, an incredibly bad photograph of the young man who was staring at him now. It had been labelled "Deserted Bridegroom." He said in his pleasant, cultured voice,

"I really think it would be better if you would tell me what has brought you here."

"I thought you would have seen it in the papers," said Oliver bitterly.

Mr Smith looked past him.

"I—er—read *The Times*. You had better, I think, assume that I—er—know nothing of your affairs."

Something clicked in Oliver's mind. "He does know something then. Why did I come? What's the good of it anyhow? She's gone."

"Yes, Captain Loddon?"

"I was to have been married a week ago today—to Loveday's cousin, Rose Anne Carew. The night before—she walked out of the house and disappeared."

"Er—what time was that?"

"I'll sing you a song of the fish of the sea," said Ananias brightly.

"Hush, Ananias!"

Ananias said "Oh Rio!" in a tone of protest and subsided.

"Yes?" said Mr Smith. "What time did you say?"

"Half past six," said Oliver. "Her old nurse lives just across the road—she's married to the man who keeps the village inn. She's got a delicate child, and she rang up at half past six to ask Rose Anne to go over. The child has had some kind of fright, and gets all worked up. Rose Anne is the only person who can quiet her."

"She—er—went over?"

"Yes, she went over. It's only just across the street—not fifty yards. She put on the coat that belonged to a dress she was wearing and ran over. She hadn't any hat. She stayed about twenty minutes at the Angel—they say she left at ten to seven. But theysay she borrowed a hat. It was one she had given the child a few days before."

Mr Smith looked vaguely at the fire.

"She borrowed a hat?"

"A bright green hat," said Oliver.

Ananias broke into song:

"Away love, away.
Way down Rio.
So fare ye well, my pretty young gel,
For we're bound for the Rio Grande."

"No, Ananias!" He repeated the words, "A bright green hat—"

"She left the Angel at ten minutes to seven, and she never reached the Vicarage. There was to be a family dinner. Most of us were staying at the Angel—I was myself, but I had driven into Malling to meet Russell who was going to be my best man."

Ananias said, "Way down Rio," in a tentative manner, and was again rebuked.

"She wasn't missed till a quarter to eight—we just thought she was late. We were out all night looking for her. Someone in a green hat got into the 7.22 at Malling—that's the nearest station—it's three miles away. Next day after we'd gone to the police they found that the ticket-collector at Claypole, which is the next stop but one, had seen a girl in a green hat get off there at 7.48. Well, I've seen the Malling porter, and I went over to see the fellow at Claypole, and they'd both noticed that bright green hat, but they couldn't give any other description. The Claypole man says she went straight through the booking office and got into a car that was waiting outside. He says the door was opened from inside and she got in and drove away. And she dropped this when she was looking for her ticket." He leaned forward with a jerky movement and pushed a torn scrap of paper at Mr Smith. "It's got her name on it. It's a bit of the envelope of the last letter I sent her."

Mr Smith looked down at the scrap of paper. He held it a long way off, and then produced a pair of spectacles from a battered shagreen case and looked at it more closely.

"The writing on the back isn't anything," said Oliver—"just the porter trying to get his girl's name right."

"Pretty young gel," said Ananias softly—"pretty young gel—way down Rio—"

"Ananias—*no!*" said Mr Smith.

"There's been no news since," said Oliver abruptly.

Mr Smith gazed into the fire. Several thousand people disappeared every year. Most of these disappearances were voluntary. The disappearance of Rose Anne Carew had a most voluntary sound. The story of the girl who runs away on her wedding eve is one of the oldest stories in the world. The girl very seldom runs alone. Really, Loveday was very impulsive—a dear child, but impulsive. This poor jilted young man would have to do what other jilted young men have done throughout the ages—he would have to get over it somehow, and presently find consolation. He said gently, "She has not—er—communicated with her family?"

"No."

"And the police, Captain Loddon—what is their—er—view?"

Oliver got up—walked to the fire—stood looking down at it with his back to the room.

"They are quite sure that she went because she wanted to go. They think—she went away—with someone else."

There was a painful pause. Ananias lifted an untuneful voice and sang:

"So good-bye to Sally, and good-bye to Sue.
Oh, Rio.
And you who are listening, good-bye to you,
For we're bound for the Rio Grande."

Mr Smith got out of his chair and went down the room, walking a little more quickly than was his wont. Having cuffed Ananias, he came back at his usual drifting pace and leaned against the mantelshelf. He had a view of Oliver Loddon's profile like a mask set sideways, stiff and pale. The case seemed plain enough. The girl had eloped, and had probably gone abroad. Presently she would write. Or perhaps she wouldn't write. There seemed to be no very strong family ties, and modern youth was casual enough.

Oliver turned on him suddenly, haggard but controlled.

"I don't believe it, you know, sir. I—I've got to the point where I would rather believe it, because it would mean she was—safe. But I don't believe it—I can't."

"Ah," said Mr Smith gently—"you don't believe it. May I ask why?"

"Yes—I want to tell you. I want to thresh it out—get it into words—if you don't mind, sir. It keeps going round in my head."

"I do not mind in the least. Will you—er—give me your reason for being unable to accept what is, I gather, the theory of the police?"

Oliver gave a short, hard laugh.

"It's more than theory—it's solid conviction. But I don't accept it, because Rose Anne is quite incapable of doing a thing like that. You see, she—cared for me." He used the past tense, as if Rose Anne were dead. There had been times in the last week when he would have given his right hand to be quite sure that she was dead.

Mr Smith looked down into the fire.

"It is difficult to be sure on such a point."

"I *am* sure," said Oliver Loddon. "But we will set that aside. I want to tell you what she was like. A police report takes no account of character, but you can't leave it out—it's got to be reckoned with. I'm going to tell you about Rose Anne. She wasn't impulsive— she wasn't what you'd call modern. She was very unselfish, very considerate and—and gentle." The last word could only just be heard. It was the thought of Rose Anne's gentleness which stabbed more deeply than anything else.

Mr Smith said, "I see—"

Oliver got his voice again.

"I must make you see. She always thought about other people. If she had been—different, she wouldn't have gone over to the Angel that evening. It simply isn't in her character to go away and leave us all this time without a word. It is a thing she couldn't do—if she was a free agent. Even, if she didn't care for me, even if she cared for someone else, it isn't in her to torture us like this."

Mr Smith said, still looking into the fire.

"Human nature is a very strange thing—very—incalculable."

Oliver straightened up.

"There's another thing. If she left the Angel at ten minutes to seven, I don't see how she could have caught the 7.22 at Malling. It's three miles and a rough road, and it was a pitch dark night. Once she got into lighted streets she couldn't have run without attracting attention. I don't say it couldn't be done, but I say Rose Anne couldn't do it."

"And the police?"

"They think there was a car. They think it was all planned. But look here, sir, if she was picked up by a car outside the Angel, why should she touch Malling at all? Why should she go by train to Claypole, which is only six miles from Hillick St Agnes, and be picked up there by another car? It doesn't make sense."

Mr Smith stooped down and put a log on the fire. There was an uprush of sparks, brilliant and wayward. He said,

"She was—er—seen at Malling and at Claypole?"

"It doesn't make sense," said Oliver.

Mr Smith stood up and dusted his hands with a white silk handkerchief.

"Might there not be a mistake as to the time she left the inn?"

"I suppose there might, but there's not much margin. You see, Elfreda—that's one of the cousins—heard her at the telephone answering the call from the Angel: Elfreda was on her way upstairs, and the clock struck half past six as she came through the hall. Rose Anne had to get her coat—she wasn't wearing it—and go across the road. She would be a little time with Florrie, getting her quiet. Then there was the business of borrowing the hat, and then they wanted to drink her health, so they asked her into their parlour. Mrs Garstnet says—"

Mr Smith was in the act of returning the white silk handkerchief to its appropriate pocket. His hand stopped in mid air. A sense of soundless shock checked Oliver on the first two words of his sentence. He forgot what he was going to say next. He forgot everything, because Mr Smith was looking at him fair and square for the first time. He also felt as if Mr Smith were looking right through him. The sense of shock still tingled. It was as if he had blundered into an electric wire. He had no idea what had happened, and stood dumbfounded.

Mr Smith's gaze removed, became veiled again and vague. He said in an abstracted voice,

"I don't know that I—er—quite caught that name."

"Garstnet," said Oliver. "Mrs Garstnet."

Mr Smith removed the spectacles which he had pushed up on to his forehead and began to polish them with the white silk handkerchief.

"Surely a most unusual name?"

Oliver supposed it was, but he couldn't imagine why this should interest Mr Benbow Collingwood Horatio Smith. He said with controlled impatience,

"Mrs Garstnet was Rose Anne's nurse. She married the landlord of the Angel about ten years ago. Florrie is their only child."

Mr Smith continued to polish.

"Ah—Florrie—" he said. And then, "Can you—er—tell me—what is the colour of—er—Florrie's hair?"

Oliver was startled into a stare. If it hadn't been for that recent impression, he might have suspected a bat or two in the upper storey. He said in a surprised voice,

"Red, sir. I think you'd call it red—a sort of dark copper."

Mr Smith took out the shagreen case and put his spectacles away in it. He bestowed the case in one pocket and the white silk handkerchief in another. Then he said,

"That—er—puts the case in—er—quite a different light."

"Florrie's hair?"

"I think we must have a very serious talk, Captain Loddon," said Mr Smith.

Chapter Eight

A SERIOUS TALK implies a talk of some length. They returned to their chairs.

Oliver wondered what was coming next. He was pricked with curiosity, startled a little out of his strained mood of grief. Mr Benbow Smith lay back with his head tilted and his gaze upon the ceiling. He appeared to be plunged in thought. On his perch in the window Ananias in deep offence continued his toilet. At intervals he glanced over a humped shoulder and emitted a slight angry hiss. Oliver was leaning back too. He had become conscious of great fatigue.

Moments passed, minutes passed.

Then Mr Smith began to speak in a gentle, abstracted voice.

"Difficult to know—er—just where to begin. There are so many threads, and they are all tangled—some of them mere gossamer— some of them perhaps—er—figments of the imagination—more perhaps—er—straws to show which way the wind is blowing. My friend Colonel Garratt has—er—no use for gossamer, and no opinion of straws, so, you see, it is all very difficult."

Oliver saw nothing, so he said nothing. Mr Smith's gaze dropped upon him for a moment and then returned to the ceiling. In that moment Oliver received a strange reassurance. He waited, and the quiet voice went on.

"All very difficult, Captain Loddon. Well, I am going to make you a present of these difficult tangled threads. Do you—er—by any chance remember the Rennard case?"

"I remember the name. Years ago wasn't it—some kind of financial smash?"

"Ten years ago," said Mr Smith. "Amos Rennard was tried at the Old Bailey on charges of fraud and conspiracy. He had played the game of fraudulent company-promoting with—er—unprecedented ingenuity and success. When he crashed he brought down a great many people with him. There was a very notable scandal—in fact a number of very notable scandals. Firms of old standing were ruined, many—er—important people had been victimised. On the fourth day of the trial, when it was perfectly evident that the verdict would be guilty, and the sentence an extremely heavy one, Mr Amos Rennard made a most spectacular escape from custody. As he was being taken out to the police van, the crowd—there was a considerable crowd—got out of hand. The people in front were pushed forward, and the police were rushed by a band of roughs. The affair was utterly unexpected and only lasted a couple of minutes, but when it was over Amos Rennard was found to have disappeared. There was a hue and cry, but he was never recaptured. The police were able to trace him to Rillingham, where he had his own private aerodrome. He took off in a fast machine piloted by a mechanic named Leyland. The aeroplane crashed in the channel, and Leyland's body was recovered and identified. There was no trace of Amos Rennard." The slight hesitation had left Mr Smith's voice. "The police," he said, "considered that the case was closed. Amos Rennard was dead, and all that remained to be done was to clear up the—er—very considerable mess. I may say that it was never satisfactorily cleared up. Immense sums could not be accounted for. The official theory was, and—er—still is, that Rennard had placed very large sums in various foreign banks under a number of different aliases—quite a common proceeding for criminals—and that as he was dead, the sums would simply continue to lie there unclaimed. The possibility of his having escaped was not neglected by Scotland Yard, but it was soon abandoned. Er—yes, Captain Loddon, I am of course aware that you must be wondering what possible connection there can be between the Rennard case and the disappearance of Miss Rose Anne Carew. I do not know that there is any connection. I am—er—offering you a number of tangled threads. The Rennard case is one of them."

Oliver sat up frowning.

"But why—"

"Just a minute," said Mr Smith. "There are more threads. Amos Rennard was a widower with two sons. They were lads of sixteen and seventeen at the time of the smash. A year later they took out a fishing-boat from Woolacombe in Devon. It was their intention to try for conger. I do not know if you know the North Devon coast. Immediately beyond Woolacombe it becomes extremely dangerous. There is a promontory known as the Norte, with a village beyond called Morthoe. The boat was found smashed upon the rocks, but the bodies of the two boys were never recovered. This was not considered strange, as the currents are so strong."

"Well?" said Oliver.

Mr Smith raised his right hand.

"Amos Rennard disappears—his two sons disappear. He was an extremely affectionate father, in fact a man to whom family ties were very important indeed—perhaps a Scottish trait coming out. His mother was, I believe, a Highland woman, Jean Mackay. The red hair may have come into the family with her."

Oliver said, "Red hair?" Florrie's red hair... Sheer lunacy this— or—a floating—gossamer—thread—

Mr Smith gave a slight vague nod.

"They—er—called him the Old Fox—Rennard the Fox. He was as red as his name and very proud of it. Please bear that in mind, Captain Loddon—he was most inordinately proud of his red hair, and of the fact that his sons inherited it. I would like you to bear this in mind."

"I don't see where we're getting to, sir," said Oliver. Red hair and a financial scandal ten years old—what had it got to do with Rose Anne—with Rose Anne?

Mr Smith changed his position. He sat up a little more and looked past Oliver at about the level of his shoulder, the effect being that he was slightly less aloof. Ananias glanced over an out-stretched wing, said "Awk?" in an enquiring voice, and was rebuked. He began to groom his tail feathers with the air of one who has proffered an olive branch and been rebuffed.

"Another thread," said Mr Smith—"another—er—family tie. There was a nephew, a boy of about fourteen, a brother's son. The brother is dead. The widow apprenticed young Ernest Rennard as a mechanic at the Ledlington Motor Works. When he was eighteen he went on a day trip to Boulogne and fell overboard. That is to say, it was opined that he had fallen overboard. He was believed to have re-embarked at Boulogne, but he was nowhere to be found when the boat arrived at Folkestone. His ticket was never given up." There was a slight pause, after which he added, "His mother bore her—er—loss with admirable fortitude."

"You mean?" said Oliver.

Mr Smith raised a hand and let it fall again.

"I am merely offering you a thread. I do not ask you to attach any meaning to it—er—yet."

Ananias chanted suddenly on a loud raucous note:

"And we're bound for the Rio Grande."

"Ananias—*no!*" Mr Smith's tone was one of unusual firmness. Ananias cocked his head on one side and dropped to a croon:

"Way—way—way—
Way down Rio—

Mr Smith said "No!" and the croon petered out.

"Four threads," said Mr Smith. "Disappearance of Amos Rennard—disappearance of two young Rennards, his sons Mark and Philip—disappearance of Ernest Rennard, his nephew. These constitute the—er—first group of disappearances. We now come to the—er—second group, and it is here that I am on the—er—ground which my friend Colonel Garratt would describe as—er—legendary. He would not, I think, use that word, but it conveys his—er—meaning. He is the head of the Foreign Office Intelligence branch, and a man of great experience and ability. That being so, you are at liberty to consider that I have a—er—bee in my bonnet. Colonel Garratt would undoubtedly tell you so. He does not—er—mince his words."

"You were going to tell me about a second group of disappearances," said Oliver. He did not know where this was leading them, but through all his fatigue he was conscious of a quickening interest.

Mr Smith's gaze passed over him. He said,

"Yes—the second group. They date from about seven or eight years ago. Several thousand people disappear every year. It is, therefore, an extremely invidious task to take some of these disappearances and—er—group them. I cannot—er—prove that this grouping is other than arbitrary. I will begin with the year nineteen-twenty-eight. From the disappearances of that year I would—er—select that of the Reverend Luke Simpson. Mr Simpson was a young Non-conformist minister. He belonged to the denomination in which Amos Rennard had been brought up, and of which he was still a member at the time of the—er—crash. Mr Simpson had recently been appointed to the chapel at Ledlington. He was an entirely blameless young man and an extremely eloquent preacher. He was an orphan and a bachelor. He had no debts, no entanglements, and no vices. He went out for a walk along the Ledstow road on a foggy Sunday afternoon in November and was never seen again. In the December of the same year Dr Harold Spenlow disappeared from Sunningdale. He was a brilliant and rising young man on the eve of setting up in Harley Street. He had gone down to Sunningdale on a Saturday afternoon to play golf. He was in his usual spirits. He drove a friend as far as Virginia Water, and parted from him at the station at six-thirty. They had been talking of their round of golf, and had made an arrangement to play again on the following Saturday. Dr Spenlow drove away from the station and was never seen again. His car was found drawn up by the side of the road on Chobham Common. He might have been taking that way back to town, but it is highly improbable. Like Mr Simpson he had no debts or entanglements—in fact no discernible motive for a voluntary disappearance. Now, Captain Loddon, it would take too long to go into all the cases which I have—er—assigned to this second group, but it contains a good many—er—professional men—a clever architect, a chemist, a photographer, an engineer, an electrician. And all these men were young, of exceptional promise, and without close ties. None of them had any reason for suicide. There are other points of similarity. I have to some extent based my groupings on these points. During the year nineteen-thirty I observe a different type of disappearance. A number of young men in the building trade were missing. In some cases, the man was out of work, but in others he had walked out of a good job and never come back. There is one feature common to all these disappearances—in no case was the young man married or a widow's only son. All were good workmen and of a steady character—bricklayers, carpenters, and painters. In the last two or three years there has been a third class of disappearance—highly spectacular. You will doubtless remember the case of the Polish violinist, Josef Piglosiewiec. He had a very successful concert tour in this country in the autumn of nineteen-thirty-four. His last appearance was at the Town Hall at Reading, where he had an enthusiastic reception. Owing to the number of encores it was past half past five when he came out. A car had been ordered to drive him to Guildford, where he had a private engagement. It appeared afterwards that this car had been countermanded by someone speaking over the telephone and using M. Piglosiewiec's name, but at the time this was not known. When he left the hall a man in chauffeur's uniform touched his hat and indicated a waiting car. It was a dark and foggy night. M. Piglosiewiec got in and was driven away. Like Mr Simpson and Dr Spenlow he was never seen again. The car was never traced. The affair created a considerable sensation."

"Yes, I remember. The accompanist went too, didn't he?"

"Yes—they were together. He was a fellow Pole. Neither was traced. Then, later in that same year—in December, I think— Violette de Parme, the brilliant young French dancer, disappeared in Paris. She was rehearsing the—er—star role in a new ballet, and a great many people were very seriously inconvenienced, but public opinion declined to take the affair seriously. People shrugged their shoulders and—er—smiled. It was considered that the lady was amusing herself, and that she would return when it suited her to do so. When she did not return she was soon forgotten. During nineteen-thirty-five I find the disappearance of two crooners, a jazz pianist, a negro saxophonist, and half a dozen variety artists. None of them in the front rank, but all clever rising young men and women with the prizes of their profession before them—not failures, Captain Loddon, not elderly discouraged men and women, but young people well on the way to success."

Mr Smith had been speaking in an inexpressive monotone, but now he changed it. Leaning a little forward, he said with some emphasis,

"It was the cases relating to the—er virtuoso class which attracted my—er—particular attention. I found myself working backwards towards the Rennard case. The threads I followed often—er—broke, often tangled, but those points of—er—similarity to which I referred a little while ago recurred continually. I became convinced of the importance of the Rennard case."

"What do you mean by points of similarity?" said Oliver.

Mr Smith looked dreamily over his head.

"I will give you an instance. There is one recurrent factor. I have not been able to—er—trace it in all these cases, but in many of them it—er—recurs. I think I—er—Amos Rennard's predilection for red hair."

"You didn't say he had a predilection for red hair—you said he *had* red hair."

Mr Smith smiled.

"I seem to remember mentioning his pride in the fact that his sons had inherited the family hair. He had, I am told, an extreme partiality for the colour, and chose a wife from a family as red as his own. It would, in the circumstances, have been surprising if the sons had had hair of any other shade."

Florrie came up again into Oliver's mind—Florrie's red hair. What was he getting at? Where were they getting to? They weren't getting anywhere.

Mr Smith said in a measured voice,

"Two of Mr Simpson's parishioners remember to have seen him in the company of a red-haired lad. Their recollection is too vague to be of much value. One of them, a Miss Lucy Thorpe, says she passed Mr Simpson on the Ledstow road. She was on her bicycle, and went past quickly. She says the minister was standing by the side of the road talking to a young man who seemed to be in deep distress. He had his back to her, so she did not see his face, but she was positive he had red hair. She is not sure which day this was, but it was not far off the time Mr Simpson disappeared. It might have been the Friday, or the Saturday, or the Sunday—she doesn't know. A very poor witness. The other, a man, is even vaguer. He saw Mr Simpson walking with a red-haired man who was a stranger to Ledlington. It was some time that autumn. In the case of Dr

Spendlow the red hair motif is very slight. The friend whom he drove to Virginia Water station remembers that they passed a very pretty girl just after they turned off the London Road. She crossed the road, and they had to brake in order to avoid running her down. She was very young indeed, and she had a very fine head of red hair. In the case of the Polish violinist the motif does not appear, but Violette de Parme was credited with a red-haired lover—a young man, very handsome, very distinguished. Several of her friends had seen her with him, but no one knew his name, and Violette refused to gratify their—er—curiosity."

"Had she red hair herself?" said Oliver.

Mr Smith shook his head.

"Oh, no. Those who disappeared were not—er—selected on that account. I should not expect it except—I have not asked you what is the colour of Miss Carew's hair."

Oliver felt a kind of tingling horror. He said,

"Not red—it's not—I suppose there is some red in it. It's a lovely colour—a sort of dark chestnut."

A moment ago he had felt that they were not getting anywhere. Now, with a violent recoil, he had a glimpse of where all this was leading them. He cried out,

"What has this Rennard business to do with Rose Anne? What possible connection is there?"

Mr Smith looked at him gravely.

"I should have asked that question myself. I had not thought of any connection. I did not anticipate any connection until you mentioned a very uncommon name."

"What name?"

"The name of the people from whose house Miss Carew disappeared."

"Garstnet?" said Oliver. "For God's sake, sir!"

"I told you Amos Rennard was a widower, but I did not tell you his wife's name. It was Garstnet—Ellen Francis Garstnet."

Chapter Nine

IN A STUNNED silence Oliver tried to think what this might mean. There was a time that passed. Then Mr Smith was speaking again.

"This is naturally a shock to you, Captain Loddon. It was—er—a considerable shock to me. While you were telling me about Miss Carew's—er—disappearance I had no other thought than that her flight was a voluntary one. Some trouble had been—er—taken to make it appear that she had not gone alone. I was entirely deceived. Then you mentioned the name of a village—er—Hillick St Agnes. It arrested my attention by its similarity to a name which I have had occasion to—er—note in connection with the Rennard case. I will recur to this presently. I was about to ask you a certain question when you mentioned the name of Garstnet. When you further informed me that little Florrie Garstnet was the possessor of a very fine head of red hair, I became convinced that Miss Carew's disappearance could no longer be accounted a voluntary one. Now, Captain Loddon—this innkeeper—is his Christian name Matthew?"

"Yes, it is."

Mr Smith nodded.

"The father, also Matthew Garstnet, kept the Bell and Bucket inn on the Exeter turnpike road. He had it from his father, and he from his father again—all Matthews. Amos Rennard met his wife there. About the time of the smash her brother Matthew sold the goodwill of the inn and went away. He was then a widower with two daughters. When did he come to Hillick St Agnes?"

"About ten years ago. He married Rose Anne's nurse. Florrie is their only child."

"And the two elder daughters?"

"Fanny is married. Mabel is at home."

"I see—" said Mr Smith. His gaze became so absent-minded that Oliver wondered with impatience whether he ever really saw anything at all.

There was a considerable silence, and then he heard Mr Smith say in a dreamy voice,

"Mabel Garstnet—I wonder—er—about Mabel Garstnet. Is—she—er—by any chance of the same—er—general appearance as Miss Carew?"

"Certainly not!" said Oliver. And then, "What do you mean?"

Mr Smith did not look at him.

"Height—build—" he suggested.

"There are thousands of girls of approximately the same height and build."

"Just so, just so. You will remember, Captain Loddon, that you—er—raised the question as to why Miss Carew should walk or drive the three miles into Malling and proceed by train to Claypole, where she was met by a car, when that car might just as easily have fetched her from Hillick St Agnes, a distance of only six miles by road. The point was, I think, very well taken. It has occurred to me that there was perhaps a reason for this train journey. Mrs Garstnet says that Miss Carew left the inn wearing a bright green hat. It may have been considered desirable that this green hat should be—er—noticed and described. It may have been very important to establish the fact that Miss Carew—er—travelled from Malling to Claypole that night. We do not know whether she did or not. A young woman in a green hat travelled that way. She got out at Claypole, dropped an envelope addressed to Miss Carew, and drove away in a car which was waiting for her. A young woman in a green hat, Captain Loddon. Not—er—necessarily Miss Carew. Just—er—possibly Mabel Garstnet."

Oliver got up. This was not a case to him. It was Rose Anne—her safety, her danger. He said harshly,

"Is it any good going to the police with this? What are we going to do about it? If you're right—if you're right, sir,—we ought to get a search warrant—we ought to be searching the inn. But the Garstnets—she was Rose Anne's nurse—she was devoted to her—I can't believe it."

"I am—er—afraid that the police would not believe it either, Captain Loddon. I do not think that you would get your—er—search warrant. I fear you would only put a very powerful and—er—unscrupulous organization upon its guard. As to the question of Mrs Garstnet's affection for Miss Carew, I think one must remember the undoubted presence of such—er—under-currents as fear, self-interest, self-preservation, hope of—er—benefits to come. All these are factors to be—er—reckoned with. There is, for instance her own child—you say a delicate child. If the choice lay between Florrie and Miss Carew, what line would you expect Mrs Garstnet to take?"

"How could there be a choice like that?"

"I don't know—there might be. We do not know what pressure might be brought to bear on a woman in Mrs Garstnet's position. And she might not think that she was harming Miss Carew. She might—" Mr Smith's tone became dreamier than usual—"she might even—er—imagine that she was doing her a service."

Oliver spoke more harshly still.

"I'm not concerned with Mrs Garstnet's motives. If the Garstnets have touched Rose Anne, she can go to blazes with the rest of them. You say it's no good going to the police. Well, what do you expect me to do?"

"I expect you to do all that any man can do who is quite willing to take his life in his hands. Try the police if you wish, but I do not think that you will get them to listen to you. I have not been able to get them to listen to me. I think you will merely put the Rennards on their guard. I do not by any means suggest that you should do nothing. I am willing to place all my knowledge at your disposal. I am willing to help you in every way that I can. I believe that I can help you. Will you sit down and listen to what I have to say?"

Oliver sat down. He knew very well that it was no use going back to the police. They had their theory, and they would stick to it unless and until he could produce some strong rebutting evidence. At present the only evidence seemed to be Mrs Rennard's maiden name and Florrie's red hair. Impossible to believe that these things would make any impression upon the police.

Mr Smith leaned back against the worn leather of his chair.

"Now, Captain Loddon, I will tell you that I have taken it upon myself to pursue some—er—investigations. I was—er—interested. I—er—employed a private detective, a clever young man who had been invalided out of the police service. His name was Gilbert Wray. He collected a good deal of the information I have given you. Then he was found dead. He had had a fall over the edge of a quarry.

There were no suspicious circumstances. He was lame. It was his lameness which had necessitated his leaving the police. The slope above the quarry was covered with short grass slippery from rain. There was a verdict of death from misadventure. I—er—wished to continue my investigations. I was in a position to put my hand on a very able man—I will call him John Smith. He took on the work and collected some useful information. Then one day he wrote to me and said he was following up an important clue. He said, 'It's much too important to be risked on paper, but in case anything happens to me there are some rough notes in my despatch-case. I'm going up to Hillick St Anne tonight.'"

Mr Smith paused for a moment and leaned slightly forward.

"You see now why I was startled when you mentioned Hillick St Agnes. Perhaps you can tell me something about the connection between these two places."

"Well, Hillick St Anne isn't really a place at all. No one lives there now. I believe there are about three hundred people in Hillick St Agnes, but St Anne's died seventy or eighty years ago. It was just a mining village about half a mile farther up the hill."

"A mining village—" said Mr Smith in his vaguest tone.

"There are old lead workings. The vein petered out, and the St Anne's people moved down to St Agnes. You can still see the remains of some of the cottages."

"And the—er—shaft?" said Mr Smith.

"There is one quite close to Hillick St Agnes, but it has been filled in. Some child got lost there about forty years ago. It was really more of an entrance than a shaft. Anyway they filled it up, and I think they did the same at St Anne's, but I'm not sure."

There was a pause. Then Mr Smith said,

"John Smith wrote his letter to me and set out for Hillick St Anne's. There is nothing to show whether he got there or not. He was riding a bicycle. It was found badly damaged at the foot of a steep drop. John Smith was lying beside it with his neck broken. There is a hairpin bend in the road above and no parapet. The place was one at which such an accident could easily have happened. I am entirely convinced that John Smith was wilfully murdered, but there is not the least hope of being able to prove it."

"But this only happened ten days ago," said Oliver. "The village was full of talk about it. I know the place quite well. The road isn't much more than a track beyond Hillick St Agnes, and if he tried to ride his bicycle round those bends, well, it was suicide, not murder."

"Murder, I think, Captain Loddon. But, as I stated, it will, I fear, never be possible to prove it. As soon as I received the—er—news I made enquiries as to the despatch-case mentioned in John Smith's last letter. I was not altogether surprised to find that it had disappeared. The landlady, a very voluble and tearful person, assured my—er—representative that such a thing had never happened in her house before, and that she was quite at a loss to account for it. I, as I have told you, was not surprised. The Old Fox leaves very little to chance."

"Amos Rennard?"

"Amos Rennard."

"You think Amos Rennard murdered those two men of yours?"

"I haven't the very slightest doubt of it," said Mr Smith.

"But why, sir—why?"

"They were—er—enquiring into his affairs. I do not think that his affairs would bear enquiry. Or shall we put it another way? Shall we say that he is of the opinion that his affairs will not—er bear investigation?"

Oliver leaned forward.

"You say he was written off as dead, but you talk of him as if he were alive."

"I am quite sure he is alive," said Mr Smith.

"And you think he would do murder?"

"I am quite sure that he would do murder, Captain Loddon."

"Why?"

Mr Smith lifted one hand and let it fall again. "My—er—conviction is the—er—result of a series of investigations. It has—er—been built up from a number of small pieces of evidence. I cannot—er—convey it to you. I can only say that I have it."

"Well then, sir, you have this conviction that Amos Rennard is alive, and that he is not only capable of murder, but that he has murdered these two men. You also believe that he has kidnapped a number of people. You suggest a motive for the murders, but what motive could there possibly be for such wholesale kidnapping? What does he want with these people? What does he do with them? You must have some theory. What is it?"

Mr Smith was silent. He looked into the fire. A long, slow minute went by. Then he said,

"I will tell you my theory. You will not believe it—I have not been able to make anyone believe it. I am willing to tell it to you because it does not—er—matter to me at all whether you believe it or not. But if you do believe it, you may perhaps find it—er—helpful."

Oliver received a second impression of power and sureness. It is the man who is sure of himself who disregards the opinion of the world. To be sure is to have power. Mr Benbow Collingwood Horatio Smith was quite obviously content to let the world go by. Its belief or disbelief was nothing to him. But if he could help he would. He cared about that.

Oliver said, "That's very kind of you, sir. I'd like to know what you believe." He leaned forward. "Why should Amos Rennard kidnap Rose Anne?"

Ananias burst suddenly into the silence which followed the question:

"So fare you well, my pretty young gel,
For we're bound for the Rio Grande."

He was not very severely rebuked, and he continued to murmur, "Rio—Rio—Rio—" under his breath.

Mr Smith looked into the fire. The new log was burning now, the old log was dust. He said,

"I have not been able to—er—discover that any of the people whose disappearances I connect with Amos Rennard had red hair. I should not—er—have expected it. You will remember that I expressed this opinion when you asked if the dancer Violette de Parme had red hair. In my view of his character Amos Rennard would not desire to see his—er—family colour made—er—common. I have a great deal of—er—evidence to show his—er—pride in his red hair and his strong desire that it should be hereditary. He married a red-haired woman himself, and I think we may assume that he would bring considerable pressure to bear on his sons to do the same."

"You haven't answered my question," said Oliver, "you haven't attempted to answer it. What in heaven's name has all this to do with Rose Anne? Why should he kidnap Rose Anne?"

Mr Smith looked at him with compassion.

"How can I answer you, Captain Loddon?"

Oliver sprang up.

"I want a plain answer. What are you suggesting?"

"This," said Mr Smith in a tired voice. "If one of the Rennard sons had met Miss Carew and—er—fallen in love with her, it would seem from your own account that there is sufficient red in her hair to warrant the supposition that she might be an acceptable bride."

"Sir!"

"It is only a theory. There may be some other reason. But if my theory is correct, I do not think that you need give up hope of being in time to rescue Miss Carew. I really mean this, Captain Loddon. From every account which I have had of him, Amos Rennard has an extreme partiality for—er—ceremony. It was, I believe, a—er— passion with him. If there was to be a wedding in the family, he would make it an affair of state. His sense of family was, even in the old days, an inflated one. In what I believe to be his present circumstances it may very easily have become a monomania."

Oliver walked to the end of the room and back. He felt as if his head would burst. He passed the parrot's perch, and caught a murmur of "Way down Rio." Then, standing directly in front of Mr Benbow Smith, he said,

"What is it you believe about him? You say, 'his present circumstances.' What are they?"

Mr Smith looked past him.

"I believe that he has made himself a State. I believe that he rules over it, an absolute dictator. I believe that he recruits for it with the utmost ability and lack of scruple. I believe that he has made himself a king."

"Where?" said Oliver Loddon. There was sarcasm in his voice, but there was horror too. The thing was unbelievable—but what if it forced itself upon his belief? He said "Where?" again, and Mr Smith answered his question with another.

"Amos Rennard was not called the Old Fox for nothing. Where does the fox go when the—er—hounds press him too hard?"

The fox goes to earth. The words said themselves somewhere in Oliver's mind. He could not say them aloud. He had no power to say anything at all.

Chapter Ten

OLIVER WENT BACK to Hillick St Agnes. He took a late train which landed him at Malling just before eight in the morning. In the interval he had slept, his first real sleep for a week. His interview with Mr Benbow Collingwood Horatio Smith had done something to him, he did not quite know what. His dull hopelessness was gone and his conviction that he had lost Rose Anne for ever. He did not accept Mr Smith's amazing theories, but they had opened possibilities of action. They had in some inexplicable way broken the tension of his mind and eased its strain. He was stimulated to argument, scepticism, protest, but he was going back to Hillick St Agnes, and in the morning he would go up to Hillick St Anne's. If there was anything there for John Smith to find, why shouldn't Oliver Loddon find it too?

He sat in the train and thought of these things, and quite suddenly fell asleep.

He got to the Vicarage in time for breakfast. They had no news there. Elfreda looked as if she had not stopped crying all the week. Miss Hortensia sniffed and primmed her lips, and said she supposed it was modern to take your own way without the least consideration for other people's feelings.

Oliver had no temptation to linger when the meal was done. He set out on foot, and once clear of the village cut across the hillside to the track which ran up to St Anne's. Just before he joined it he could look down and see the place where John Smith had gone over the cliff. He frowned at it, and wondered. Impossible to believe that any man with a brain in his head would have ridden a bicycle down that shaly slope and round the double bend. If the man had really been murdered, it was Oliver's opinion that the murder had been over-staged. The place was just a bit too dangerous for the accident theory to ring true. People don't ride bicycles down that sort of track unless they are contemplating suicide.

He walked on to Hillick St Anne's, and found it a sufficiently depressing spot. There must have been twenty or thirty cottages built of the local stone. Not one had a roof, and only one a wall more than three feet high. In the one exception an end wall stood entire with a window in it. The rotting frame sagged away from the stone. The glass had been gone for half a century. All the people who had ever lived here were dead and gone, their houses a heap, the gardens coarse with weed. There was nothing for John Smith to see here, and nothing for Oliver Loddon. The rusted remains of some winding gear showed him where the shaft had been, but it was all crumbled away and overgrown. He looked over the edge, and saw a tangled mass of weed and bramble. He could not see if it was quite filled in, but there was no path here for a man to climb.

He stayed about half an hour, and having scrutinised every part of the ruin, came back again to Hillick St Agnes. Why should a man have been killed just to prevent him from seeing the things which Oliver had seen? It was blithering nonsense. John Smith hadn't been murdered at all. He had tripped over his own feet and carried his bicycle with him down the cliff because he had been a fool to try and take a bicycle along a path like this. But most people were fools anyway. This one had paid for his folly.

As he came into the village street, Mabel Garstnet emerged from the post office. At any other time Oliver would have lifted his cap and passed on. Mabel was one of those girls who needed no encouragement to catch your eye and giggle. Fanny, the one who was married, had been quite different, not so good looking but much nicer. He remembered her as a cheerful, friendly creature with a nice clear skin and amazing red hair. Mabel's was darker— and all at once it came to him that it was not so very much unlike Rose Anne's in shade. And it came to him that it might have been Mabel who had worn the green hat and travelled from Malling to

Claypole. He found himself staring at her, and under his gaze Mabel coloured, giggled, and rolled a fine pair of eyes.

"Oh, Captain Loddon—what a surprise! I'm sure we never thought we'd see you here again. Oh dear, I oughtn't to have said that—ever so stupid of me, I'm sure, but you know what I mean. I was ever so surprised, but that's not to say I wasn't pleased. There's pleasant surprises as well as the other sort, and I'm sure everyone'll be pleased to see you back."

Well, he'd let himself in for it by staring at her. He said "Thank you," and, to get away from the personal note, asked after Florrie.

"I hope she's all right again."

Mabel turned her shoulder and looked sideways at him. She had admired this pose on the screen and practised it nightly before her looking-glass.

"It's ever so nice of you to take an interest, I'm sure. Mother'll be ever so pleased when I tell her. She thinks a lot of you, Mother does."

"Florrie is all right then?"

"Oh, no, Captain Loddon, indeed she isn't, poor little thing. Mother's had to send her away."

So Florrie had been sent away. What did that mean? What should it mean? It did mean something. In a bored, casual tone he said,

"Oh, I'm sorry to hear that. Where has she gone?"

Mabel threw him a glance which said, "*Aren't* we on confidential terms!"

"Ever so bad her nerves were, poor Florrie—kept awake crying and carrying on something dreadful, you've really no idea, so Father, he said 'Give her a change and see what that'll do.' And I must be hurrying along, Captain Loddon, or whatever will everyone say—you and me standing talking in the street! Dreadful how people gossip in a village, isn't it?" She giggled, wriggled, and departed. He thought her one of the silliest girls he had ever met.

He went back to the Vicarage and got hold of Elfreda.

"Look here, did you know they had sent Florrie away?"

Elfreda stared. She had cried so much that her eyes were quite swollen up. She looked heavy and plain, and she sniffed continually.

"Oh, yes—Mrs Garstnet couldn't do anything with her. You know she was awfully, awfully fond of Rose Anne."

This had not been Oliver's impression. Florrie had struck coldly upon his mood of grief and strain. She had seemed to care more for the loss of her green hat than for the disappearance of her dear Miss Rose Anne. He said so, but Elfreda shook her head.

"That's because you don't understand children. They're like that, but it doesn't mean they don't care. She just didn't realise that Rose Anne had gone, but afterwards Mrs Garstnet told me herself that she didn't know what to do with her."

Oliver frowned.

"Would you send a delicate child away to strangers if it was really in such a state of distress?"

"I don't know. The Garstnets did."

"Where did they send her?"

"I don't know that either. Why do you want to know?"

"I want to see Florrie. I want to ask her some questions."

"Oh, well, Mrs Garstnet would tell you."

"I don't want to ask Mrs Garstnet—I don't want her to know."

Elfreda's eyes opened as wide as their swollen lids would allow.

"Oh, well, I could find out easily enough—at the post office. Mrs Tweddell loves talking about how often everyone's relations write to them and all that sort of thing. I could go and buy some stamps at once if you'd like me to."

Oliver walked up and down the garden and smoked a cigarette.

It took Elfreda twenty minutes to buy her stamps, but she returned full of information.

"Just fancy—Fanny Garstnet has only written home twice since she was married—isn't it queer? They weren't married here, you know, and Mrs Tweddell says people in the village are wondering whether she was ever properly married at all. Only two letters in a year—it does seem odd, doesn't it? And Mrs Garstnet never writes to her, and Mrs Tweddell says—"

"Did you find out about Florrie?"

"Of course I did. She's with an aunt at Oakham."

"Where's that?"

"About ten miles from here, over the hills. It sounds rather a grand address—The Place, Oakham. Mrs Garstnet has written three times already. She just worships Florrie, you know. And, Oliver, Aunt Hortensia told me to find out tactfully how long you are going to stay, because of joints and things like that. She's had a row with Midstock, you know, so she's getting everything from Malling, and it's driving us all to drink. Her temper was quite bad enough before."

"I'm not staying," said Oliver abruptly.

He departed after a most uncomfortable lunch. Elfreda was visibly cheered by his presence, and was therefore singled out for such a snubbing from Miss Hortensia that she burst into tears and left the table. The rest of the meal was a monologue on the subject of modern girls, during which Oliver ate in silence and the Reverend James Carew neither ate nor uttered.

Chapter Eleven

OAKHAM HAS NO station of its own. There is a halt at Sindleby, which is three miles away by road but only a mile by the footpath which runs steeply up to Gibbet Gap and as steeply down again on the other side.

Oliver took the footpath. He was surprised at his own determination to see Florrie. He seemed to himself to be catching at straws and pursuing shadows, yet his determination to see Florrie remained.

He found Oakham a pretty, tiny village standing in the circle of oaks to which it owed its name. They were very old trees, relics perhaps of the forest which had once clothed these slopes. The cottages were old too—picturesque, insanitary, and about to fall beneath the weight of years. The church had an archaic look. It stood upon rising ground with its grave-stones about it. The Place was beyond the church, an old stone house with a high stone wall, and within the wall a dense screen of trees.

At the inn, he learned that the Place was empty. There was a caretaker there, a Mrs Edwards. This explained the grand address.

Mrs Edwards had been there a long time, "getting on eight years"—a very quiet woman, but she had a little girl staying with her just now, her niece, a poor peaked little thing. A lot of red hair she had too. Oliver took his opportunity.

"Who—Mrs Edwards?" he said, and got a shake of the head.

Mrs Edwards' hair had been grey when she came to the Place getting on eight years ago. A woman of fifty she'd be or thereabouts. No, it was the little girl's hair that was red, and to be sure, it must be in the family, because Mrs Edwards' son that come to visit her once in a way, he had red hair, and the wife he brought along the last time he came, she'd got hair like a Guy Fawkes bonfire so she had, so 'twas bound to be in the family.

Oliver walked up past the church, and wondered about Mrs Edwards. Florrie's aunt might be Mrs Garstnet's sister or she might not. She might be a married Garstnet, or she might be only an aunt by marriage. He supposed that the Mrs Rennard whose son had gone overboard between Boulogne and Folkestone and of whom all trace had afterwards been lost—well he supposed this Mrs Rennard would be aunt to Florrie Garstnet in some sort of way—a very far-fetched sort of way. He couldn't think why it should have come into his head, but there it was, and there he was bolstering it up with the thought that this remote village and this long deserted house would be an excellent hiding-place for a woman who wanted to disappear. Only why should Mrs Rennard want to disappear, and what possible reason was there for identifying her with Mrs Edwards?

He came round the corner of the churchyard upon stone pillars green with age and heavily overshadowed by low, sweeping boughs still brown with autumn leaf. Between the pillars hung an iron gate, a rigid affair like a section of park paling, and on the other side of it, holding to the bars and peering at him through them, was little Florrie Garstnet. He was irresistibly reminded of a monkey in a cage, perhaps because he had always thought that there was something of the monkey about Florrie. She had the long hands— the long, pale hands. Her small face was pressed against the bars. Her eyes regarded him in just the kind of stare with which an animal peers from its cage world into yours.

He said, "Hullo, Florrie!" and Florrie just went on staring.

He came right up to the gate, tried it, and found it locked, as indeed he had expected. Florrie edged away from him sideways, still holding to the bars. When she had reached the left-hand pillar she turned a little so as to face him and said,

"You can't come in."

Oliver laughed shortly.

"I don't know that I want to come in."

Florrie said, "Ooh!" and then "What do you want?" Oliver leaned on the gate. He was fond of children, and as a rule they were fond of him. What he wanted was to win this odd little creature's confidence and get her to talk. If you could get a child started, there was as a rule no stopping it. But the very urgency of his need was a handicap. A child is as quick as an animal to sense fear or pain. As he hesitated, Florrie struck in.

"I know why you've come."

"Do you?" He managed a friendly smile.

Florrie nodded so vehemently that her copper curls came bobbing down across her eyes. She took a hand from the bars to push them back.

"Yes, I do. And Mother said I wasn't to say a word to no one, no matter how they arst me."

Oliver's heart gave a jump. He said as carelessly as he could,

"You haven't told me why I've come. I don't believe you know."

Florrie nodded again.

"Yes, I do. And Mother said—"

"All right then—you know why I've come. Now suppose you tell me."

Florrie stared at him.

"My auntie says people did ought to mind their own business."

"Well, this is my business," said Oliver. "Do you like chocolates?"

Florrie said, "Ooh!" Her mouth opened a little way, her eyes brightened.

Oliver produced from his coat pocket a most exciting bright blue box tied up with silver ribbon. He held it in one hand, balancing it, and looked at Florrie.

Florrie looked at the blue and silver box.

"Ooh! Is it for me?"

"Perhaps. I just want you to tell me about the night Miss Rose Anne came to see you."

"My mother said I wasn't to tell no one," said Florrie.

Oliver had a qualm. If it had been for anything except Rose Anne's safety, Rose Anne's life... He said quickly,

"What did she say you weren't to tell?"

Florrie looked sideways.

"I wasn't to tell nobody nothin' about Miss Rose Anne."

"Florrie," said Oliver, "if you loved someone very much, and they went right away and you didn't know where they were, or what they were doing, or whether they would ever come back, wouldn't it make you very unhappy?"

Florrie stared.

"Fanny went away," she said.

"Your sister Fanny?"

She nodded.

"But I wasn't unhappy—I didn't cry."

"You know Miss Rose Anne has gone away?"

A scared look went over her face. Then she said in a sort of sing-song,

"Miss Rose Anne's run off with a gentleman, and I expect they're married by now."

"Florrie—who told you that?"

She stared without speaking.

"Someone taught you to say that. Who was it?"

No answer.

"Florrie, when you saw Miss Rose Anne, did she tell you she was going away?"

The red curls were shaken.

"What *did* she say to you? You were ill, weren't you?"

The curls were shaken again.

"I wasn't ill. I cried."

"Why did you cry?"

"For Miss Rose Anne to come."

"And when she came, what did she say to you?"

"She put her arms round me, and she said, 'Oh, Florrie, don't cry,' same like she always does."

"And then?"

"Then I stopped."

"And then?"

"She sat on my bed and sang to me."

"What did she sing?"

"She sang 'Pussy's a Lady.' But I'm not really a baby now. Shall I sing it to you?"

She piped up in an untuneful little voice:

"Hush-a-bye, baby. Pussy's a lady.

Mousie's all gone to the Mill.

If baby won't cry, she'll come back by-and-bye.

So hush-a-bye, baby, lie still and don't cry."

"Now can I have my chocolates, please?"

"In a minute," said Oliver.

Why should Florrie have been forbidden this innocent recital? Why should she have been sent away to prevent her telling people that Rose Anne had sat on her bed and sung her a nursery rhyme? There was more—there must be more. Or was he merely mare's-nesting? He said as gently as he could,

"And then, Florrie—after she had sung to you?"

"She kissed me good night, and she said, 'Bye-bye blessings,' like she always does, and she went away, and now can I have my chocolates, please?"

"Not just yet. You say she went away. Do you mean she went out of the room?"

"Yes—out of my room."

"And you didn't see her again?"

Florrie shook her head. The curls played bob across her face.

"Did you hear her ask for the green hat that she gave you?"

Florrie shook her head again. Her little peaked face began to quiver.

"It was my hat."

"And Miss Rose Anne borrowed it?"

Florrie shook her head again.

"It was my hat. She give it me for my very own. She give it me for my own self. It was my green hat."

"Who took it away?" said Oliver.

She gave him a secret look.

"Florrie—who took it away?"

"It wasn't her hat—it was mine," said Florrie in a small, determined voice.

"Who took it away from you, Florrie?"

He got another of those looks—wary, secret—and something else—was it afraid? He said,

"Miss Rose Anne wouldn't want to take your hat away, Florrie." And all at once Florrie's tongue was loosed. She began to pant as if she had been running, and to sob, and to say between those panting breaths,

"She didn't—she didn't—oh, she never! She give it me—for my very own—and it was my hat—and—Mabel—didn't—ought—to have—took—it—away!"

"Mabel?" said Oliver. "Mabel took the green hat?"

Florrie stopped crying, stopped half way through a sob, looked sideways, her eyes still bright with tears.

"I didn't say Mabel—I didn't say nothin'."

"You said Mabel took your hat."

Florrie gave a rending sniff, caught her breath, and recited in the same sing-song as before.

"Mabel came into my room and took my green hat to borrow for Miss Rose Anne that was going to run away with a gentleman and I expect they're married by now."

"That's what your mother told you to say if anyone asked you?"

Florrie nodded.

"And now may I have my chocolates, please?"

Oliver opened the box.

"I'm not going to give them to you all at once. Look here, you can have six, and if you want some more you must come back for them. See?"

"When shall I come?"

"Tomorrow morning—ten o'clock."

She shook her head.

"There's school."

"Two o'clock?"

She nodded.

"But I don't know nothin' about Miss Rose Anne," she said.

Chapter Twelve

OLIVER WALKED back to Sindleby. Had he learned anything from Florrie, or hadn't he? Had she anything to tell, or was he merely wasting time that was the most precious thing in the world? As he went over his interview with Florrie, the thing that stuck out a mile was that the child had been coached. She had been taught the answers to two of his questions, and when they came along she was pat with her sing-song. Someone had taught her to say, "Miss Rose Anne's run off with a gentleman," and someone had tried to explain why Mabel Garstnet had come into her room and taken the green hat—explain, or explain away. When Florrie, between violent sobs, accused Mabel of taking her hat, Oliver was convinced that she was speaking the truth. When she recited an explanation of why the hat had been taken, she was saying a piece that had been put into her mouth. It was a very good piece, and the explanation was a completely plausible one. But why had Florrie been coached with it, and why had Florrie been sent away from home? The more he thought about it the less he liked it. If there is only the truth to tell, why should it need so much dressing up? What need is there to coach a child unless the child knows something which must at all costs be covered up or explained away?

Mabel—and the green hat—Rose Anne's own hat which she had given to Florrie, and which Mabel had borrowed on that horrible evening. Mabel Garstnet had borrowed it, and Florrie had been taught to say she had borrowed it for Rose Anne. Mabel—Mabel and the green hat... She might, so far as description went, have passed for Rose Anne in a half light. They were of the same height, the same build. Mabel in the green hat might quite easily have been so described that the description would fit Rose Anne Carew, especially if she had worn Rose Anne's coat.

This last thought stabbed into his mind like a knife. He had not known that he could feel a keener pain, but this struck very deep. Rose Anne stripped, Rose Anne defenceless—and in whose hands?

His own extreme helplessness filled him with despair. How could he go to the police and say, "I believe Rose Anne has been kidnapped by Amos Rennard, who has been officially dead for ten years. So far as I know, he never saw her or heard of her, but his late wife's brother married her old nurse, and they keep the inn at Hillick St Agnes. I want a search warrant." Well, he supposed that, if he was sufficiently insistent, the search warrant might be forthcoming. Did he even dream that Rose Anne was hidden away at the Angel, where the house had been full to overflowing with her relations? He didn't think it, he didn't even dream it. Then what would a search warrant effect? Mr Smith's words came back—"I fear you would only put a very powerful and unscrupulous organization upon its guard." Did he believe in this organization? He didn't know. Did he believe in Amos Rennard? He didn't know that either. He only knew with a deadly certainty that Rose Anne would never have left them all of her own free will. She was either dead, or she was under some restraint. If there was the slightest chance that one of Mr Smith's tangled threads might lead him to her, what did it matter what he believed or didn't believe? There was no chance that he dared neglect.

He went back to Hillick St Agnes, and put up at the Angel. They gave him his old room and a very good welcome. Matthew Garstnet was bluff and hearty, and his wife kind and attentive.

"You know we've had to send our little Florrie away, sir. Poor child, she took on so, and we thought a little change—she was that fond of dear Miss Rose Anne."

Oliver hadn't noticed Florrie being very fond of anyone except herself. He tried a cast.

"Where have you sent her, Mrs Garstnet?" Now—if she lied—if she lied—

But Mrs Garstnet did not lie. She said in a grateful voice,

"I'm sure it's so very kind of you to take an interest, sir. It's my husband's sister-in-law she's gone to, and most kind of her it is, but the doctor we took her to—you know we took her to a London doctor a matter of a few weeks ago—he said most particular that it would be the best thing in the world for her to be away from home for a bit, only I couldn't bring myself to it, not till now, Florrie being my only one. And I'm sure it's most kind of you, sir, to ask when you're in such trouble yourself—I suppose you've no news, sir?" Her voice broke on the question, and when Oliver had said, "None," she wiped her eyes and hurried from the room. It seemed to him impossible to suspect her. She was so entirely the concerned family servant, the doting, anxious mother. And on that he got an echo of Mr Smith's hesitant, cultured voice saying, "If the choice lay between Florrie and Miss Carew, what line would you expect Mrs Garstnet to take?" How could there be a choice? He had no answer to that. He had no answer to the hungry clamour of questions which filled his mind.

Later he went over to see Elfreda. She took him into the schoolroom after ten minutes or so of difficult conversation with Miss Hortensia and James Carew.

Elfreda banged the schoolroom door.

"I've got to stay here for another week because Daddy won't be back till then. Isn't it grim? I think aunts ought to be abolished—don't you—except some of them are rather lambs really. I think Aunt Hortensia must have been frightfully badly brought up. I mean, why doesn't Uncle James tell her to hold her tongue and go to Timbuctoo?"

"Elfreda, I want to talk to you," said Oliver. "I suppose you really knew Rose Anne better than anyone else."

The tears rushed into Elfreda's eyes.

"I suppose I did—I mean I do—I mean I'll do anything for her."

"Well, I want you to tell me something—which might be a help—in looking for her." The words stuck and wouldn't come out. It wasn't so easy to ask questions about Rose Anne.

Elfreda stared.

"But I can't think of anything, Oliver."

"Wait a minute—I haven't asked you yet. Did she ever speak of anyone—any man? Was there anyone who—who—anyone with red hair?"

"Oliver, she wasn't like that. She wouldn't—she didn't—I mean we just laughed about him. It wasn't the least bit serious—I know it wasn't."

Oliver's heart gave a thump. He said quickly,

"Then there was someone—with red hair?"

"But it wasn't anything in the world. Oliver, it wasn't—she wouldn't."

He put his hand down hard on her shoulder.

"I know she wouldn't, but I want you to tell me about it all the same—everything, please."

Elfreda blinked, and blinked away a couple of tears.

"It was when she was staying with us last summer in the Isle of Wight. There was a big fancy dress dance—you know, we wanted you to come, and you couldn't get leave—and Rose Anne went as a white rose. Nannie made the dress. She really did it beautifully—all big cut-out petals. It was a lovely dress."

"When you say 'Nannie,' whom do you mean?"

"Oh, Mrs Garstnet. Rose Anne still calls her Nannie. Well, she really did look like an angel in the dress, and she had a great success. And about half way through I saw her dancing with the most frightfully good looking man—he really was. He was all in white too, a kind of eighteenth-century court dress, only instead of a powdered wig he had his own red hair."

Oliver's hand closed on her shoulder. She cried out,

"Oh, you're hurting me!"

"I'm sorry." He took his hand away. "You said this man had red hair—"

"Too marvellous—the dark red sort. And as soon as I got the chance I asked Rose Anne who he was, and she said, 'Well, he calls himself Mr Octavian.' So I said, 'How do you mean, he calls himself?' and she laughed and said, 'Well, he says he's the Rosenkavalier.' And of course the Rosenkavalier's name was Octavian, and I suppose what he meant was that he was Rose Anne's cavalier— anyhow that's how he behaved. But it was only a joke to her—it really was, Oliver, because we all teased her about it, and she just said that their dresses went together and their steps went together, so why shouldn't she?"

"Why shouldn't she what?"

"Oh, dance with him. And she did, quite a lot, and I don't blame her, because he was easily the best dancer in the room."

Oliver said, "Go on," and got a frank, surprised look.

"But there isn't anything—there really isn't."

"Do you mean she didn't see him again?"

"No, of course she didn't. He just blew in and blew out again. I think he must have come ashore from one of the yachts. The amusing thing was that everybody thought he was with somebody else's party. Personally I believe he gate-crashed—he looked as if he'd got nerve enough to do anything. He told Rose Anne he had come there to dance with her, and as a matter of fact he didn't dance with anyone else—at least I don't think he did—and we ragged her about it. And then he just faded away, and no one ever saw him again."

"You're sure Rose Anne didn't see him again—quite sure, Elfreda?"

"Oh, yes, I'm quite sure."

"Or hear from him?"

"No, I'm sure she didn't." She paused, hesitated, and said in a dragging voice, "Unless—there was that telephone call."

"Which telephone call?"

Elfreda gulped.

"You know—the one they've all badgered me sick about."

"Yes. Just run over it again, will you?"

"Well, you know—it was that afternoon, and you were in the garden. We were talking about people flirting, and you said she didn't need to flirt. You said, 'She just looks, and we fall down flat,' and she got up—and went away—and looked round over her shoulder and said, 'Did anyone call up for me?' "

Oliver said, "Yes, I remember." Had Rose Anne at that moment remembered someone, not Oliver, who had fallen down and worshipped at a single look? Had she expected a call, a message? She had looked over her shoulder and smiled. Of what had she been thinking—of *whom* had she been thinking?

Elfreda swallowed a choking sob.

"Then, when Aunt Hortensia was scolding me about the wreaths, there was that telephone call—and it's no use anyone asking me any more about it, because the only single thing I know is that there was a man on the line, and he said, 'Is that Miss Carew?' And I said, 'Miss Hortensia Carew—or Miss Rose Anne Carew?' and he said, 'Miss Rose Carew.' So of course I thought it wasn't anyone who knew her, because no one ever calls her Rose. And I said she couldn't come, could I take a message? And he said no, I couldn't, and it didn't matter and he'd ring again—only he didn't."

Oliver stared straight in front of him. "No one ever calls her Rose."... But the Rosenkavalier—the Cavalier of the Rose—who had met her, seen her, just that once in her white rose dress—he might think of her as the Rose, and ask for her as Miss Rose Carew...

With an abrupt movement he turned away. It was all madness. Because they had nothing to go upon, they were trying out of this nothing to make something—to force a shape upon it—clothe it with empty theories. Could he ask himself or anyone else to believe that this man, this red-headed gate-crasher who had met Rose Anne once four months ago, had only to ring her up on her wedding eve for her to throw everything to the winds and go to him? No, he hadn't ever rung her up. He had said he would ring again, but there had been no second call—only Mrs Garstnet telephoning from the Angel begging Rose Anne to come to Florrie—to Florrie.

He turned back to Elfreda.

"Thank you very much, my dear. I shouldn't cry any more if I were you—it doesn't do any good."

He went back to the Angel. It was in his mind that he must go to London and see Mr Benbow Smith again. He had left his car in a Malling garage, so he would have to make an early start if he meant to do the three miles on foot and catch the 8.20. He would miss his appointment with Florrie, but that couldn't be helped. He doubted very much whether there was anything to be got out of her. Anyhow she could wait.

He went in by the back way, because he didn't want to meet anyone. Anyone really meant Mabel Garstnet, who was showing a tendency to linger in his path and giggle at him. The back way was the one he had commonly taken when coming in from the garage. It led past the kitchen, and the parlour used by the Garstnets. It occurred to him that he might knock on the parlour door and notify his early start. He was just about to do so, when he saw that the door was ajar, and it went through his mind that this probably meant the room was empty. And then, hard upon that, he heard the sound of a sob. He had just come from one weeping woman, and he was in no mood for another. He drew back as Matthew Garstnet said "Shut up!" on a low growl of anger.

Well, if there was a family row going on, he had better go up to his room and ring. But before he could pass he heard Mrs Garstnet say in a choking voice, "It's her face—the way she looked at me. Oh, I can't get it out of my mind!"

This time Matthew Garstnet swore. He may have struck her as well, for she cried out sharply. He certainly struck the door, for it slammed to not a foot from Oliver's shoulder.

He went softly up to his room, and thought about what he had heard.

Chapter Thirteen

"Now I wonder what the young man will have to say," said Mr Smith. "What do you think about it all, Ananias?"

The grey parrot sidled along his perch, bobbing a sleek head and repeating in a cooing whisper the words of a curse learned long ago in unregenerate foc'sle days. It was now forbidden, and Mr Smith reproved him, tempering his rebuke with a gentle ruffling of the feathers at the side of the bobbing head.

"No—no, Ananias! I have no doubt that you are perfectly right, but you must restrain yourself. And I was not asking you whether you thought there had been—er—dirty work, because I am tolerably sure on that point myself."

The parrot lifted an arched claw and stepped off the perch on to his master's wrist.

"Now you know, Ananias, I am expecting Captain Loddon. He said two o'clock, and it will be two o'clock in exactly half a minute from now, so you had better get back to your perch."

The sound of the front door bell and the sound of the parrot's loud "Awk!" of protest came together. Then the door opened and Miller was announcing Captain Loddon. Mr Smith advanced to greet him with the parrot still upon his wrist. Perhaps he wished to see how Ananias and his guest would react to one another. He had had visitors before now who had blenched visibly at grasping a hand within reach of such a very sharp beak. Mr Smith's opinion of them had not been enhanced by this behaviour. It had occasionally been confirmed.

Oliver took the hand that was offered to him.

"How do you do, sir? It is very good of you to see me." His eyes went to Ananias. "That's a very fine parrot."

Mr Smith nodded.

"Shake hands, Ananias."

And coyly sidling, Ananias stretched out a cold, horny claw. There were some very loud "Awks" when he was put back on his perch again. When they had subsided, Mr Smith waved Oliver to a chair and took the one beside him.

"Well, Captain Loddon, what did you find at Hillick St Anne's?"

"Nothing," said Oliver—"nothing at all. It's just a completely derelict village. There isn't one house with a roof on it or a place where you could hide a cat."

"And did you—er—come to tell me that?"

Oliver said bluntly, "No, I didn't. Look here, sir, I haven't really got anything to tell you at all, but I want to tell it to you all the same. There's nothing that would be any good to the police, but—"

"You may tell me anything you like, Captain Loddon."

"It's so little," said Oliver in a restless voice—"and what there is can be so easily explained away."

"Yes?" said Mr Smith on an enquiring note.

From his perch Ananias regarded them with disfavour. He had an urge to make himself felt. Rising upon his toes, he flapped his wings and declaimed:

"Three jolly admirals all of a row,
Collingwood, Nelson, and bold Benbow."

"No—no—*no!*" said Mr Smith.

His voice meant business. The wings dropped again, the rose-coloured linings were hidden. Ananias sulked.

"Well, Captain Loddon?" said Mr Smith as if there had been no interruption.

"I've got three or four—well, scraps," said Oliver. "First of all, sir, I'd like to tell you that no one who wasn't a lunatic, and suicidal at that, would have attempted to ride a bicycle down that track from Hillick St Anne's. I shouldn't have thought anyone would even try to wheel a bicycle on it, but if your man was wheeling one, he might have tripped and gone over the edge. On the other hand it doesn't seem very likely."

Mr Smith nodded gently.

"And that—er—leaves us just where we were before."

"Well then, I went back to St Agnes, and Mabel Garstnet told me her mother had had to send Florrie away. She said they couldn't do anything with her, she was so upset. She didn't say where they'd sent her, but Elfreda found out from the post office."

"Elfreda?" murmured Mr Smith.

"Elfreda Moore. She's a first cousin, and she was Rose Anne's greatest friend. She was going to be her bridesmaid."

"Yes? Go on."

"She found out that Florrie was at Oakham. It's only about ten miles away, so I went there. It's right off the map—just cottages, and a few outlying farms, and one big house they call The Place. It's empty, and Florrie's there with the caretaker, who is Matthew Garstnet's sister-in-law. Mrs Garstnet told me that."

"You asked her?"

"Not about Oakham. She doesn't know that I've been there, or that I know where Florrie is. I just asked after the child, and she thanked me and said Florrie had been so upset about—about Rose Anne that they had sent her away to a sister-in-law of Matthew's, but she didn't say where, and I didn't say anything more."

"That was wise. Go on, Captain Loddon."

"Well, I saw Florrie. She was down at the gate. But I didn't get anything out of her—at least I don't know whether I did or not. She's frightened about something. She's been coached. She said a piece about Rose Anne."

"Yes?"

"She said, 'Miss Rose Anne's run away with a gentleman and I expect they're married by now.' Regular parrot stuff—you could tell she'd been coached. And when I thought she'd let something out, she did the same stunt again."

"What did she—er—let out?"

"She said her sister Mabel came into her room and took the green hat, the one Rose Anne is supposed to have borrowed to go away in. She said it was her hat and Mabel had no business to take it, and then she got scared and let off a piece about Mabel having borrowed the hat for Miss Rose Anne, and I thought she'd been taught that too. Only you see, sir, if she got an idea in her head about Mabel taking the hat, it would be quite natural for Mrs Garstnet to explain to her that she had taken it for Rose Anne—if she really had."

"Yes," said Mr Smith—"suggestive, but—er—inconclusive."

"Well, that's all about Florrie," said Oliver. "I was going to see her again this afternoon, but I thought I'd like to talk to you first."

"Just one moment, Captain Loddon. I am—er—wondering about this sister-in-law of Matthew Garstnet's. You see, he has no such—er—relation."

"You're sure about that?"

Mr Smith nodded.

"The present Mrs Garstnet may have a sister, or sisters—I do not know. But she would not allude to a relative of her own as her husband's sister-in-law."

Oliver agreed.

"The first Mrs Garstnet had no near relations. Matthew Garstnet had no brothers. He had one sister who married Amos Rennard. Strictly speaking, he could not be described as having a sister-in-law, but people are not always exact. His sister Mrs Rennard certainly had a sister-in-law, the widow of her husband's brother Joseph. I—er—mentioned her to you before. It was her son Ernest who was reported missing on a pleasure trip between Boulogne and Folkestone. I told you that I had not been able to trace her whereabouts. I find myself wondering whether she is—er—residing at Oakham."

"The name," said Oliver, "is Edwards—Mrs Edwards. She keeps herself to herself."

"Yes," said Mr Smith, "I think that very likely. I should certainly go back and see Florrie again—Florrie and—er—Mrs Edwards. If she is—or was—Mrs Joseph Rennard, she has a noticeable red scar upon her left cheek. I should certainly go back if I were you."

Oliver assented. He had no great hope of Florrie, and he was not at all interested in Mrs Joseph Rennard. He said a trifle abruptly,

"Well, sir, there are two other things, and I'll tell you the last one first, because it's about the Garstnets too. It's just something I heard Mrs Garstnet say when I came in last night. I was passing their parlour—as a matter of fact I was just going to ask her to have me called early—when I heard her crying. And then she said, 'It's her face—the way she looked at me. Oh, I can't get it out of my mind!' And then Matthew Garstnet swore at her and banged the door—it had been a little bit open. It—it's nothing of course—or—it might be something. She may have been talking about Florrie, or... It's just another of the things which you can easily explain away, but it seems to me that there are rather a lot of them. Then there's something else. After you told me about the Rennards I thought—mind you, I don't feel that I can accept your theory about Amos Rennard—I don't feel as if the thing was possible—all those disappearances—but I'm ready to follow up anything, any shadow, because if I don't do something I shall go mad. So I thought I'd follow up what you said about the red hair, and I asked Elfreda about it."

"Yes?" said Mr Smith. "Yes?"

Oliver told him about the fancy dress ball and the red-haired Cavalier of the Rose whose dress had matched Rose Anne's.

"And who," said Mr Smith, "may I ask—who would be in a position to know what Miss Carew's dress was going to be? That is an important point. Also you have not told me what it was, Captain Loddon."

"She went as a rose," said Oliver shortly—"as a white rose. Mrs Garstnet made the dress." His heart broke in him at the thought of Rose Anne in her white rose dress.

There was a little silence. Then Mr Benbow Smith said quietly,

"I think that is very important indeed. Miss Carew goes to the ball as a rose, and there appears, to match her, Octavian, the Rosenkavalier. It could hardly be—a coincidence."

Oliver said in a low, hard voice,

"He came there to dance with her. He told her so."

"Miss Moore is your informant?"

"Yes, Elfreda Moore. Rose Anne was staying with them."

"Then you will please tell me everything that Miss Moore told you. Do not leave anything out."

Oliver repeated Elfreda's story as he had heard it from her the night before.

When he had finished, Mr Smith got up out of his chair and drifted over to the window, where he stood looking out upon the street. It was a grey November afternoon of drizzle and mist. The streets were wet, umbrellas were up, and the rainy sky seemed to touch the roof-line of the tall houses over the way. Not much to look at, yet Mr Smith looked long and earnestly before he came back to the hearth, walking slowly. That he should have passed Ananias twice without so much as a glance was in itself a matter of some significance. But Oliver Loddon was not to know this. He got up because Mr Benbow Smith did not return to his chair but came to rest upon the hearth, looking down into the fire in very much the same manner as he had looked out into the mist. When he spoke, it was to repeat his former words.

"I think that this is very important. You say that you do not accept my—er—theory, but you have told me a story which fits that theory in a very remarkable manner. Can you believe for a moment that it was chance which brought this Octavian to the ball in a dress which was the complement of Miss Carew's? Why, he even told her that it was no accident when he said that he had come there to dance with her."

Oliver bit his lip.

"Does a man meet a girl at a dance in July, make no further attempt to see her, and then carry her off by force in November?"

Mr Smith looked up for a moment and then down again. "A normal man, acting within the limits of—er—civilization and under the restraints of civilized law—er—no. An abnormal man, freed from these restraints and knowing no law but his own desires—er—yes, Captain Loddon."

"And you believe that we are up against such a man?"

Mr Smith looked at him again.

"We are dealing with—er—facts, not beliefs. It is a fact that Miss Carew has disappeared. You have said that you are—er—absolutely certain that her disappearance was not a voluntary one."

"I am absolutely certain."

"You have known her—a long time?"

"I met her three years ago. I fell in love with her then. I didn't ask her to marry me, because I was on the point of going abroad, and she was—very young. I came back just over a year ago. We became engaged in May."

"So that, taking into account the—er—exigencies of your profession, you have, I suppose, only seen her at intervals and not for very long at a time. Are you quite sure that she did not meet this man again?"

Oliver said, "No." And then, "Don't misunderstand me, sir. I am quite sure of her—her loyalty. I am quite sure that she did not go of her own free will."

Mr Smith said, "I see—" He looked down into the fire. After a while he went on speaking. "You asked me a question a little while ago. I did not answer it, but if you wish, I will answer it now."

Oliver said, "Yes?"

"You asked me if I believed in the man I had—er—described to you. I do. I believe him to be one of the Rennards, probably one of Amos Rennard's sons. There were two of them, you know, and I have never believed that they were really drowned. The Old Fox is said to have been a very affectionate father, and an affectionate father would naturally wish to have his sons with him. At the time of the—er—accident they were sixteen and seventeen years of age. They would be twenty-six and twenty-seven today. Both had red hair. Their names were Mark and Philip. Philip is said to have been a remarkably handsome and talented youth. His hair was of an unusual copper shade. I incline to think that he may be the—er— Rosenkavalier. And now I would like to leave the—er—region of fact and—er—theorise for a while. The Octavian of that fancy dress ball was someone who knew Miss Carew was going to be there and what her dress was going to be. Do you know whether she was making a long stay in the Isle of Wight, or did she go down just for the dance?"

"Just for the dance. I was asked too, but I couldn't get leave."

"And she brought her dress with her—the dress that Mrs Garstnet had made. How could a chance—er—gate-crasher have known anything at all about Miss Carew and her dress? But Mrs Garstnet's nephew might have known—Philip Rennard might have known. You say that you fell in love with Miss Carew at first sight. Another man may have done the same thing."

"Sir!"

"One moment, Captain Loddon. If this man was one who for ten years had known no law, no curb, no restraint, is it difficult to suppose that he might endeavour to take what he coveted?"

"You are asking me to believe that this man has kidnapped Rose Anne?"

"You have just reiterated your conviction that her disappearance was not voluntary."

At the other end of the room Ananias could be heard muttering, "Pretty young gel—pretty young gel—pretty young gel—" Then, on a loud squawking note,

"So fare ye well, my pretty young gel,
 For we're bound for the Rio Grande."

"No, Ananias!"

Ananias dropped to a murmur of "Rio—Rio—Rio—"

"Think, Captain Loddon—" Mr Smith's voice took on a rare quality of earnestness—"think. If she did not go voluntarily, who was responsible? Someone. Think whether the drama of a disappearance on her wedding eve would not appeal to the flamboyant young man who had walked uninvited into that ball-room in the Isle of Wight and presented himself to Miss Carew as the Cavalier of the Rose. Then think again—Philip Rennard is the Garstnets' nephew, the son of Matthew Garstnet's sister. Miss Carew runs over to the Garstnets' house to see their child and—disappears. The Garstnets say that she left the inn shortly before seven o'clock. I say there is no proof that she ever left it at all."

"They would never have dared to keep her there," said Oliver. "The house was full. We were all there—Russell and I—all the relatives."

"Yes—yes—that would be—er—very good camouflage, you know. And they would not have kept her there. They would have—er—conveyed her as soon as possible to a place of safety."

Oliver said, "Where?"

"That," said Mr Smith, "is what we have to find out."

Chapter Fourteen

THE LETTER came next day.

Oliver went back to Hillick St Agnes, and arrived late at the Angel. He left his car in its Malling garage and walked the three hilly miles for the sake of the exercise. He had been in trains and houses all day long, and the keen air was grateful to him. He slept that night in the fumed-oak bed which had replaced the archaic four-poster he remembered on a previous visit. He slept, but the sleep was full of dreams in which he searched for Rose Anne. She was there but he could not see her, within reach but he could not touch her, round the next bend of the road, lost in a shadow, whirled from him by a sudden and terrifying wind, a wind that shook the world and left him dizzy and blind.

Blind—in his dream he was blind—no glimmer of light, no faintest ray, only a thick, pressing darkness, heavy upon his eyes, upon his thoughts, upon his heart. There was no Rose Anne. She had never been, and the dream he had had of her was done, most utterly done. She was gone, and he would never find her again, because there was no Rose Anne. The sweat of anguish broke on him, and suddenly he heard her voice. It came sweetly into his dream and broke it. She said his name, just the one word, just "Oliver," and the darkness broke. He came up into the light again, and saw a grey dawn strike between the curtains.

The dawn is not so very early in November, and he had no mind for sleep again. He wanted in any case to make an early start. He was going to St Anne's again, he was going to see Florrie. What he had to do was to get enough evidence to put before the police, enough evidence to support Mr Smith's theories or to explode them. He had to get facts, and he had to get them quickly.

He dressed, breakfasted, and walked over to the Vicarage. He could not leave Hillick St Agnes without seeing the Carews and Elfreda. And just as he came up to the gate, he met the postman coming away. He was an old man and very friendly. He beamed at Oliver and said,

"Morning, Captain, morning. There's a letter for 'ee, and I hope it's got good news in it, that I do."

Oliver went in, and found James Carew in the hall with a letter in his hand. He was staring at it, and when Oliver spoke to him he stared at him too. Then he took him by the arm and into the study, and when the door was shut he put the letter into his hand. It was addressed in Rose Anne's writing to

CAPTAIN OLIVER LODDON
AT THE VICARAGE,
HILLICK ST. AGNES

and it had the Paris postmark.

Oliver walked to the window, opened the letter, and read at the top of the sheet his own name.

His own name. Just Oliver. That was how it had been in his dream—just his own name. But this was different. There was no sweetness here. The letter said:

"OLIVER,

You must please try and forgive me. When it came to the point I could not marry you. It would not have been fair to either of us, because, you see, I love someone else—"

There was a queer little blot here, as if the pen had stopped and so stayed until the ink ran down and made a round black bead. The letter went on, as Rose Anne must have gone on after making that blot:

"I love someone else, and I am going to marry him as soon as it can be arranged. Give my love to them all and say I

shall write again when I am married. Tell them not to worry.
I can't give any address, because I don't know how long we
are going to be anywhere.

"ROSE ANNE."

Oliver read the letter twice. Then he turned round and put it
into James Carew's hand.

Later he was walking down the hill towards Malling. He
wanted to get away from tears, and grieved, shocked faces, and
Miss Hortensia's moralities. He had planned to go to Malling, but
when he was half way there it occurred to him that there was no
longer any reason for his plan. Since Rose Anne was in Paris with
the man she loved, he had all the facts he needed, and the theories
of Mr Benbow Collingwood Horatio Smith were blown sky-high
and scattered to the breeze. There was nothing for him to do in
Malling or anywhere. His dream came back upon him, cold and
staring. *There was no Rose Anne.*

He had been so sure of her. He would have pledged himself to
the uttermost for her loyalty and her love, and she had not had so
much of either as to come to him and say, "I've made a mistake. Let
me go." He had loved an imagination of his own heart. There was
no Rose Anne.

Half way down the hill he walked into blinding rain—very cold
rain, driven before a stinging wind. He was wet through by the time
he reached Malling. He had only a small suit-case with him, but
there was a larger one in the car, and the car was in the garage of the
Rose and Crown. He had no notion what he was going to do next,
but it seemed a good idea to put on dry clothes.

When he looked back on this time, he thought his mind had
quite stopped feeling anything at all. His body was cold and wet. It
had a most extraordinary sensation of fatigue. It wanted to lie down
somewhere and sleep for a very long time.

He came into the Rose and Crown, and asked for a room, and
a fire, and his suit-case, and a hot drink. After that he was not very
clear about anything, but he must have peeled off his wet things
and got into bed, because when he awoke, there he was, the clothes
hanging on a chair and an empty tumbler on the small table at his

side. He did not know how long he had been asleep, but he thought it must have been a long time, because the light had changed a good deal. He sat up, and found that he was in his dressing-gown. His watch told him that it was three o'clock. After all, he had only slept five hours. It must have been about ten o'clock when he reached Malling.

He got out of bed, and found the fire burning brightly. Someone must have been in to make it up. All the King's horses and all the King's men might have clattered through the room without rousing him, so deeply had he been drowned in sleep. He stood by the fire now and remembered what lay on the other side of that sleep. Everything seemed a long way off and a long time ago. It was in another life that he had been going to marry Rose Anne. Her letter was an old story.

The letter—where was it? He had put it in his pocket. He ought to have burnt it at once. He frowned at his own carelessness, because his wet clothes might very easily have been taken down to be dried. Odd that he couldn't remember undressing. He wondered if the drink they had given him had been double strength, and he wondered whether he had hung his clothes to the fire himself, or whether someone had picked them up from where he had dropped them in a sodden heap. He reached for the coat, felt in the nearest pocket, and found the letter safe. The pocket was still clammy, the letter in its envelope quite damp. He took it out, because before he burned it he must read it again. It was the only one of Rose Anne's letters he would ever read again. They must all be burned, but he would not read them first—only this one he must read before it went into the fire. He still felt nothing. He could say her name and handle her letter without any feeling at all. It was rather like having a limb that had gone to sleep. Better get through with the business before it woke up and began to hurt like the devil.

The sheet stuck when he would have unfolded it, and he leaned down to hold it in the warmth over the flame. Paper dries very quickly. The letter gave off a little cloud of moisture and crackled stiffly as he opened it.

His first thought was that the paper had smudged with the wet. There were brown marks between the lines of writing. And then he saw that the brown marks were writing too. His heart beat hard against his side as he held the paper close to the fire again and watched the brown deepen as the heat caught it. The black writing said, "You must please try and forgive me." The brown writing stumbled beneath it, and said,

"My darling, I love you—I do love you. Don't believe this letter. There will never be anyone but you."

Between all the lines the brown writing went, trembling and uneven—Rose Anne's writing, shaken with the haste and fear which were shaking her as she wrote. It went as far as the blot and broke off there. He held the page to the fire again. There must be more. There must be something to tell him where she was and how he could reach her. The paper scorched his hand. He drew it back and scanned it eagerly, but there was no more brown writing after the blot, only the black writing with its lie that Rose Anne loved someone else. He went on trying, as if an intensity of effort could compel unwritten words from the paper, but it was no use, the words were not there. All the numb places in him had come awake and were crying out in anguish for those unwritten words—for any one of them which would give the slightest clue as to how he could reach and help Rose Anne.

There was a time when the sense of her helplessness and his impotence broke him down. What had they done to her to make her write that lying letter? He had a picture of her, gentle and lovely, moving amongst the flowers in her father's garden, and the sun on her hair. It broke him down.

Chapter Fifteen

SOMEONE CAME knocking at the door. He went to it, shot the bolt, and spoke through the panel.

"What is it?"

A girl's hesitating voice murmured something about the fire and faded out.

Oliver switched on the light, went over to the window, and drew the curtains. He occupied himself in putting his things together.

He took particular pains over folding the clothes which had been wet, and whilst he moved about these tasks he was getting a grip on himself again. When he had shut the suit-case down he was ready to think. He was to decide what he would do next, and it seemed to him that it must be one of three things.

He must take Rose Anne's letter to the police,
or
He must take it on to Mr Smith,
or
He must follow the broken threads which he already held in the hope that one of them would bring him to Rose Anne.

He sat down on the side of the bed and weighed these courses one against the other.

If he took the letter to the police, the search for Rose Anne would be transferred to the other side of the Channel. It occurred to him with a good deal of force that the letter might very well have been written—no, dictated—with this very object. He did not believe Rose Anne was in Paris. He did not believe she had been taken out of England. He did not believe a word of the lying letter. He tried to imagine what the police would make of it, and he thought that it would be quite possible for them to read it as the effusion of a girl who, having eloped, was now in two minds about it and inclined to regret what she had done. He thought they would be very likely to read it that way.

He decided that he could not spare the time to go and see Mr Smith. He could not incur the danger of being too late. With those piteous, straggling words calling him, he must attempt whatever could be attempted—now, without any delay at all.

It was the third course. Well, where was it going to take him? His first impulse was to return to Hillick St Agnes and force a search of the Angel. These old inns had cellars. Why had they not been searched already? The Garstnets must co-operate, or plead guilty. This impulse spent itself. This crime was not the work of some boggling amateur. Mr Smith's words recurred again: "You will place an unscrupulous and powerful organization on its guard."

He was admitting now that he believed in such an organization. Rose Anne was not the first to disappear, and of the others not one had ever come back. It was not a mere matter of Matthew Garstnet and his wife, and the cellars at the Angel. There were dark depths— His thoughts broke off in horror.

What then?

There came into his mind Oakham—small, remote Oakham, with its one big house lying deserted behind stone walls, and Matthew Garstnet's sister-in-law keeping a solitary guard there— Matthew Garstnet's sister-in-law who might be Amos Rennard's sister-in-law too. Sparks went to and fro in his mind. Florrie had been sent there to be out of the way. What if Rose Anne had been sent there too? It was only ten miles by road.

The sparks flashed. A plan began to form. Hillick St Agnes must be assured that the letter had done its work. If anyone was watching for his reactions, they had better be given something to keep them quiet.

He went down to the telephone-box and rang up James Carew. He actually got Elfreda, and as she would do equally well, he informed her that he was returning to London, and that his club would find him there till further notice. The Angel got the same message, and here it was Mrs Garstnet who answered. She went away in the middle and fetched pencil and paper to write down the address, although she had had it when he was away before. He thought he heard a muffled whispering—somewhere. Was she asking Matthew what she should say? He wondered. And then there she was, rather curiously out of breath.

"Oh, yes, Captain Loddon—I'm quite ready now."

He dictated the address, and when she had written it down she said,

"Then you won't be coming back again?"

"I don't think so. There isn't anything to come back for—now."

He heard her catch her breath. There was a sound as if the receiver had knocked against something.

"I'm sure I can't say, sir, how very sorry we are." Her voice broke. "Miss Elfreda—tells me—there was—a letter."

Oliver said, "Yes." He paused, then added, "She's in France. She's going to marry someone else. Good-bye, Mrs Garstnet."

He came out of the box with a sense of satisfaction. He thought he had done that well. By closing-time tonight every man, woman, child, cat, dog, and mouse in Hillick St Agnes would know that Miss Rose Anne had run away to France to be married, and that Captain Oliver Loddon was taking himself and his disappointment to London and wouldn't be coming this way again.

He wondered in his own mind whether he had really said good-bye to it all, and then winced away from the thought, because if he found Rose Anne—if he found Rose Anne—they would come this way not once but many times. An old song began to ring in his head:

"Bring back, bring back,
 Bring back my bonnie to me, to me.
 Bring back, bring back,
 Oh, bring back my bonnie to me."

As he paid his bill and had his cases brought down, the tune was still there, and when he drove away it fitted itself to the purr of the engine. What was he going to do next? Drive to Oakham. Well then, what was he going to do with his car when he got there? There are times when a car can be a nuisance. To leave it in Malling was to inform all and sundry that he was expecting to return. To put it up in Oakham was to advertise his arrival there. He would very much have preferred to come hiking over the hill. In the end he decided to drive to Oakham and leave the car somewhere off the road whilst he had a look at The Place. It would be late enough by the time he got there, and dark within another half hour.

He drove on through the grey weather, and wondered if it would turn to fog. It was cold enough and still enough. No rain now, but trees and hedgerows black and dripping, and the light failing momentarily. In his mind the pretty, plaintive old tune took words again:

"Last night as I lay on my pillow,
 Last night as I lay on my bed,
 Last night as I lay on my pillow,

I dreamed that my bonnie was dead.
Bring back, bring back,
Bring back my bonnie to me, to me.
Bring back, bring back,
Oh, bring back my bonnie to me."

Chapter Sixteen

HE RAN the car up under one of the oak trees which stretched out their branches over the wall. They were still in leaf and made a perfect screen. He was twenty yards off the road, and it would be dark in less than no time.

He made easy work of getting over the wall, with the car to give him a leg up and a convenient bough to take hold of, but once he was over he was not so sure what he was going to do next. Something very unpleasant about skulking round someone else's house in the dark. It really was quite dark in here under the trees. He began to move along on the inside of the wall in the direction of the gates. He had a torch in his pocket, but it must be kept for emergencies. Meanwhile he thought his best plan would be to follow the drive.

It was very neglected. Bushes crowded in upon it, and trees hung low overhead. What had once been gravel was now moss, and very slippery. It seemed to be a long drive. And then all at once he was out of it, with some light still coming from the sky. There was enough anyhow to mark the difference between sky and house. The Place stood right in his way, a great square block, all black, with no light showing anywhere. He supposed that Mrs Edwards kept to the kitchen premises, and he had a not unattractive picture of a glowing fire and a teapot on the hob. This homely image increased his discomfort. He was probably the world's champion fool, wandering round spying on a caretaker and a child. Anyhow, fool or not, he was going to have a stab at it.

He crossed the front of the house, grateful for the moss, which deadened the sound of his feet, and came to steps which led up on to a terrace. The terrace ran round two sides. There was not a gleam of light anywhere. The ground must have risen, for it took only a couple of steps to bring him down from the terrace at its far end. He came to a wall with an arch in it, and a wooden door which swung in when he pushed it. There were flagstones under foot, and the feeling of being in an enclosed place. He made out that he was in some kind of court or yard. All right, in about half a minute he would probably run into a water-butt, tread on a rake, or take a header over a chopping-block. Back yards were always littered with booby traps, especially old back yards like this. The place fairly reeked of neglect and decay. The flagstones were slimy, and there was a smell of fungus and rotting wood.

Well, what on earth was he going to do now? His idea that Rose Anne might be here seemed fantastic in the extreme, but even the most fantastic imagination boggled at the suggestion that this back yard held any clue to her whereabouts. No, if there was any such clue, it would be within the house itself. He picked his way back to the arch and regained the terrace. If he was going to do any breaking and entering, he had better get as far away from the kitchen as possible.

He reached what he took to be the main front, and considered ways and means. Hopeless to expect such a godsend as an open window. Caretakers don't leave windows open after dark on a cold November night. It is easy enough to get into a house if you don't mind breaking a window, but he would have preferred that his breaking should not be of this technical kind. Also he had a horrid feeling that there might be shutters inside the glass.

In the end he had to chance it. He selected the smallest window, wrapped his coat about a hand, and stove it in. The falling glass made a most daunting noise, and he remembered too late that all the best burglars use brown paper spread with treacle. Anyhow there was nothing to be done about it now except wait and see whether Mrs Edwards had heard the crash. He consoled himself with the reflection that it was very improbable, as the kitchen was miles away and his guilty conscience had certainly made the most of the noise.

After letting the longest ten minutes on record tick away he enlarged the hole gingerly and climbed in. He had thought of it as dark outside, but it was a great deal darker here, in a room whose size he could not guess. He had expected it to be small, but it didn't feel small. There was a wooden floor under his feet, but his second step took him bumping into a large upholstered chair, and he realised that the room was furnished. It was quite irrational, but it surprised him. He had somehow expected the deserted house to be empty too—just a shell, with bare, echoing walls and stripped rooms.

Nothing stripped about this room anyhow. You couldn't move a foot without barging into something—the glass front of a cabinet, a damp billowing sofa back, the sharp corner of a chair. And there were tables everywhere. He was no sooner clear of one than he was into another. Lord—what a room! He supposed it was the drawing-room, and his little window a mere accessory to the big ones he had rejected, but it felt more like a jumble sale. By good luck he came to the door without knocking anything over, and opened it a crack at a time upon a pitch-dark hall. There was no sound of any kind, no stirring of the cold air, no point of light. The place smelt of cobwebs, and mildew, and dust. It occurred to him that Mrs Edwards was no housewife.

He left the shelter of the doorway with reluctance, and found the hall large, and bare of any covering under foot. A board creaked, and the sound seemed to ring through the house. Then his groping hand touched the newel-post of the stair, and as it did so he saw it, and the line of the baluster running upwards, and the other newel the width of the stair away.

Light—light shining down, very faint, but getting brighter. And not only light, but sound—the sound of footsteps somewhere overhead, coming nearer. The stair ran up some dozen steps and divided, going away to right and left of a wide landing. The light came from the left. Someone was coming along a corridor towards the stair, someone who was carrying a light, and who almost certainly intended coming down into the hall. The light was like candle-light, very faint and flickering. It served to show him where he was—too far from the half open drawing-room door to get back to safety there. He retreated along the side of the staircase as the footsteps began to descend.

Every properly constituted stair has a cupboard under it—but of course the door might be on the other side. He had begun to think that his luck had petered out, when his hand found the knob it was feeling for. A door swung in, and Oliver followed it, praying inwardly that the place wasn't a receptacle for empty bottles or old fireirons. It seemed to be quite empty. He left the door ajar, and waited for the steps and the candle-light to go past overhead.

That was just where they were now, right over his head, only instead of passing they stood still, and there came to him through the chink which he had left the most undoubted sound of a sob. And then Florrie's voice whispering, "I don't want to—oh, I don't want to."

It surely wasn't Florrie with the candle. He had only just time to feel surprised, when another voice said, "Come along now, there's a duck—Auntie'll be waiting tea."

Oliver pricked up his ears, because he knew this voice very well. If he wasn't mistaken, this was Fanny Garstnet. That is to say, she had been Fanny Garstnet, and as he didn't know her married name, he thought of her as Fanny Garstnet still. She had rather a nice voice, round and full, with none of Mabel's finnicky accent. Well, here was Fanny trying to pacify her little half-sister, and to judge by the bump he had just heard, Florrie had sat herself down on the stair and was refusing to budge.

"Oh, Florrie, you promised you'd be a good girl."

He heard another of those sobs.

"If I'm good, you'll go away."

"Oh, Florrie!"

Florrie drummed with her heels on the stair.

"When I'm good, I don't get nothin'. I cried and cried and cried, and then you came. You wouldn't have come if I hadn't. If I'm good, you'll go away again." Then, with a change of voice, "Oh, Fanny, I *want* you."

From the sounds above him Oliver thought that Fanny had sat down on the stair and taken Florrie on her lap. It sounded as if she were rocking her to and fro.

"Flo darling, I can't stay. I'm—wanted."

"Who wants you? I want you too. Is it—Miss Rose Anne?"

The name came in a whisper. The stair creaked. Fanny Garstnet said in a hurry,

"Florrie, whatever put such a thing in your head? You mustn't say things like that."

She made a movement to get up, but Florrie began to sob again.

"If you go away, I'll cry, an' I'll go on cryin' all day, an' all night, an' all of next day till you come back again, so I will."

"Oh, come along with you and have your tea! There's Ernie waiting for his, and me waiting for mine, and Auntie waiting for hers."

Florrie gave another sob.

"I don't care about Auntie—I don't care about whether she gets any tea."

"Well, if that isn't naughty!" said Fanny, but he heard the sound of a kiss. And then quite suddenly there was a torrent of sobs, and Florrie's voice gasping out,

"Don't let her—open—the black hole an'—put me in! Oh, Fanny, don't let her!"

Fanny was kissing the child and petting her.

"Why, duck, of course she wouldn't. Whatever made you think of such a thing?"

But Florrie's sobs increased.

"Oh, Fanny—she said it—she did. I cried—in the night—like I told you—an' she came—an' I said it was acause of the black hole—what I saw—up home—an' I thought they'd put Miss Rose Anne in it—an' she said if I didn't hold my noise—I'd find there was a—black hole here too—an' if I ever said a word—about Miss Rose Anne—they'd put me in it—oh, *Fanny*!"

Horror touched Oliver's heart with ice. The broken words and their possible meaning came into his mind and froze there. A black hole—a grave—Rose Anne—hidden away—buried... The dreadful word murder spoke itself in the cold places of thought.

Then Fanny Garstnet's kind, comfortable voice:

"Honey duck, hush! What are you talking about? Miss Rose Anne isn't in any black hole."

"Oh, Fanny—but she is! I seed the hole! That's what—frightened me—only—I wouldn't—never say. Whisper an' I'll—tell you—" Her voice went away and he lost it. That is, he lost the words. The faint sound of sobbing breath went on, and every now and then he heard Fanny say,

"No, lovey," and, "You didn't," and then again, "Oh lord, Florrie, don't you say such things!"

Oliver stood in the dark and listened. He knew now why he had come to this house. It was to hear a death sentence—not his, but Rose Anne's. And faintly among his frozen thoughts there rang the tune which had been ringing there for hours: "Last night as I lay on my pillow... I dreamed that my Bonnie was dead—"

Overhead Florrie's frightened murmurings rose again into words.

"She said—she'd put me—in it—Oh, Fanny, she did!"

"Well, she won't," said Fanny Garstnet with decision. "What an idea, to be sure! Now look here, honey duck, can you keep a secret?"

Florrie gave a great sob.

"Yes—I can."

There was the sound of a kiss.

"You always was a close little thing. If I tell you something, will you promise you won't tell no one at all—never? Cross your heart?"

"Cross my heart, I won't, Fanny."

"Well then, come close and I'll whisper."

Oliver pushed back the cupboard door and leaned out. He'd got to hear what Fanny Garstnet was whispering now—he'd got to hear it. He heard her say close to Florrie's ear,

"So you see it's nothing to be frightened of—only a door. Why, Ernie and I come through it regular. We come through it today. It's nothing to be frightened of, honey duck, only you mustn't say a word, not ever."

Florrie gave a deep satisfied sigh.

"You're sure it's not a hole?"

"Ssh—ssh! Don't you talk about it—ever! *Mind!*"

"Cross my heart, I won't," said Florrie. She gave another sigh. Then, in a voice that was suddenly brisk and interested, "Will there be currant buns for tea?"

Oliver heard Fanny laugh.

"Well, his mother does make them for Ernie, but he'll eat them all if we don't hurry. Ernie's terrible hard on buns."

Chapter Seventeen

THE STEPS died away and the light faded. Oliver came out of his cupboard and leaned against the wall of the stair. His mind, which had been cold with horror, was suddenly alive and alert again, with every thought centred on what he had just heard Fanny Garstnet say.

He went over it word by word. Florrie had seen something that frightened her at Hillick St Agnes, and that was why she had been sent away. She had seen what she called a black hole. Perhaps this was the original fright which had started the screaming fits that only Rose Anne could pacify. Perhaps there had been more than one occasion when she had seen something which she wasn't meant to see. She described it as a black hole. She associated it with Rose Anne. And she was dithering with terror because Mrs Edwards— he supposed that "Auntie" was Mrs Edwards—had threatened her with the same thing here. And then Fanny—he did his best to recall exactly what it was that Fanny had said... She was trying to comfort Florrie, and she said, "It's nothing to be frightened of—only a door." And she was speaking about Florrie's black hole. There was nothing else she could have been speaking about. And it wasn't a hole at all—it was a door. A door—where? Florrie's original fright had been at Hillick St Agnes, and the black hole that had frightened her—the black hole which was really a door—must be in the Angel, because Florrie had said "Up home." But then Fanny said, "Ernie and I come through it regular. We come through it today." Ernie and Fanny were here at Oakham Place, and Mrs Edwards, who was "Auntie" and seemed to be Ernie's mother, had threatened Florrie with a black hole here. It must be this black hole which was the door through which Ernie and Fanny came "regular."

Ernie... One of Mr Smith's ravelled threads came suddenly to his hand, because Ernie was short for Ernest, and Amos Rennard's nephew, the young motor mechanic who had disappeared between Boulogne and Folkestone, was Ernest Rennard, and he was a widowed mother's son. Another thread fell into place beside the first. Mr Smith had suggested that Matthew Garstnet's sister-in-law

Mrs Edwards was really not so much *his* sister-in-law as his sister Mrs Amos Rennard's sister-in-law, widow of the Old Fox's brother Joseph and mother of the disappearing Ernest. This would make her "Auntie" to Fanny and Florrie Garstnet in a family as clannish as the Rennards were supposed to be. Had Mr Smith mesmerised him with all these threads which kept leading to the Rennards? Or was it true that it was the Rennards who had carried off Rose Anne? He didn't know. He only knew that something had brought him to this house, and that behind reason and argument lay the deep instinct that here there was a clue to what had become of her. Florrie's black hole—Fanny's door—must be found. A hole—into what? A door—leading where? He was here to discover these things, and it came to him that two men had died on this trail already, and that Mr Smith had not been speaking lightly when he had said, "I expect you to do all that any man can do who is willing to take his life in his hands." It seemed ridiculous to think of extreme and imminent danger in a house tenanted by a couple of women and a child, but he had a stronger conviction of it than he had ever had before in his life. Ernie—to be sure there was Ernie, the young motor mechanic with a passion for currant buns. He did not sound at all sinister, but the sense of danger persisted and increased. He arrived at the certainty that he would need all his resource and all his courage if he was to find Rose Anne.

He moved across the hall very cautiously in the direction in which the light had disappeared.

There was a door in the far corner, difficult to find because the walls were panelled and the door felt like any other panel until his hand encountered the knob. He need not have been so careful about opening it, as there was a baize swing-door on the other side of it, horrid and damp to the touch and the stuff peeling off. What sort of place was this, and what except hard necessity would drive any mother to send a delicate, nervous child here? He guessed at some strong compulsion, and wondered the less that Mrs Garstnet should have betrayed Rose Anne.

He came through the baize door into a flagged passage. This was one of those houses with a perfect warren of small rooms, cupboards, and what are usually described as offices. He looked into one in which a very old smell of apples still lingered, and another which was vaguely haunted by an aroma of boot-blacking, and presently he located the kitchen. A line of light showed under the door, and there was quite a cheerful buzz of conversation. There was the sound of a young man's hearty laughter and Fanny's voice chiming in. A pleasant time was being had by all over Mrs Joseph Rennard's currant buns—if she *was* Mrs Joseph Rennard, and not plain Mrs Edwards entertaining son and daughter-in-law in all innocence. Anything less sinister than this family tea-party could hardly be imagined.

Oliver laid his ear to the crack of the door and heard the hearty young man say,

"Well, Mother, your buns just about take the cake, and I can't say fairer than that—can I, Florrie?"

"Please I'd like another," said Florrie with her mouth full.

Then there was more talk of buns, Ernie counting up how many Florrie had eaten, and Fanny saying it was a shame. And then he heard Mrs Edwards' voice for the first time, and it was a voice which matched with the damp, gloomy house, and not with the cheerful family tea—a dreary voice and hard behind its dreariness. Yet the words were what any mother might have said.

"I wish you didn't have to go back, Ernie."

Ernie went on being hearty.

"Well, I'm not going till I finish my tea anyway."

Oliver cast about in his mind for a plan. If Ernie and Fanny, who might be Ernest and Fanny Rennard, were going back as soon as they had had their tea, it was imperative that he should know how they went. If it was through the door which had frightened Florrie, and which she described as a black hole, then he must without fail follow them. Because he was more and more sure that Rose Anne had been taken through such a door. From behind it had come her piteous message written between the lines of a dictated letter.

He retreated into the apple-room and waited for what would happen next. With the door a little ajar he could watch the line of light from the kitchen and hear the voices come and go, though he could only catch a word here and there. The black hole wouldn't be in the kitchen, he felt quite sure about that. It was much more likely to be in one of the cellars, and wherever it was, Florrie would be got out of the way before it was used. He had found a flight of steps leading to the cellar floor at the end of the flagged passage. He could do nothing now but listen and wait.

He had to wait for nearly an hour before the kitchen door opened. He was a witness of an affectionate farewell between Ernie and an austere middle-aged woman with iron grey hair and a mouth like a trap. He looked for a scar on the cheek, but the light was behind her and he couldn't be sure. Ernie certainly did not get his looks from her. He was a very large young man with a pleasant freckled face and hair of a particularly cheerful shade of red. Oliver stopped believing in a Mrs Edwards. Ernie's hair finished that. Here was an authentic Rennard, and, if he was any judge, a thoroughly good chap. He and Fanny looked as pleasant a young couple as you could find.

The farewells broke off in a hurry because Florrie began to cry. Fanny gave her a hug and was hurried off.

"You take her back into the kitchen, Mother," said Ernie. "Florrie, you go and look behind the cushion in my chair and see if you don't find a box of chocolates there. Come on, Fan! Good-bye, Mother."

And then the kitchen door was banged on Florrie's sobs and the young Rennards went off down the passage to the light of a good strong electric lamp. It dangled from Ernie's left hand and made bright patches and very dark shadows as it swung. Oliver let them get away down the steps before he followed. He had taken his shoes off, and carried them knotted together by the laces, so he was counting on being able to move as quickly as he liked without making any noise. Stone has its advantages. It doesn't creak.

He reached the bottom of the steps, and was in a sort of hall from which a passage ran away to the right. He saw the passage because the light flashed round and showed it, but everywhere else it was dark, and when the flash was gone he lost the passage too. He ought to have followed closer. What if he had missed them— lost his chance of getting through to Rose Anne? He blundered into the mouth of the passage, started to run along it, and discovered by bumping into the wall that there was a sharp-angled turn. He bruised a shoulder, saw the light again, and the shadow of Ernie's hand, huge and black, reaching back towards him on a stretch of lighted wall, and he heard Fanny say,

"Oh, Ernie, I do hate to leave her, poor little thing—she does take on so."

If they had looked round at that moment, they must have seen him. The light flickered across his eyes and then swung off and left the passage between them dark again. They were about twenty feet away. Difficult to judge distance in a place like this, but he didn't think it was more than that. Whatever it was, he must risk getting nearer. He began to edge forward an inch at a time and kept his eyes on Ernie and the lamp. Wherever the Rennards were going to, they were not in any particular hurry. They talked about Florrie, and about Mother, who was Ernie's mother and a problem, and about Mabel, who thought a lot too much of herself, and presently they kissed each other and said wasn't it nice to get a bit of a time off.

"You know, Ernie"—Fanny had her head on his shoulder and spoke with a good deal of wistfulness—"you know, Ernie, I do think it would be downright heaven to have a little place of our own—a nice little garridge business. And I could run a tea-room, you know. That would be fun—wouldn't it? And all this—I don't see any end to it, and what's the good of it anyway? I tell you it frightens me."

Ernie put his arms round her. He didn't seem to have anything to say. The two red heads leaned together, while the light made a pool on the floor and the silence of this underground place came into its own again.

Oliver was just wondering whether he dared go a little nearer, when Ernie's head came up with a jerk.

"Well, we must go," he said, "or there'll be trouble."

Oliver heard Fanny sigh.

"Do you think they'll ever let us go—really?"

"I dunno, Fan. Best not think about it. Here, hold the light." He pushed it into her hand and she held it up. A square yard of wall was brightly lit.

Ernie seemed to be counting. Oliver heard him mutter under his breath, "Three up—two along—one down. Here goes." And he saw him push with both hands against the squared stones in front of him. There was a click, and a piece of the wall slid out of sight. It looked exactly as if Ernie's big hands had stove it in. And what was left was a black irregular hole—Florrie's black hole. Oliver wasn't surprised that it had frightened her. The thing had a strangeness, because the wall had been so solid, and then all in a moment there was the hole. These things came to him, not as consecutive thoughts, but as part of an impression compounded of hope, shock, excitement.

There was no time to think. Fanny stepped over the edge of the hole and was gone, and the light with her. Ernie followed, his shadow thrown for a moment, monstrously distorted, upon the opposite wall. And then with a click there was darkness again, darkness complete and absolute.

Oliver stood there and waited. They wouldn't come back, but he must let them get well away. It was either that or follow them close and quick, and this he decided was too risky. They might hear him, or he might blunder into them. No, what he had to do was to find the spring or whatever it was that opened the door in the wall—find out what lay beyond it—find out whether Rose Anne was there. Rose Anne—he had hard work to stand there waiting when he thought about Rose Anne.

He gave them five minutes, and never in all his life had five minutes seemed so long. The hands on the luminous dial of his wrist-watch seemed to have stopped, yet where they had pointed to five they now showed five minutes past.

He got out his electric torch and switched it on. Then it came to him that there was nothing to mark the place where Ernie and Fanny had stood. Or was there? He tried to think, and got the picture of the two red heads leaning together and Fanny saying, "Do you think they'll ever let us go—really?" Think—think—think... Fanny's hair—and the lamp dangling from Ernie's big left hand and making a circle of light on the stone... light on the stone—big blocks like paving stones—old—worn—cracked—that was it—cracked. He hadn't noticed it at the time, but he saw it quite distinctly in the picture now, a crack running across the circle of light—a very old crack, green with slime.

He went forward, casting about with his torch, and found what he had seen in the picture, a flagstone split across the corner and the broken edges of the crack mildew green. Well, this was where they had stood, Ernie here and Fanny just beyond him. Ernie had pushed the wall.

Oliver tried pushing it now. It was like pushing the side of a house. Nothing happened. It seemed quite incredible that this solid wall should have broken under his eye and let the Rennards through, but, incredible or not, he had seen it happen, and where they had gone he could follow.

There was a spring to be found, and Ernie had found it by counting three up—two along—one down. Three up—well, presumably that meant three up from the floor. He harked back to the picture in his mind again. Fanny had the lamp now, and Ernie was counting with his left hand. That meant three up from the broken flagstone. This brought him to a point about six feet up the wall, which was built of big two-foot blocks. Two across—he shifted the torch and reached out with his right hand. One down, and he was pressing on a spot about four feet above floor level. But press as he would, nothing happened. His other hand—Ernie had taken two hands. But then Ernie had had someone to hold the light. Oliver had to put it down on the ground, where it wasn't a great deal of use. He pressed with both hands now, keeping the right on the slab he had reached when he counted one down, and experimenting with the left. Ernie hadn't stooped at all, he was sure of that, so the right place must be somewhere fairly high up.

He thumped every inch of the wall within his reach, and found it solid as a hillside. An exasperating sense of helplessness came over him. He reached out sideways and slipped. His left foot went from under him, throwing him forward against the wall. His right foot scrabbled and stumbled on the slimy stone. Scrabbling and stumbling, it must have chanced upon the spring. The wall gave, went from him, swung in. There was empty space under the thrust of his hands. He pitched forward and fell sprawling across the threshold of the black hole.

Chapter Eighteen

UP AGAIN, he had a look at the thing. It certainly bore no resemblance to a door. It followed the irregular spacing of the stone flags. The mechanism which moved it was of the simplest, but it required a simultaneous pressure upon floor and wall, and he was lucky to have chanced upon the right combination. Under this pressure a section of the wall pivoted and swung in. He had it at right angles to him now, and his immediate concern was to find out whether he could open it from the inside. If he found Rose Anne, he would have to get her away, and the probabilities were that they would have to make a bolt for it.

He pushed the slabs back into their place and investigated. Thank goodness the thing was quite easy from this side. No need to count stones and feel about for the right one, with a lever ready to one's hand.

He turned from the wall with relief, and found that he was standing above a flight of rough stone steps. They went down almost as steeply as a ladder, and he was glad to see that there was an iron handrail. He switched off his torch and went down backwards— cautiously. He had no intention of stepping off into space.

The steps seemed solid enough. There were a hundred of them. He had to put his torch on again at the bottom, and saw a long passage running away down hill on a fairly steep incline. As there was no choice of ways, he followed it. There was no mistaking where he was now. This was a gallery in a mine. The steps had been cut to connect the house with the gallery, when and by whom he had no knowledge. He had to keep the torch on for fear of blundering into a side passage and losing the way back. He had to chance the light being seen. He had, in fact, to take so many chances that on any reasonable forecast he was bound to come to grief. Only, as it happened, he was in no mood for reason. The long strain, the long agony of the days since Rose Anne's disappearance, had brought him to a point where a sudden hope took him beyond the cool probabilities of the case. He could not think dispassionately of turning back and going to the police or letting Mr Smith know what had happened. He could only go forward. Nothing mattered if he could reach Rose Anne. To know that she was alive seemed enough. When he knew that—if he knew that—then it would be time to think and plan for her escape.

They wouldn't let her go easily.

This was present in his mind, but he withdrew his thoughts from it. Find her—find her—find her—that was what mattered. Everything else could wait.

Within the limits of this frame of mind he was alert and capable. After letting the torch illumine a stretch of passage he would switch it off and cover the distance in the dark. The slope went on and on, and down and down. A tingling impatience made his slow progress irksome. He would have liked to run, and it came to him to wonder whether caution was worth while where danger was at once inevitable and unescapable.

His fingers pressed the switch for perhaps the twentieth time, and he saw the passage divide. Two black galleries fronted him, one inclining to the left and the other to the right, and now of course he had no clue as to which one the Rennards had taken. He turned right because, with nothing to choose between right and left, a right-handed man is slightly biased in that direction. After turning on his torch three times he came to more steps, and descended them as he had done the others, backwards and without a light. The air was clammy now and warm. His temples were damp and the palms of his hands. A kind of horror of the darkness came upon him about half way down. The place was heavy with silence and old gloom. It was difficult to believe that light had ever passed this way. A man might fall here, and die, and his bones whiten and never be found.

He went on climbing down until the steps ended and his feet were upon the level stone. Now he would have to put the torch on again. Quick on that thought came another. Suppose the battery failed, suppose when he touched the switch there was no bright, leaping ray, suppose—He felt for the switch, found it with his thumb, and pushed.

Whether he released his own weak beam, he never knew, for with the very movement light broke, intense and blinding. A great arc-light drenched him with its glare. He threw up an arm to shield his eyes, was aware of hurrying feet, and dropped his guard again. Someone struck him from behind, and he went down and lay like a log.

Chapter Nineteen

HEARING came back first. He heard Fanny say in a weeping voice, "I don't care what you say." The words floated round in his mind. They didn't mean anything. They floated in his mind like coloured balloons. They didn't mean anything at all. But he knew that it was Fanny Garstnet who had set them floating there—Fanny Garstnet— Fanny Rennard—and she was crying—her voice sounded as if she was crying—Fanny Garstnet—

And then someone said Rose Anne's name—"Miss Rose Anne." That was Fanny too—"Miss Rose Anne." And then, "She'll never look at you if you touch him, Philip, and that I tell you straight."

Oliver opened his eyes. The blinding light was gone. He was in a room—ordinary room—ordinary light—one of those dangly things with a shade on the end of it—nice soft light—not that hideous glare. He blinked at it and looked again. No, not ordinary room— odd room—green curtains—lots of green curtains—curtains all round—must be a lot of windows—Fanny—Fanny with her red hair flaming under the light—Fanny saying, "All right, Philip, you just try it and see."

Oliver woke up. What had gone before was like a dream— coming and going—all queer and muddled—but now he was awake. Someone had fetched him a crack on the head and laid him out, and here he was, on a very comfortable couch, looking through half closed lids at two people on the other side of the room. One of them was Fanny Garstnet who was certainly Fanny Rennard, and the other, the man she called Philip, must be Philip Rennard, the Old Fox's son who was supposed to have been drowned. He was also beyond any shadow of doubt the man who had masqueraded as the Rosenkavalier.

Oliver kept his lids down and took stock of him. He saw an amazingly handsome young man attired in light flannel trousers and a silk shirt open at the neck. Dark red hair, rather like mahogany, worn much too long with a most offensive wave in it. It might be natural, it probably was natural, but civilised man doesn't go about with a wave in his hair just because nature has put one there.

"The fellow looks like a film star." This was Oliver's first impression. And then something happened to change it. Philip Rennard, who had been staring moodily at his own feet, lifted his head with a jerk and looked full at Oliver. He had the dark eyes which sometimes go with red hair—eyes the colour of deep peaty water. Just now they were bright with a dancing spark of hatred, and behind the hatred there was something else—conscious power. The image of the film star registering this and that emotion for effect was wiped out. Here was a very dangerous enemy, who hated him, who had the power to give effect to his hatred.

The look stayed upon him for an intolerable dragging minute and then was turned away. Without another word Philip Rennard lifted one of the green curtains, opened the door behind it, and went out. The door fell to, but Oliver saw Fanny run to it to make sure that it was latched. Then she came over to him and slipped her fingers under his wrist. He felt them tremble a little. He thought she had been crying. He opened his eyes and said,

"All right, Fanny. What happens next?"

Fanny dropped his wrist and backed away. She opened her mouth and clapped a hand upon it. A frightened gasp came through the muffling fingers. And then she said,

"Oh, Captain Loddon! Why ever did you come?"

Oliver sat up.

"To find Rose Anne. Fanny—she's here? Fanny—tell me!"

Fanny's eyes were brimming over.

"Oh, yes. Oh, yes, she's here, poor lamb."

He caught her by the wrist.

"Fanny—for God's sake—is she—safe?"

The tears were running down her face.

"Oh, yes, Captain Loddon—the way you mean—she's safe—poor lamb."

A weight like the weight of the world was lifted from Oliver. He crushed Fanny's wrist so hard that she cried out.

"Why do you say poor lamb—if she's safe? Fanny—Fanny, tell me! I've been nearly mad!"

She caught her breath.

"I'll tell you. Oh, it doesn't matter what I tell you now."

He was too intent at the moment to take the meaning of that "now," but it came back to him afterwards—ominously. She pulled away from him, ran to the door through which Philip Rennard had gone out, and opened it, holding the curtain away with an unsteady hand. When she had shut that door he thought she looked less frightened, but a second curtain was pulled aside and another door disclosed. He could not see where it led to, but he heard her say with relief, "It's all right, Ernie—I just wanted to see if you were alone." Then she shut that door too and came back to him, drawing a stool to the side of the couch and leaning so close that her words needed only the merest breath to be audible. She began by repeating her first question in a tone of distress.

"Oh, Captain Loddon! Why did you come?"

And Oliver said, "I came to find Rose Anne. Don't waste time, Fanny—tell me."

"I don't know how you found out she was here."

"That doesn't matter. Tell me about her."

She looked up at him and then away.

"You know Philip took her?"

Oliver said, "Yes."

She swallowed a sob.

"I don't know how you found out. I don't know how you came here, but it's no good. No one gets away from here—no one's ever got away. It's been no good since the very first time Philip saw her photograph, and that's what makes me feel so bad, because he wouldn't never have seen it if it hadn't been for me marrying Ernie and coming down under. And Miss Rose Anne gave me the photo herself, and wrote on it too. We're the same age, you know, and we always played together, and I'm sure there isn't anyone in the world who's fonder of her than I am."

He had to restrain his impatience. If he didn't let her run on he wouldn't get what he wanted.

She ran on tearfully—"Ernie and me got married just above a year ago. He used to come to the Angel to get the stuff away. There's a lot of food and stuff that has to be got down under, and—that's Uncle's cleverness—he gets it sent where it won't make talk. There's hotels all up and down the country where he has stuff delivered for him in different names. They don't know a thing except that it'll be fetched. Well, Ernie does the fetching with a lorry, and the stuff comes down here by one of the back ways."

Florrie's black holes! He said quickly,

"There's a back way in through the Angel, isn't there?"

Fanny nodded.

"And that's what I found out," she said. "Ernie didn't show it to me—I came on it same as poor little Florrie did and got a fright that nearly killed her, and lucky for me it was Ernie I ran into, or I wouldn't be here now. Well, after that we used to meet there. And then it was found out. Oh, Captain Loddon, it was awful, because I thought they was going to do me in—and they would have too if it hadn't been for Ernie being a Rennard and no end useful, and me being Uncle's niece. So they let us get married instead, but I had to come down under, and they never let me out, not a step, not till my baby was born. And they won't let me take him, not when I go up with Ernie—no, they keep him here to make sure I'll come back and not talk. That's more of Uncle's cleverness. They don't call him the Old Fox for nothing, and Philip takes after him."

"Rose Anne—" said Oliver. "Fanny—Fanny—tell me about Rose Anne!"

The tears ran down over Fanny's face.

"I wish I hadn't got to," she said in a weeping voice.

"Fanny!"

"It was the photograph she gave me. Philip saw it, and he never said a word, just stood looking at it for ever so long. But afterwards he asked about her—who she was, and where she lived, and all. That was somewhere about last May, and then it seems he got Mother to manage so that he could see her. Poor Mother—you mustn't think too hard about her, Captain Loddon. She's been fair broken-hearted over this, but they work on her about Florrie—say they'll take her away and put her somewhere where she'll never see her again—all that kind of thing. And she can't bear it, Mother can't, so she give in. She sent for Miss Rose Anne to see Florrie, and she let Philip stand in one of the rooms where he could see her go by, and from that minute he laid his plans to get her. He found out there was a dance she was going to with Miss Elfreda—somewhere down in the Isle of Wight it was. It was a fancy dress affair, and he found out what she was going to wear and got his own dress made to match, and he went there and danced with her and come away with his heart that set on her that nothing wouldn't move him. He was bound to have her, and the way he planned it was the way that would make the biggest stir. Philip's like that, you know—he'd rather do a thing dangerous than do it safe. It was just what he wanted, to snatch her away the very day before her wedding and leave everyone talking. And the way he planned it you'd be bound to think she'd run off with someone else."

The agony of that touched Oliver again. He said,

"Fanny—where is she?" And even as the words passed his lips he heard a hand move on the door behind the green hangings.

Like a flash Fanny was on her feet, the stool picked up and swung out of reach, Fanny herself away on the farther side of the room. All this while the door was opening.

It was Philip Rennard who held the curtain back, but it was Rose Anne Carew who came first into the room, and the sight of her brought Oliver to his feet. His head was dizzy and his heart knocked at his side. The room swam before his eyes. Rose Anne's face came and went.

And then his sight cleared. They were facing one another in the little room. Philip Rennard had come in and shut the door behind him. He was aware of this, and of Fanny breathless in the background, but his eyes were for Rose Anne.

She had come a little inside the door and stopped there. She had on a white dress which he had never seen before. It hung heavy and straight to her feet, and it made him think of a shroud, because she might have looked like this if she had risen up from a grave. Her hair hung loose. There was no colour in her face, no colour at all. Her eyes were fixed, not on him nor on anyone in that room, but on some distance of her own imagining. He did not think she saw him, or any of them. She stood there quite still, her lips set in the faint smile of sleep or death. Through the dreadful intensity of his own watching gaze he was aware that Philip Rennard watched her too—watched with a like intensity, a like passion. And Rose Anne between them, walking and breathing, but as unaware, as withdrawn, as the lovely marble figure from a tomb.

The ground rocked under Oliver's feet. Fanny had said she was safe—but what had they done to her to make her look like this? He said her name in a voice which sounded strangely in his own ears.

"Rose Anne—"

Rose Anne said, "Yes?" She turned her eyes upon him and looked at him as sweetly and indifferently as a child might look at a stranger.

"*Rose Anne*—" He came forward, and would have taken her hand, but she went back a step.

Philip Rennard laughed.

"We're in the same boat, you see. She doesn't like me to touch her either. She doesn't like being touched—do you, my lovely Rose?"

And like an echo Rose Anne said, "I don't like being touched, do I?"

Oliver stood where he was. He heard Fanny catch her breath. He said,

"Don't you know me, Rose Anne?"

She gave him a clear, blank look.

"Oh, yes—you are Oliver."

In his mocking voice Philip said,

"And isn't it kind of Oliver to come and see you? He's taken a great deal of trouble about it, you know. Aren't you going to say thank you?"

Rose Anne said, "It's very kind of you, Oliver. Thank you very much."

She wasn't there at all, not his Rose Anne. This was a simulacrum, an empty echo. There was no life or breath. It wasn't Rose Anne at all. No use to touch her, not under Philip Rennard's eyes—to see her shrink away and hear him laugh. It was no good, and it hurt too much.

Philip Rennard came and stood beside her.

"Come, Rose, you're disappointing Captain Loddon. I'm afraid he expected a warmer welcome. It's a pity to have come so far and risked so much, and then be disappointed in the end—isn't it? This is Captain Oliver Loddon, you know, and if I hadn't run off with you, you would be Mrs Oliver Loddon by now, and so I think he expects you to say something a little more—effusive."

She turned her head and looked at him with a faintly puzzled air.

"I did say, 'Thank you very much.' "

"Perhaps he thought you would be pleased to see him."

She turned back.

"I'm very pleased to see you."

It was quite heart-breaking. Her words were like wind blowing through an empty room. There was nothing there but an empty blowing wind. She said what was put into her mouth to say, and it meant nothing at all.

Fanny Rennard broke in.

"What do you want to torment her for? I won't have it, Philip! Why can't you leave her alone? Anyone can see she isn't herself, poor lamb. Why can't you let her be?"

"Am I tormenting you, Rose?" said Philip.

She was a yard away, and he made no movement to come nearer, but his eyes dwelt on her and his voice caressed her. She said,

"No, Philip."

"*There*, Fanny—you see! I don't torment her—I'm very kind to her. Don't you think I'm very kind to you, Rose?"

She echoed him again—"Very kind."

"You're very fond of me?"

She echoed that too—"Fond of you."

"Well then, what about a kiss? Or are you still not liking to be touched?"

She shook her head.

"I don't like being touched."

He laughed. It was not a merry sound.

"You're very fond of me. Well then, what about Captain Oliver Loddon? Are you fond of him too? I expect he'd like to know."

"I'm very fond of him," said Rose Anne in the voice of a docile child.

"Perhaps you'd like to kiss him. Would you, Rose?"

She went back a step.

"I don't like being touched."

That ended the intolerable scene. Philip Rennard pulled the curtain back with a jerk and opened the door.

"All right, my lovely Rose, you needn't be afraid—he shan't touch you. Fanny, take her back to her room! Tell Marie she's not to be left—not for a moment!" He went out with them, but turned on the threshold to say, "You see, we take good care of her here, Loddon. Nobody has any chance of annoying her."

Chapter Twenty

THE DOOR was locked upon him. He had started towards it, but checked at the sound of the key in the lock. He went back to sit on the edge of the couch with his head in his hands. His head ached and his heart too. He had found Rose Anne, and she was more lost to him than in his most despairing dreams, because in the very worst of them there had never been a moment when she had not cried out for him, as he cried out for her—with all his body and soul, with every impulse, every purpose, every thought. He was left to a sense of frustration past bearing. What had they done to her to drain her of her lovely life, her living intelligence, her quick responsive love? It was as if he had seen her bled to death—under Philip Rennard's eyes.

He had a moment of fierce and primitive regret. The fellow had been within reach of him. He might have had him by the throat and stopped that mocking breath. He might have choked him dumb, and battered that filmstar face of his to a pulp.

That was folly. Even if he hadn't still been giddy from the blow on his head, he had no more chance of getting Rose Anne away than he had of flying. They might be any distance from the place where he had been knocked out, and even if they were on the very spot, he could not have forced her to the ascent. He heard her say again in that gentle voice, "I don't like being touched, do I?"

He had never suffered as he did now. To have found her, and to have found her like this. It was unbearable, and yet it had to be borne. For a time he could not think. He could only set himself to endure.

He looked up when Fanny came in, and said,

"What have they done to her? For God's sake tell me!"

She dropped the green curtains over the door and came to him.

"It's not what you think. No one has hurt her—no one has laid a finger on her. It isn't that. It's—it's—well, when they bring anyone down under they give them some stuff to—to keep them quiet."

The strain relaxed.

"You mean they've drugged her? You're sure—it's only that?"

Fanny looked away.

"Oh, Captain Loddon, I don't know. None of them know. You see, they gave her the stuff—to keep her quiet, and then Philip told them to stop it, but it didn't go off, not like it does as a rule."

"You mean the effect didn't go off?"

She nodded.

"It ought to go off in a few hours, and it's days since she had any. Philip stopped it. He's in love with her—really and truly in love, I mean. He doesn't want her like she is now. He wants her like she was, and he wants to make her in love with him, and to have her come to him because she wants to come. And now he's got you here, what he'd like best of all is to cut you out and have her choose him of her own free will."

Oliver threw up his head and laughed, while Fanny stared at him.

"Oh, Captain Loddon, don't!" She came closer, and said in a hurrying whisper, "You don't know—how dangerous it is—for you. He meant to kill you right away—only then he thought of this, and he'd rather—he'd rather have you alive and see her in love with him and marrying him, and you out in the cold."

Oliver laughed again and said,

"I'd take my chance of that, Fanny. He's got a bit of wind in the head, hasn't he, your Mr Philip Rennard?"

"Oh, *don't*!" said Fanny again. "You don't know Philip or you wouldn't talk like that. He's always had everything he wants. Uncle won't cross him, and there isn't anyone else who can. Mark's too fond of him—"

"And who's Mark?" said Oliver.

He got rather a shrewd look from Fanny.

"You know such a lot, I reckoned you'd know that too. Uncle's got two sons—"

"And Mark's the other one?" said Oliver.

She nodded.

"He's the eldest—Uncle's right hand. He doesn't make a show like Philip, but he runs all the outside business—there's a lot of it. And Mark's not a bad sort, but he won't put out a finger to hinder Philip—none of them will—so if you don't watch your own step, no one's going to do it for you."

"I see—" said Oliver.

"You'd better," said Fanny in her earnest whisper. "Better get it right into your head and keep it there. There's no law down under except what Uncle makes and what Philip chooses. Anything he does is good enough law. If he was to walk into this room this very minute and shoot you dead, nobody wouldn't take any notice except to see that you was cremated and to get the stain out of my carpet." She began to cry again. "It sounds awful, but it can't sound a bit more awful than what it is. The only thing that's keeping you alive this minute is what I told you. The way Philip's made, he'd rather get Miss Rose Anne away from you when you were alive than when you were dead. He's proud and he's cruel, and he wants you to see her turn her back and come to him and marry him as if she liked doing it—and he's quite sure he can make her."

"All right," said Oliver—"let him try."

"He can't," said Fanny—"not with her like she is, poor lamb. She's just like that all the time—says yes when you say yes, and no when you say no. It just makes your heart ache. But I'll tell you something. He wasn't sure about her till just now, and that's why he brought her in on you like that. He thought maybe she was putting it on, so he brought her in and watched to see how she'd take it."

"And what does he think now?" said Oliver. Something stirred in him. Was it hope?

"I don't know," said Fanny in a dejected voice. "Philip doesn't let on. I think he'll wait. The doctor goes on saying she's so highly strung and you never can tell how it'll take people like that."

"The doctor?" He caught up the word.

She gave a little angry laugh.

"Oh, yes, we've got a doctor, and a parson, and what you might call every modern convenience. If Uncle wants anyone, he has them fetched down under, and one of the first things he did was to get his own doctor. Spenlow's the name—Doctor Harold Spenlow. And Uncle says he ought to be happy, because he's got the finest laboratory that money can fit out and no one to interfere with him. And he fetched the parson he wanted, the Reverend Luke Simpson. He says he ought to be happy too, because it's a parson's business to preach against sin, and there's plenty down here to keep him happy."

"I'd like to meet Uncle," said Oliver drily.

Fanny gave an angry little laugh that was half a sob.

"I shouldn't worry—you'll meet him all right. He always sees everyone new, and if you want to please him, you'll tell him he's not forgotten up there. There's a straight tip for you. And you needn't be afraid to pile it on—he'll swallow anything. Why, he was as pleased as Punch for weeks when someone put him in a book of famous trials the other day. That's the only thing that worries him about being down under—he can't get up on his hind legs and tell everyone how clever he's been, which is what he'd like. So he always has the new ones up one at a time and brags about it—" She broke off suddenly, ran to the door, and looked out, holding the green curtain up in a loop over the shining red of her hair. Then she came back again and said more soberly. "Do everything you can to please him, Captain Loddon. It might make a lot of difference." She went away after that, and he was alone again.

He found three doors, and found them locked. He found out why the walls were hung with curtains. Stone is cold comfort to live with, and the room he was in had been cut out of solid limestone. There were no windows, but he discovered a ventilating shaft with a grating fixed across it. One of the doors opened upon a gallery. He had caught a glimpse of it when Philip Rennard held the curtain back, and when Fanny looked out just now. The other doors were in the two side walls.

He looked at his watch, and found that it was eight o'clock. There was a good sized lump on the back of his head, and he could have done with something to drink. The air was hot, and his mouth dry and parched. He wished he had thought of asking Fanny for some water.

It was nearly nine o'clock before she came back—out of breath as if she had been running.

"He wants to see you now."

"Who does?"

"Uncle. He's sent for you. Oh, Captain Loddon, you'll be careful, won't you?" And with that there came in Ernie Rennard and a man with a dark, clever face and restless eyes.

"Dr Spenlow," said Fanny—"and Ernie, my husband, you know. They'll take you along."

Dr Spenlow gave a crooked smile.

"We have all to do as we are told down under. It will save you a lot of trouble if you get hold of that right away."

Spenlow—Dr Harold Spenlow—Mr Benbow Collingwood Horatio Smith in his book-lined study talking about unaccountable disappearances—the Reverend Luke Simpson for one, and Dr Harold Spenlow for another... Well, here was the man himself—eight years later. What would eight years down under do to a rising young specialist? Oliver, walking along a lighted gallery beside him, glanced sideways once or twice and thought, "He hasn't gone to seed, and he hasn't got used to it. I should look out for him if I were Amos Rennard." Then, with a feeling of repugnance, he remembered that it was this man who had drugged Rose Anne. He said on the impulse,

"I've seen Miss Carew. Why is she—like that? What have you given her?"

Dr Spenlow's eyebrows lifted, making him look a good deal like Mephistopheles.

"Well, you don't lose much time, do you? Do you expect me to give my professional secrets away?"

"What did you give her?" said Oliver in such a tone of fury that Ernest Rennard walking ahead of them swung about and said uneasily,

"Now, Captain Loddon, it's no good talking like that, and it won't do Miss Rose Anne any good either."

"It's a pretty name, isn't it?" said Dr Spenlow in his mocking voice, "and she's a pretty creature, but there's really no need for you to get yourself into trouble by murdering me. Quite natural you should feel an urge that way, but better not to indulge it. Don't you agree, Ernie?"

Ernie's pleasant face wore a frown of disapproval.

"There's no call for anything of the sort," he said. "And I'm sure Captain Loddon's too sensible to think of any such thing, and you ought to know better than to bait him, Doctor. Why can't you set his mind at rest and tell him Miss Rose Anne's all right."

"Perhaps my professional conscience won't let me. Perhaps I'm not sure whether she's all right or not, Mr Ernest Rennard." His glance raked Oliver as he spoke.

Oliver thought, "Damn him, he doesn't know whether I've heard the name before. He *wants* to know." He could trust himself with his temper now. If he was to get Rose Anne away, he must ride it on the curb. He said,

"Would you mind telling me just what you mean by that?"

There was a flicker of something in the dark, restless eyes. The voice lost some of its mocking tone.

"I don't mind in the least. Mr Amos Rennard is a very humane person and the soul of hospitality. He likes to feel that his guests are enjoying themselves. If there is any doubt about it, he enlists my professional assistance."

"You mean he gets you to drug them?"

Ernie looked over his shoulder and said,

"Give over, the both of you! What's the sense of talking like that?"

Dr Spenlow laughed as if he were amused.

"You stick to your last, Ernie. You're a first-class mechanic, and I'm not—I shouldn't dream of interfering with you."

"What have you done to Miss Carew?" said Oliver.

Dr Spenlow shrugged his shoulders.

"Nothing to make you want my blood. As I told you, I assist new-comers to settle down here by giving them small doses of a drug which is my own secret. The usual dose for a man is two grains, and for a woman one and a half. Miss Carew has had two half grain doses. The effect should have been very slight at any time, and it should certainly have worn off in a very few hours. She had the last of her two doses a week ago. I am therefore quite at a loss to understand her present condition, but I do not really think it should cause you any anxiety. She seems quite happy." He said these words with a curious drawling inflection, then added with considerable briskness, "It doesn't suit Philip's book, of course, but you don't have to worry about that."

Ernest Rennard fell back and pushed his big shoulders between them.

"Look here," he said, "I won't have it, and that's all there is about it. You shut up, or I'll shut you up! Captain Loddon's got one bump on his head, and I shouldn't think he'd want another. As for you, Doctor—"

"Oh, I don't want one either," said Spenlow laughing. "All right, Ernie, we'll change the subject. What shall it be? There's no weather to talk about—your politics are dangerous. I can think of nothing but the story of our lives. I'm sure Captain Loddon would be interested to hear how Fanny lured me here."

A brick-red flush spread upwards from Ernie's neck. His large ears glowed with it. He looked very angry indeed.

"That's something you've got to take back, Doctor. You know as well as I do that Fanny hadn't the least idea what was going to happen. She was only a child, and she did what she was told, and they didn't ought to have made her do it."

"Very sad," said Spenlow—"*and* bad, I quite agree. And if I hadn't been a fool, it wouldn't have happened." He turned to Oliver. "I'd gone down to Sunningdale for a round of golf with a fellow called Paton. We played, we lunched, we yarned, and at four-fifteen I drove him to Virginia Water station. It was just about dark when I came away. I put my headlights on, and there was Fanny in the middle of the road, a vision of loveliness, with her arms out and her hair a regular blaze. Well, I stopped, which I was bound to do—I could hardly run her down in cold blood—and I got out, which I needn't have done, and the next thing I knew I was down here with a buzzing head and a hearty smell of chloroform hanging around. They must have fairly deluged me with it, and a bit of luck for them that I survived. One of Philip's early efforts—quite well planned, but carried out in a grossly clumsy manner. I believe Fanny cried her eyes out after seeing my corpse borne away."

Ernie set his mouth in a glum silence and said nothing.

It was in Oliver's mind to wonder about Dr Harold Spenlow. Was it just his pleasant way to discover your pet corn, and then stamp on it, or was there some purpose in his talk? And where did he stand in the politics of this underworld? Much too soon to say, too soon even to hazard a guess. He thought he would see what he could get from Ernie.

They had emerged upon the low gallery of an old mine. The roof cleared the tallest head by a bare foot. The walls were rough, but the floor had been levelled. It was quite well lighted.

Oliver said, "Was this part of the old mine? It looks different."

"Oh, it's different all right," said Ernie. He seemed pleased to change the subject, and glad to talk again. "That's one of the old mine workings where we live, but hereabouts they run into a lot of caves and such like. I expect you've seen the ones in the Cheddar Gorge, and at Wookey. I went there once on my holiday when I was about sixteen, and I thought them something wonderful, but they're not a patch on what we've got here. Why, these run, one way and another, more miles than you'd believe."

"All the way to Hillick?"

Ernie's frown came down again.

"I didn't say that."

"No—Captain Loddon said it." Dr Spenlow's tone was now extremely affable. "Captain Loddon said it, and Captain Loddon was perfectly right. An old mine here, and old mines at Hillick St Agnes and Hillick St Anne's, and between them our unrivalled, our unexampled, our truly magnificent caves. Don't be so shy about it, Ernie. Why not respond to a natural thirst for knowledge?"

"Mocking devil!" thought Oliver. He said aloud,

"How do you keep your ventilation going?"

Ernie relaxed. This was a subject on which he felt free to talk.

"Shafts," he said—"like they have in mines. Most of them were here already—they only wanted clearing out, and when you get farther in there's a system of fans. It's quite simple, and it's never given any trouble. Of course Uncle got a really good man on to it."

"He means," said Dr Spenlow, "that Mr Amos Rennard, who is our beneficent dictator, spared no pains in kidnapping a highly competent electrical engineer. His motto has always been 'Get the best—it pays in the end.' That, of course, is why I am here. We are mostly very carefully hand-picked, but you, I gather, are in rather a different category—something more in the nature of a gate-crasher—our first, I believe. It will be interesting to see what happens to you."

"Now look here, Doctor," said Ernie.

Dr Spenlow laughed.

"All right, all right—I am on my best behaviour. We approach the Presence."

A pair of wrought-iron gates barred their way. The tracery showed black against a glare of light beyond. Someone on the other side called out, "Who goes there?" whereupon Ernie went forward and gave a password which they did not hear. The gates were swung back, and there appeared in the opening an enormous negro in a very odd uniform. It was made of scarlet cloth, with the baggy trousers of the Zouave, a belted Russian blouse, and a commissionaire's flat cap. The man stood to attention as they passed in.

Chapter Twenty-One

THE GATES were sunk in a recess. Oliver had to take a dozen steps forward before he could really see what lay beyond. That it was a hall of some size had been, of course, apparent, but as he came clear of the bay which held the gates, he stood still in amazement. The place was not only large, it was vast—a great natural cavern stretching away into the distance and rising to dim heights above the huge arc-lamps which lighted it. The place was the most extraordinary mixture of natural majesty and crude modernity, a blend of the cathedral and the factory—virgin rock and arc-lights—rough unhewn contours—bright jazz carpets in shades of orange, emerald and brick—walls gilded to a height of twenty feet—gilded but not smoothed, so that the inequalities of the stone caught the light and flung it sparkling back. The effect was barbaric in the extreme. The light, the space, the height above them, gave Oliver a feeling of dizziness. It was as if he had stepped on to some unknown plane where all the values were different. The sound of blaring music was taken up and repeated from the echoing rock. A wild rhythm beat its way through a crescendo and then suddenly ceased. A voice shouted at stentorian pitch, "That is the end of our programme of dance music," and for a moment the great place fell quiet.

Dr Spenlow broke the silence with his laugh.

"In the loss of everything else, we still have the B.B.C.," he said.

It seemed to Oliver the maddest thing that had happened yet.

They began to walk up the horrible carpet with the arc-lights picking out every detail of its infernal pattern. Oliver's head hurt him a good deal. He had never felt less inclined for jazz. It seemed quite a long walk to what Dr Spenlow had called "the presence."

At the far end of the hall, raised by four steps, was a kind of dais—only the word dais suggests something small, and this must have been forty feet across. The steps which led up to it, and the dais itself, were carpeted in crimson. In the middle of this expanse of crimson stood a large gilt arm-chair with six negro guards on either side of it, and in the arm-chair there sat quite the most amazing figure that Oliver had ever beheld. He didn't know quite what he had expected Amos Rennard to be like, but he certainly hadn't expected what he saw. The dictator of this under-world must have weighed a generous eighteen stone. There was no grey in the opulent wave of his fiery hair or in the flaming masses of the beard which hung down over his knees. The hair did stop short of his shoulders, but the beard appeared to go on for ever. He sat there on his gilt chair with its crimson velvet cushions in a bulging pair of grey flannel trousers and a dressing-gown of red and blue silk. His beard kept the secret of whether he wore a collar or not.

As Oliver mounted the steps, a pair of shrewd, twinkling grey eyes were fixed upon him—little piggy eyes under bristling red brows. Oliver had never seen so much red hair in his life. Tufts of it projected from the wide nostrils. Sporadic hairs encroached upon the sanguine cheeks. The backs of the hands were covered with a thick growth. What a king beaver! The words slipped through his mind as he stood a couple of yards away and gave Amos Rennard back stare for stare. Unlike most fat men, the Old Fox had a hearty voice.

"Well, Ernie my boy," he said, "and how's the youngster? Going strong? Good! Harold, you run away to your lab—you're not on in this scene. Yes, I know I sent you, but that was because they said his head was stove in. I can't see much wrong with it myself, so you can run away and play. Ernie, you needn't wait neither. Two's company and three's none. You go and put the wireless on nice and soft. Switch off the amplifier. Captain Loddon and me will be talking, and we'll want to be able to hear what we say." He jerked his great head round to right and left and dismissed the guards.

"Get down into the hall! You're off duty for half an hour. And now, Captain Loddon—I'm very pleased to see you, and I'd like you to sit down and have a talk."

The guards melted away. Dr Spenlow turned on his heel, and Ernie followed him. Oliver sat down on a horrid little gilded chair, and wondered what sort of polite conversation he was supposed to make.

"Well, well, well—" said Amos Rennard. "And what kind of wind brought you here, Captain Loddon?"

"I think you know that," said Oliver.

"Philip stole your girl, didn't he? You'd better have put up with it and got yourself another. Lots more up there, but not so many down under, so that's where the shoe pinches. It's a pity you didn't stay at home."

Oliver said nothing. The Old Fox pulled at his beard.

"Well, I'm pleased to see you anyhow, and I daresay we can make some use of you if you don't set out to give trouble. We don't waste time over people who give trouble down here, you know. If they don't fit in they have to go."

"Where?" said Oliver.

Amos Rennard gazed piously at the distant roof.

"That depends on their way of life. We do our best. The Reverend Luke is very particular about the funeral service." He twinkled cheerfully at Oliver. "No need to talk about funerals—yet. We've all got to come to 'em, but no need to hurry things on. You mind your step and make yourself useful, and I'll hold Philip off you. See?"

Oliver saw. He said,

"I don't quite know what use I could be."

"Well, you can talk to me for a start. I like to hear how things are going on up there. Philip and Mark, they come and go of course, and Ernie too. They're the only ones I can trust, being my own flesh and blood. But it's not like hearing the news from a stranger. Philip and Mark and Ernie, they're not interested in the things that interest me, so when anyone fresh comes down under I always have him up here for a talk. So that's the first way you can make yourself useful—you can talk."

Oliver couldn't help laughing.

"What in the world do you want me to talk about, Mr Rennard?"

The little piggy eyes brightened.

"Start by telling me how you know my name, young man."

Oliver laughed again, carelessly.

"Well, you made a bit of a splash in the world, didn't you?"

The Old Fox grinned.

"I should just about think I did. But it's a long time ago—ten years is a long time. They still talk about me?"

"I shouldn't be here if they didn't," said Oliver.

"And what do you mean by that, young man?" The little eyes were blank and steady. They weren't giving anything away.

"Well," said Oliver, "a friend of mine was talking about you— the case, you know, and how you tried to get away by aeroplane. He didn't believe you were dead. He said they'd found the pilot's body after the smash, but not yours, and he didn't believe you were dead. He'd made a regular study of the whole thing, and he'd got amazingly near the truth—near enough to set me looking for you."

He had glanced away. Now, at a sound, he looked back to see Amos Rennard's face convulsed with rage. So sudden was the transition from an easy good nature to this mask of rage that it fairly took his breath.

"Near enough—near enough—" The words came on a deep growl. And then suddenly oath followed oath in a torrent of language as foul as Oliver had ever heard. "Near enough! I'll teach him to come nosing after me, blast him! By this, and by that, and by the other, I'll teach him! If he's near enough, he'll come nearer still, and I'll teach him same as we taught the poor fool, the blank, blank, blank dashed fool, who came messing about the shaft at Hillick St Anne's, blast him! Dashed, blank clever he thought himself, I'll be bound! He heard the dynamo, you see—or thought he heard it—and came back to make sure. And they picked him up at the bottom of the cliff with a broken neck—and lucky to get off with that." He leaned forward suddenly, shot out a hairy hand, and caught Oliver by the forearm. "What do you know about John Smith? Here—out with it!"

The man was a human conflagration. The redness of his face, his hair, his beard, the heat of his gross body and clutching hand, affected Oliver. He felt giddy and sick. It was like being pawed by a gorilla. He must be careful what he said... it didn't matter what he said... it didn't matter, because they were doomed already—he and Rose Anne. In the midst of his physical distress his mind had a moment of fearful clarity. He had butted in upon Amos Rennard's private kingdom. Amos Rennard would squeeze him dry and throw him away... That was a mixed metaphor. The image of the gorilla cropped up again—great hairy hands clutching at an orange, squeezing out the pulp, and chucking the rind away. Through the mist of his giddiness he heard himself repeat the name of John Smith.

Amos Rennard said it again with a snarl.

"John Smith—that's what I said! What do you know about him?"

Oliver heard his own voice a long way off.

"He had a bicycle accident—"

"And you believe that?"

His head throbbed horribly, but the mist was clearing. He said, "No, I don't think so."

He was released. The little piggy eyes stared.

"How do you mean, you don't think so?"

"Well, just that. I looked at the place, and I didn't think anyone in his senses would have tried to ride a bicycle down a track like that."

Amos Rennard sat back.

"I've no business to lose my temper—it's bad for me. Do you know what I weigh? Eighteen stone and a half last Monday." He shook his head. "No, I'm too stout to lose my temper, and I've got to be careful—the doctor says so. So you knew about John Smith breaking his neck? You'd be bound to of course—I'd forgotten that. But you didn't know why he broke his neck—you didn't know he'd heard one of our dynamos."

"No," said Oliver, "I didn't know that."

Amos Rennard looked at him sharply.

"It was all Ralston's fault. I always told him he'd got that dynamo too near the shaft, and he said there wasn't anyone to hear it, and he'd got it where he wanted it and he wasn't going to put it anywhere else. You can take a bit of notice about Ralston, young man. Obstinate—that's what he was—a good engineer, but pigheaded. Well, he had to go."

Oliver said, "Where did he go?" because there was a pause and it was the easiest thing to say.

"I wouldn't like to say. We had his funeral a week ago. He'd got above himself, and it don't matter how clever they are, if they get above themselves they've got to go. We'll be put to all the trouble and expense of getting another. That's the worst of your clever ones, they don't care a dash what trouble they put you to, or how much you're out of pocket over them." His red bristles drew together in a frown. "We've got to have someone good," he said. "Philip'll have to look into it. Well now, you haven't told me how you got here, and that's a thing I'd like to know."

Oliver told him quite baldly. It didn't seem to matter what he said or did. Whether he pleased the Old Fox or put him in a rage, the end would be the same. He could think of no way in which he could become indispensable, and only the indispensable had any future here.

His head was getting worse all the time. Once or twice he did not know whether he had spoken or not. The mist got thicker. Amos Rennard's voice came booming through it.

"Hold up, young man—what's the matter?"

Oliver put a hand to his head and touched it gingerly. It didn't seem to belong to him at all. He said in a slow, careful voice,

"I don't know. Can I have something to drink?"

A rift in the mist showed him a red, reproving face.

"Not if you mean alcohol, you can't, young man. Now a good cup of cocoa, or tea—I've no objection to tea."

Oliver heard himself asking for tea, heard the hall echo with a stentorian order, and for a moment or two heard no more, because the mist seemed to have got into his ears. When it cleared, he was being treated to a lecture on the advantages of total abstinence.

"How do you suppose we'd manage down here if we'd liquor knocking about? Keep 'em sober, keep 'em safe—that's been my motto all along. And how are you going to keep 'em sober if there's liquor knocking about where they can get at it? No, no, no, young man, we're all blue-ribbon down here, and that ought to be a great consolation to the Reverend Luke. When he gets low in his mind I put him up to preach a real good rousing temperance sermon— none of your namby-pamby pulpit essays, but real good meaty stuff with plenty of hell fire about it. It don't hurt us, and it does him a power of good. That's the type of sermon you want, something that makes you feel good. You haven't met the Reverend Luke yet, have you? He's not a bad fellow, and he's a pretty good preacher. Of course there's a sameness about sitting under the one minister Sunday in, Sunday out, but I don't see my way to getting round it. It'd make a bit too much talk if too many of our ministers went missing, so we just have to put up with the Reverend Luke."

Someone brought tea in a china pot with a gay pattern of roses on it. The cup was a satisfactorily large one. Oliver drank thirstily.

The conversation had become a monologue. He listened with imperfect attention to Amos Rennard's views on such diverse subjects as education, religion, horse-racing, and the culture of mushrooms. Amos thought children were brought up all wrongly. If he had his time again, he'd bring his up differently, but Oliver did not discover wherein the difference was to lie. Religion he liked strong, with plenty of pulpit thumping, and flaming penalties for all the sins to which he himself was not inclined. Horse-racing was the parent of betting, and betting was the curse of the country. "Believe it or not, young man, I've never had a bet on anything in my life." What the Americans call "Playing the markets," did not apparently come under this heading. Mushroom culture was an interminable topic. Oliver leaned his head on his hand and stopped listening.

At long last the audience was ended.

He walked beside Ernie through lighted passages which rocked beneath his feet till they came to a room with a bed in it. Oliver sat down on the edge of the bed and looked stupidly at his feet. He ought to take his shoes off, but he seemed to have forgotten how. He stared at the laces until Ernie's big hands interrupted his view. His shoes were taken off, his coat and trousers were taken off, he was pushed down upon the pillow and covered. The light went out with a click. He went to sleep.

Chapter Twenty-Two

OLIVER WOKE with a feeling that a long time had passed. He had, in fact, slept for twelve hours almost without moving. Fanny stood by his bed hoping he felt better, and asking him whether he preferred kipper or eggs and bacon for his breakfast—"And it's gone ten o'clock, Captain Loddon." He might have been in his old room at the Angel. He chose eggs and bacon, and tea instead of coffee. His headache had gone, and he was hungry.

The bacon was deliciously crisp, and there were fresh rolls. When he remarked on them, Fanny told him they were Philip's fancy—"Austrian, the baker is—come over from Vienna before they tightened things up so that you couldn't, and had a little shop in Soho, and Philip he took such a fancy to the bread he had him brought along."

"Look here, Fanny, don't any of these people cut up rough?"

She nodded.

"Mostly—at first. They drug them for a bit, and then they settle down."

"Suppose they don't?"

Fanny looked scared.

"If they've a grain of sense they do."

"And if they haven't?"

"They go on the scrap-heap," said Fanny in a small, hard voice.

"I seem to remember your uncle telling me that."

"Then you'd best take it to heart, Captain Loddon."

Oliver stopped half way through his first cup of tea.

"And when do they begin to drug me? There isn't anything in this, I suppose? Or is there?"

Fanny's colour flamed.

"No, there isn't! And I'll thank you not to think things like that about me! I don't drug people!"

He begged her pardon, and she went away, he thought in a huff.

Presently she came back with her baby in her arms. There was no doubt about his being a true Rennard. The little frowning face with the downy red eyebrows and the thatch of orange-coloured fluff bore a most comical resemblance to the old Red Fox.

Fanny sat down with the baby in her lap and chattered away about him—his strength, his weight, his appetite, and his likeness to Ernie. All of which Oliver endured politely.

"Only I don't want him to grow up here. I can't help thinking about that, you know. It don't seem right to say that a child's never to see the sun, and moon, and rain, and trees, and all the other things that we was brought up with." She hugged the baby up under her chin and looked at Oliver over the top of his head. "What Ernie and me would like would be a little garridge. There's one going that would do us a treat in Ledlington. Ernie did his training there, you know, in the Ledlington Motor Works, and he says it'd be a real nice place to live, and real nice people there, and you can get out into the country as easy as easy, and that's what I'd like. I wasn't brought up in a town, you know, and I like being near the shops and a cinema, but I don't want to be where I can't get the sight of a field if I want to. That's what I hate about being down under—nothing but a lot of dark passages and electric lights. But I don't expect they'll ever let us go—I don't expect they'll ever let any of us go. Come to think of it, how can they? We all know too much. It'd be safer for us if we didn't." Her lips trembled. Then she jumped up. "Stupid—that's what I am. There's lots worse off than what we are. I don't know what made me get talking like this to you."

"Fanny," said Oliver, "how can I see Rose Anne?"

She had been moving towards the door, but she turned now, startled, with the baby in her arms. She said, "You can't," and backed against the door and stood there as if she would bar the way.

"Fanny, I've got to see her."

She threw up her head.

"And I tell you you can't, Captain Loddon."

"Fanny—"

"What's the use anyway?"

"I've got to know—"

She finished the sentence for him,

"Whether she's shamming or not? That's what you mean, isn't it? Now you just listen to me. Suppose you see her, and she's like she was yesterday—that won't do you any good, will it?"

"But—"

She interrupted vehemently.

"But suppose she isn't like that—suppose she's her own true self. Suppose she's been putting this on to keep Philip off, and you break her down—and I don't see how she could help but break down if you were alone with her, and you begging and beseeching and being loving to her like you would be—well, what would happen? You'd be playing into Philip's hands, neither more nor less. Do you think anything goes on here that he doesn't know? Do you think you could see Miss Rose Anne without his knowing? Why, the whole place is wired, and fixed up with microphones so they can listen in anywhere, and you never know who's hearing what you say. Why, I wouldn't dare be talking to you like I am now if it weren't that Ernie won't stand it, and he's told them so, and he knows enough to find out if there's anything fixed, and to cut it out. Why, he told them straight, Ernie did, when he brought me here—he told them bang out if we couldn't have a place where we could be private and say what we liked without every chance word being taken notice of and picked over—well, he said, 'Tisn't worth it, and 'tisn't what I call life anyway, so if that's the way it's going to be, you can put us away and have done with it, because we'd rather. Ernie's right down easy-going, but rouse him and he don't care what he says or who he says it to—and of course he knew well enough they couldn't do without him. So after that they left our rooms alone, but he keeps a bright look, Ernie does, just in case." Her colour flamed and her blue eyes shone.

Oliver said, frowning,

"You're sure—about this listening in?"

"Of course I'm sure. How do you suppose they could run this place if they didn't know what was going on? I tell you a mouse can't squeak down here without its getting to Uncle, and if it isn't the kind of squeak he likes, well, it's so much the worse for the mouse."

"Fanny—isn't there any way I can see her? Fanny, I've *got* to see her."

"Oh, you'll see her all right," said Fanny. "There's a do tonight in the big hall. Uncle's sent word for you to go. Dinner first and a show afterwards. Everyone's to be there, so you'll see her then— and for mercy's sake look out, because Philip's going to watch like a cat at a mouse-hole. He isn't one that misses much, Philip doesn't." She went out of the room on that, and left him with plenty to think about.

He dressed, tried the door, and found that it opened on to the room with the green curtains. After some groping he discovered the door which led to the gallery. Ernie loomed up as he opened it, with a suit-case in his hand.

"Feeling better this morning?"

Oliver said, "Oh, yes—quite all right." His eyes were on the suit-case. It was one he had left in the car, and that meant... He said bluntly, "That's mine."

Ernie grinned, and then looked embarrassed.

"I thought you'd be wanting your things. I brought them along for you. You'll find everything all right."

Well, they were thorough. He gave them marks for that. Any hopes he had built on his car being traced to Oakham Place died a natural death. He said,

"Very thoughtful. Did you bring the car along too?"

Ernie grinned again, less sheepishly this time.

"What do you think? She's a nice little bus. I did the best part of a hundred miles in her last night."

Well, that was that. Oliver changed the subject.

"Is there any objection to my going out?"

"Well, you might lose yourself."

Oliver laughed.

"Does that matter?"

"You might starve."

"Are there a lot of passages?"

"A good few. You're all right if you don't get away from the lights. There's a lot of old mine-workings outside of what we've got wired, and if you got off into them you'd lose your way and be lucky if you ever found it again. If you'll shut that door, I'll give you a word of warning."

Oliver shut the door.

"I'm sorry for you," said Ernie with simple directness—"and so is Fanny. We're both sorry for you, but there it stops. We can't do a thing for you, and it's best for you to know that and bear it in mind. That's one thing I want to say, and here's another. Don't you go thinking you can get away out of here or get Miss Rose Anne away, because you can't. There's just the two ways out, one that Fanny's told you about that comes out at the Angel—and she'd better have held her tongue—and the other you know already, because it's the way you came in through Oakham Place, and there isn't any man alive can get out either way except he's got the word from Uncle."

Oliver repeated this, "The word?"

Ernie nodded.

"There's a steel door that fills the passage either end, same like the door of a safe, made special to Uncle's order by Grimshaws, the big safemakers. They shut with one of those letter locks—well, you can set it to letters or figures whichever you like. It's a seven letter combination, so the chances against your hitting on the right word are a million to one or thereabouts. I used to have the word for the door to the Angel, but they've changed it since—after it came out I'd been courting Fanny—and now they don't give me the word at all. It's Mark or Philip that opens the door for me, and when I come back I have to ring through so that one of them can come along and let me in. I suppose you thought you'd got into this place when you followed Fanny and me through the hole in the wall, but if you'd gone a dozen steps farther you'd have found the steel door in front of you, and you couldn't have got through that, not without half a ton of dynamite."

"Then who knocked me out?" said Oliver.

Ernie got red about the ears.

"Well, as a matter of fact it was me."

Oliver laughed.

"And who turned on the light?"

"Well, that was Fanny. You see, when you want to get in you've got to ring through. They don't open the door till they know who's there, so anyone that's all right has got to switch the light on and stand right under it. There's a spy-hole in the door, and when they're quite sure who it is they open, and not before. So when Fanny put on the light and I saw you standing there, well, I just naturally knocked you down—and I'm sure I hope you're none the worse for it. You see, it gave me a bit of a start to think we'd been followed."

"Yes, it would. Well, thanks very much. You say it's all right for me to wander about?"

Ernie looked doubtful.

"Well, nothing's been said, but if you'll take my advice you'll go careful, and you won't do anything like trying to see Miss Rose Anne, which is bound to lead to trouble." He paused, and added, "For her sake as well as for you."

Chapter Twenty-Three

AMOS RENNARD'S feast was set. Except for the great cavern arching overhead and stretching away in all directions the scene might have been a City banquet of the nineties, for the long table was covered with the finest of linen damask and ornamented by massive plate, gold or silver-gilt. Places were laid for twenty, and the service was of silver. "Nasty scratchy stuff," as Dr Spenlow remarked at Oliver's ear.

"Well, it can't get broken," said Oliver, "and I suppose that's a consideration down here." He had had a hearty reception from Amos Rennard, who had exchanged his flannel trousers for black ones, and his patterned dressing-gown for a garment rather like a Lord Mayor's robe carried out in crimson velvet and dark fur. Some dozen people who had already collected were standing about silently at a discreet distance from the dictator's chair. Three of them were women. All had a dull and listless look. The men wore dinner jackets, and the women that kind of evening dress which is to be seen in hotels of the family type. One of the men wore a clerical collar and dark vest.

"Poor old Luke!" said Dr Spenlow. "Luke Simpson, you know. He's the only one who's been here longer than I have—beat me by a month, poor devil."

Oliver looked at the Reverend Luke Simpson and wondered what had happened to the keen, eloquent young man described to him by Mr Benbow Smith. Had he died suddenly, or fallen to a gradual decay? This was a fat man with a pale, hairless face and dull, unhappy eyes. Oliver felt sorry for him. He lifted his eyebrows and allowed his lips to form the word "drugged."

Dr Spenlow appeared to be amused.

"How angry he'd be. He has a very fierce sermon about drugging in general and the use of tobacco in particular, with excursions into the evil of strong drink. He preaches it at me once in three months or so. We attend his ministrations by order, you know, so he gets a good run for his money."

"What about the others? They all look drugged to me," said Oliver bluntly.

Dr Spenlow surveyed him reprovingly.

"A little bit free with the tongue, aren't you? Your affair of course, but in your place I should be careful—yes, very decidedly I—should—be—careful." He strung the words out, laying a strong emphasis upon them. Then, with a sudden change of manner, "What's the odds? Why not be indiscreet? *Dulce est dissipere in loco*, and so forth and so on. We drug everyone here—a little. You'll be for it yourself. I don't know why you've been let off up till now. No, that's not true—I do know, and I expect you do too. You're Philip's bait. He's using you to fish with, or he's going to use you. Queer chap, Philip—*and* deep—*and* dangerous—and *quite, quite, quite* determined to cut you out with Miss Carew. But to get the full flavour out of the situation neither you nor she must be drugged. Philip's got to think well of Philip whatever happens. Anyone can take a drugged girl by force. That's not good enough. Anyone could disgust a girl with a drugged rival. That's not good enough either. He wants to be able to say 'She chose me.' That puts Philip at the top of the tree. And at present he's not sure whether she's drugged or not. I believe he suspects me." He laughed. "I've a conscience like the driven snow—I told him so just now. So there you are. Watch out—he'll be up to something pretty soon. Like to know who all these people are? You'd better—and we've talked long enough about Philip."

Oliver said, "Yes, tell me."

"The thin, dark woman in black is Mrs Simpson."

"But he wasn't married."

He got a keen look.

"Who told you that? Well, he wasn't, but he is. She was a girl he'd had a fancy for, and the Old Fox had her fetched down under to pacify him. Poor old Luke, she nags his head off."

"What on earth does he want a parson for? He's not religious surely?"

He got Dr Harold Spenlow's reproving look again.

"I wouldn't let him hear that if I were you. He fairly oozes religion. You know—the sort which makes him feel quite sure that whatever he does is right. He can't be happy a minute unless he does feel sure, so that's what poor old Luke's here for, to bolster him up—make him feel good, and pious, and respectable. It's some job!" He laughed sardonically. "I'd rather have my own—and I'm not in love with that."

"Who are the others?" said Oliver.

"The fat woman with the grey hair is my assistant's wife. He's the little man with the bald head. He does the routine work of the laboratory. They were supposed to have been killed in an aeroplane smash. They brought her along instead of scrapping her, because she once took a science degree. If they knew how completely useless she was they'd scrap her now, but I'm a humane man, so I hold my tongue—as a rule. The thin, melancholy man is a fiddler, and the one behind him with two chins and a lot of hair is a crooner, and the one beyond him is a jazz pianist—Philip's taste. And there's Fanny—you know her—and the earnest, valuable Ernie. And that's Mark just coming across the hall."

Mark Rennard was taller than his brother Philip, and broader. In middle life he would almost certainly resemble his father. He had the ginger hair, the sandy lashes, and the heavy build, but he was pale where the Old Fox was florid. He wore a frowning look, and passed through the group on the dais without a word or a glance for anyone till he came to his father's chair and stood there bent down and talking low. Dr Spenlow gave his faint sarcastic laugh.

"A serious soul, Mark. He runs the commissariat, and it weighs on him like lead. A serious, efficient soul. That's why his father prefers Philip. Well, are you wise to our politics now?"

Oliver gave him a very direct look.

"I don't know where you stand."

The dark face twitched with something which might have been amusement.

"And you'd like to?"

"Very much."

"You won't miss anything for want of asking—will you?"

"I hope not."

"And free with the tongue, as I said before. How do you know you can trust me?"

"I don't."

Dr Spenlow laughed.

"Well, there's your answer in a nutshell—they're all in the same boat with you. They don't know if they can trust me, but they've got to, and sometimes it keeps them awake at night. You see, they can't do without me. The old man is as strong as a horse, but he thinks he's going to die if he gets a finger-ache, and he's quite sure he'd die if I wasn't there to keep the finger-aches away. Poor old Luke Simpson is his fire insurance, and I'm his life insurance, but he isn't sure he can trust me, and he daren't drug me, because nobody wants to be attended by a drugged doctor. Besides, the stuff is my own secret, and he needs me to keep the others quiet. Pretty, isn't it? Why, the only reason I'm here at all is because I treated him for an attack of gout just before the crash, and he's been obstinately convinced ever since that I saved his life."

Oliver dropped his voice and said,

"It's damnable. Why don't you dope the lot of them and get away?"

Dr Spenlow smiled with a bitter twist of the mouth.

"My dear Loddon, if you are out for information, here's something you'd better get by heart—no one has ever got away from here, and no one ever will. If anything happened to the Rennards, the rest of us would be left to starve quietly to death behind steel doors which only they know how to open. I really prefer my present existence to death from starvation. There are compensations, you know. I have an excellent laboratory, and some day, perhaps, my notes may reach the world." His eye kindled for a moment. Then he said in a different voice, "You probably won't want my advice, but here it is. Trying to get away is suicide. Trying to get Miss Carew away is suicide *cum* murder. If you've no objection to this, go ahead by all means, but you can take it from me that it's certain death. There's no way out. Do you suppose plenty of people haven't had a shot at it in the last ten years? Do you suppose I didn't have a shot at it myself? Some poor devils try the old mine-workings, and they starve or go mad. There's no way out there. No, all you can do is to make the best of it, and—there's always the drug."

A surging revolt rendered Oliver speechless. He was to accept an existence without aim, without work, without hope, without Rose Anne. Every drop of natural blood in his body said no.

He turned abruptly from Dr Spenlow, and saw Rose Anne coming across the hall. She wore a white dress that glittered as she moved. Her neck and her arms sparkled with brilliants. Her bright hair was almost hidden by a diamond wreath. Philip Rennard walked beside her. They made, as Dr Spenlow murmured, a very handsome couple.

Everything had apparently been waiting for them, for as soon as they arrived on the dais a gong boomed and the guests took their places, with Amos Rennard at the head of the table and his son Mark at the foot. There was a name-card at each place, and whilst Oliver was looking for his own name he was touched on the shoulder, and turned to see Philip Rennard with a stranger on his arm.

"You are lower down—next to Miss Carew. You don't need an introduction to her, but let me introduce you to Mademoiselle Violette de Parme." Voice and manner were those of the conventional host.

Oliver looked with interest at the lady as he acknowledged the introduction. She was very fair, very vivacious, very French. She wore her hair wreathed in the Medusa-like curls which he knew to be the latest fashion. Her black dress exposed a great deal of admirably modelled back, and was slit very nearly to the thigh to show a diamond garter, her only ornament. Her lips were as scarlet as her nails, her lashes as black as Mascara could make them. She hung on Philip's arm and looked at Oliver with a lazy allure. When she spoke her English was perfect except for the accent which no French woman ever loses. She said,

"Monsieur Loddon will be a great acquisition to our little society—n'est-ce pas, Philippe?"

To which Philip in his agreeable voice,

"I hope that will be a consolation to him."

"A great consolation," said Oliver.

He saw Mademoiselle Violette's grey-green eyes flicker sideways between their black lashes. There was some current running strongly here. He felt the pull of it, and wondered if it was dangerous. It might be—

Rose Anne was half way down the table. He wondered why he was to sit beside her, and what she would say to him, and he to her, under Philip's watching eyes, and what would be the outcome of it all.

A servant pulled back his chair and he sat down. Rose Anne's head turned towards him. The diamond wreath glittered above her smooth, white brow and candid, innocent eyes. Her look rested on him, blankly at first and then with a faint tinge of recognition.

"You are Oliver?"

And Oliver said, "Yes, Rose Anne."

She turned with a little nod and tasted the small fanciful savoury which had been set before her. Having tasted it, she laid down her fork.

"Do you think I need eat it? I don't like it very much. You know, I never did like olives."

Oliver's heart was wrung. She spoke like a confiding child. And she remembered that she disliked olives, but she had forgotten their love.

He looked across the table and saw Philip Rennard and the fair-haired French girl in the two opposite places. So that was Philip's game. Rose Anne and Oliver were to be under his microscope for an interminable hour. Not a word, not a look, not a quick-drawn breath, scarcely a beat of the pulse, but would be his to dissect, to weigh, to use.

The plates were changed. A mulligatawny soup was served to them. Rose Anne leaned back in her chair. Across the table Philip spoke to her.

"No soup, Rose?"

She shook her head and said, still in that childish tone,

"I don't like hot things."

He had her plate taken away and a cup of bouillon brought instead. And there was a fuss about that, because Amos Rennard from the head of the table wanted to know why what was good enough for him wasn't good enough for his guests. He thumped the board and made a lot of noise about it, but Rose Anne sat there pale and smiling, and when the bouillon came she sipped from it and said, "Thank you, Philip," and left most of it in the cup.

Mademoiselle Violette said in her sharp, high-pitched voice,

"And if I say that I do not like the fish, what will you do for me, Philippe? Will you serve me a fish of paradise in a gold dish, *mon ami*?"

Philip said without any attempt to lower his voice, "What a hope!"

The colour stung her cheeks, burning through the rouge that was there already. She said something quickly in French on a dropped note. And Philip, as loudly as before:

"You'll get no more from me, my dear."

The drugged faces on either side of the table showed no sign. Their jaws moved as they ate. They looked at the food on their plates. It made no difference to them whether Mademoiselle Violette de Parme had her nose put out of joint or not.

Oliver looked past them and caught Dr Spenlow's eye. Then from beside him Rose Anne spoke, reproving Philip.

"I think that's rather rude," she said. "I don't think you ought to speak to her like that."

Philip let his eyes dwell on her as if they were alone. He said,

"I'm sorry."

And Rose Anne:

"You ought to say that to her, not to me."

He smiled, and was Prince Charming to the life.

"I will if you want me to, Rose."

"Yes, please, Philip."

He turned at once and spoke to Mademoiselle Violette.

"I am reproved, you see. I was unpardonably rude, but I am sure you will forgive me."

She had turned perfectly white with rage. The artificial colour stood ghastly on her cheek-bones. Her lips were so drawn in that the shape of the skull could be seen. Oliver was horrified and dismayed. His apology was more of an insult than the original offence, and Rose Anne had lent herself to it. He was afraid for her with all his heart, and there was nothing that he could do. The current he had felt before was carrying them all away. Philip sat there smiling.

Violette did not speak. She stared across the table at Rose Anne with a stinging hatred in her eyes. The service of Amos Rennard's feast went on.

If the chef was drugged, it did not affect his skill. The Old Fox liked good food and plenty of it. He sat in his red velvet robe at the head of the table and disposed of the menu plateful by plateful. Mark appeared to be a good trencherman too, but Philip ate little, and Mademoiselle Violette nothing at all.

Oliver turned to Rose Anne in the silence which followed Philip's apology. Since this appeared to be the Palace of Truth, he might as well be in the mode. He touched one of her gleaming bracelets with the tip of his finger.

"Diamonds?"

She moved her arm. He was to remember that she must not be touched. Having moved it, she said in her gentle, distinct voice,

"Yes."

"And your necklace? You used not to have any diamonds, Rose Anne."

"No. Philip gave them to me. They cost a great deal."

Oliver wondered whether Philip had paid for them, or whether he could be made to pay with a really satisfying term of penal servitude. He said,

"I'm sure they did."

The necklace was a double chain of brilliants linked here and there with a diamond rose. The wreath in her hair repeated the pattern. She lifted the chain to catch the light and let it fall again.

"They are very beautiful, but I don't like wearing them—really." She leaned forward and spoke to Philip, who was watching her. "Don't you think I might take them off now?"

"Why, Rose?"

"Cold," said Rose Anne. She unclasped one of the bracelets and laid it down on the white table-cloth. "Hard." A second bracelet was laid beside the first. "Very—very—heavy." She slipped them all off and pushed the glittering pile towards him.

Philip Rennard's smiling gaze rested on it for a moment, then went to her bare white arms. He said in a low, intimate tone,

"Quite right, Rose—your arms are too beautiful to be hidden."

But she turned to Oliver.

"Do you like that better?"

"Much better, Rose Anne."

"But I like the chain round your neck," said Philip across the table—"and the wreath in your hair. It ought to be a crown, but you shall have a crown too some day."

She lifted the chain over her head and laid it down. Then her hands went to the wreath.

"Rose—" Philip's voice had an insistent note, but the wreath was lifted from the bright hair and laid beside the chain. Rose Anne met his dark gaze with the blue innocence of her own.

"Thank you, Philip. It was so kind of you, but they hurt."

Philip picked up the diamonds gravely.

"I wouldn't have you hurt for all the diamonds in the world. Shall I give them away?"

"Yes, please."

"To Violette?"

"If you like, Philip."

He dropped the glittering handful into the French girl's lap.

"A present from Rose," he said in a light laughing tone.

Oliver expected an explosion, but none came. Violette's dreadful pallor remained unchanged as death. Her black lashes flickered up and down again. The drawn-in lips moved and said,

"Thank you, Philippe."

It was at this moment that the lights went out. Through the whole hall the great arc-lamps flickered once and died. Like a curtain darkness fell. And with it something else. Oliver's vague fear of what this hour might hold for them became an agony of terror for Rose Anne. His arm was round her before he had time for conscious thought, and his lips were at her ear.

"Rose Anne!"

She turned. Her lips touched his. He felt them move, and felt her draw away. Her open palm pressed hard against his shoulder, holding him off. The bright beam of an electric torch struck between them like a dividing sword. She said in a sweet, cool voice,

"I don't like to be touched."

At her last word the lights came on again. They shone down on Amos Rennard's amazing tangle of hair and beard, on Dr Harold Spenlow surveying the scene with a sardonic eye, on Fanny flushed and frightened, on a dozen dull drugged faces, and on Philip Rennard. He had pushed back his chair and was standing. His left hand held the electric torch. With his right he had Violette de Parme by the wrist. She too had risen—perhaps she had risen first. The diamonds which he had flung her lay unregarded at her feet. The hand whose wrist he had caught held a small, sharp dagger, a mere toy for size, with a razor edge which caught the light. The torch went into his pocket, and he had her in a grip in which she could not move. The telling spins it out. In the acting it all went by in a flash as the lights came on. The girl shrieked as he twisted her wrist. The knife dropped, and he put his foot on it. He shook her with such violence that she had no more breath to scream with, and threw her back into her chair.

"Sit there and behave yourself!"

The knife joined the torch in his pocket. The diamonds lay where they were. The ordered service of the feast went on.

Chapter Twenty-Four

THE INTERMINABLE MEAL was over at last. If the servants were drugged they were amazingly efficient. As soon as Amos Rennard rose the table was cleared, broken into leaves and carried away. The chairs were ranged in a semicircle, curving to right and left of the Old Fox's seat. The guests took their places.

Rose Anne was between Philip and his father. The French girl sat in a brooding silence with Luke Simpson on one side and his wife on the other. They spoke neither to one another nor to her. Oliver found himself last but one on the left, with Dr Spenlow beyond him, and Dr Spenlow's assistant on his other side. He said,

"What happens next?"

Harold Spenlow had a trick of the voice which took his words just as far as he meant them to go and no farther. He used it now.

"Music—to soothe our savage passions."

"What kind of music?"

Dr Spenlow laughed.

"Good—bad—indifferent—and, to my mind, damnable. According to your taste. Philip has the most catholic taste—Josef Piglosiewiez for a start. He was the rage of Europe, I'm told, before Philip lifted him. The affair made some stir."

One end of the dais had been raised to form a stage. There was a grand piano, a screen or two, and some palms—enough to call up the illusion of a concert platform. To this stage the thin, melancholy man whom Harold Spenlow had pointed out before dinner advanced, violin in hand. A much older man with a bush of grey hair opened the grand piano and sat down to it.

Josef Piglosiewiez lifted his violin to his shoulder. There was a chord, a murmur of accompaniment, and the faint sweet notes of a lullaby came upon the air. It was the softest, most ethereal playing, like something remembered, like something heard in a dream. When it was over, the violinist bowed as gravely and conventionally as if from the platform of Queen's Hall. Three bows, and then a racing tarantelle, inconceivably swift, every note perfect. At the end he bowed again without a smile and came back to the chair he had left.

"Is *he* drugged?" said Oliver at Dr Spenlow's ear.

"You don't think he could play like that? But it doesn't work that way. They don't have enough to spoil them for their jobs, only enough to take the fight out of them, to keep them from kicking against the pricks. They go on doing the thing they know, and they go on doing it as well as ever, but they don't start anything new. We've no revolutionary dare-devils down here, and no go-getters. Now sit back and listen to our nice tame crooner."

The crooner had two chins and a lot of hair, and fat white fingers which were marvellously agile upon the keys. He sang in a meltingly effeminate voice:

"Lost—a heart as good as new,
Lost the moment I saw you—"

Oliver turned and looked at Rose Anne. It had been that way with him. He had seen her, and he had loved her once for all. But it had been that way with Philip Rennard too—and what was to happen to her between them?

"Finders keepers—losers weepers," wailed the crooner with dismal appropriateness.

Amos Rennard broke into a hearty, coarse guffaw and slapped his knee. Oliver could not hear what he said, but he could guess it well enough. He turned away sick with hopeless rage, and heard the song go on:

"Lost—two lips that look like mine,
Found—two lips that are divine.
I lost my heart, but I was lucky too,
Because I lost my heart—to you."

One of the women sang after that, an old-fashioned sentimental ballad of the *Just a Song at Twilight* type with a super-sugary tune. The voice was pretty, the words, the tune, the sentiment all as pretty as could be. Amos Rennard enjoyed it thoroughly. He beat time, he wagged his beard to it, he hummed the refrain.

Followed a jazz pianist who exhibited the most remarkable gymnastic feats and slammed, banged, thumped and bumped his way through a lively collection of the latest dance hits.

There was a little hitch after that. It appeared that Mademoiselle Violette was to dance, and that she refused, not in so many words but in a pose of sulky languor, head against the back of her tall chair, hands laid open in her lap, feet passively resistant.

Philip got up, went over to her, offered his arm. She looked at her reddened finger-tips. He bent and spoke to her. She slapped his face. It was over in a flash. He straightened himself.

Amos roared with laughter, and Mademoiselle Violette sprang to her feet, blew a kiss to the audience, and ran up on to the stage, where the pianist sat staring.

Her dance was an amazing thing, spirited, vicious, alluring. Oliver could well imagine that Paris had mourned for her. She had a daring technique and a wild, wilful grace. He guessed her to be at the top of her form. He said to Harold Spenlow, "You're not going to tell me that girl's drugged," and got a shake of the head.

"Not much! Philip wouldn't get any kick out of it if she were. It amuses him to go around striking matches in a powder-magazine, but if the powder was wet, there would be no fun about it. He likes to get a kick out of things."

Philip Rennard stood watching the dance with the red mark of the dancer's hand across his cheek. He leaned on the back of Rose Anne's chair, and sometimes he bent down and spoke to her, but only she could hear what he said. Whatever it was, it did not move her from her gentle silence or change the faint smile about her lips.

Violette de Parme flung back her fair hair and bowed.

"Why do you not all dance?" she cried in a shrill, ringing voice. "Why watch me? Why not dance yourselves and get your blood to run again, and your feet to move again, and your hearts—perhaps—to beat again?"

She ran down from the platform, smiling, animated.

"Well, Philippe, what do you say? Did I dance well? Let us see if anyone can dance better. You shall have Miss Carew for a partner and I will have Captain Loddon, and we will see who dances the best. Jacques shall play, and we shall dance—Oh, all of us, for this once—even your Reverend Luke, and the Mrs Reverend Luke, and the scientific Dr Spenlow, and the serious Monsieur Ernie. Let them all be a little mad for once, and dance, and forget that when the dance is over there are no streets outside, no lights, no taxis, no gay world waiting to applaud!" She had dropped her voice, and only Philip heard the end. Rose Anne might have heard it too, but if she did she made no sign.

Philip laughed.

"Now I wonder whether you would really like the key of the street. I think not, somehow. And now, as you suggest, we'll dance."

The crimson carpet was rolled up, the chairs removed, Amos Rennard's throne set in state upon the platform, and the dancing began. Curious and melancholy to see these lethargic people revolving to the strains of the *Blue Danube*. Luke Simpson did not dance, but his wife did. In her high-necked black silk, with a string of very white artificial pearls and a straggle of mouse-coloured hair slipping down from under the net which failed to control it, she made her small, neat steps, talking all the time in a colourless monotone to the little bald-headed Professor, who never spoke at all. Fanny and Ernie danced together, and looked happy.

Rose Anne went round in Philip Rennard's arms. He held her lightly and talked low, and if she did not hear him nobody else did. She did not speak. She suffered his arm at her waist and permitted her fingers to rest on his, and that was all. Step matched step as they swung to the perfect rhythm.

Mademoiselle Violette said, with her hand on Oliver's arm,

"They go well together—*hein*? You don't like that? Nor do I. Philippe is a good dancer, is he not? He should be, since he has practised with me for—I don't remember how long. Come—we are to dance together. Let us show them what we can do."

"Please don't expect very much," said Oliver. "I haven't had Rennard's advantages, you see."

She threw back her head and laughed. Her laughter had the same ringing sound as her voice when she called on them to dance.

"No, it is he who has taken the advantage of you." Then, as they slid into the dance, "What is going to come of it, *mon brave Capitaine*?"

"I don't know," said Oliver. "Do you?"

"That depends—"

"Upon what?"

"Upon how brave you are, *mon Capitaine*."

"Oh, enormously," said Oliver.

She was so light in his arms that he could hardly feel her there, yet in some mysterious way she imparted her own movement and grace. She imparted too a sense of adventure, a quickening of the pulses.

She looked up at him between those amazingly dark lashes, and he saw a little green devil there. It winked and beckoned to him. The lashes went down again. He was in no mood to follow little green devils, and in no mood to play with fire in Philip's private powder-magazine. He thought he had enough on hand without that.

Violette said softly, "I think you are brave. You will need to be. All these people whom you see, they have no courage any more. If they ever had any, it has been stolen away from them by Dr Spenlow's drug. Now they are not brave any more, nor sad any more, nor happy any more, nor anything any more at all. Oh, *mon Dieu*, Captain Loddon—do you want to be like that? For me I would rather die. And you?"

Oliver said, "Yes," and felt it very sincerely.

Mademoiselle Violette went on, low and quick.

"Just now if I had stabbed your Miss Rose, Philippe would have killed me—I would be dead—it would be all over—finished. It is a pity, is it not?"

"You don't expect me to say yes to that, do you?" said Oliver.
She laughed.

"Perhaps not. You love her very much, your Miss Rose?"

"Yes."

"What a block of ice you are, *mon Capitaine*! One cold word—is
that all you have for her?... Well then, I am to understand that you
love her very much—all in this one cold word. Now, my brave, my
very brave Captain, what will you do for her? Anything? Nothing?"

"Anything."

"*Je te crois bien!* Well then, listen to me. If you are to do anything
at all you will have to do it quickly. Philippe has waited, but he will
not go on waiting. It has intrigued him this pose of the patient lover,
but it is only a pose. He is not patient at all, he is cruel—like a cat
with a mouse. If he can make anyone suffer, that amuses him very
well. It has amused him to make me jealous, to insult me, to drive
me if he can into some folly which he can laugh at. But now—I
know him so well—he is getting tired of all that. He looks for a new
pose—he will be the strong man who takes what he wants." She
laughed a little hysterically. "It will be all most *comme il faut*, most
respectable. The Reverend Luke will marry him to your Miss Rose.
That is another slap in the face for me, do you understand?"

Oliver's hand closed hard on hers.

"Do you know this, or is it guesswork?"

She looked up at him defiantly.

"I know what I know. I am not clever enough to guess."

"How do you know?"

"You do not believe me? What an unamiable disposition you
have, *mon Capitaine*! Very well, I will tell you how I know. Do you
see that woman there? No, not dancing—the one in black. She is a
compatriot of mine. Her name is Louise Couperin, and once she was
Louise and a famous *couturière* in Paris. Philippe had her brought
down here because he did not wish that I should lose my *chic*. He
said all these women were too dowdy." She laughed. "Louise herself
cannot make the Reverend Mrs Luke anything but dowdy. Well—*à
nos moutons*! Louise has told me tonight that she is to make the
wedding dress for your Miss Rose—*and she is to make it quick*.
Philippe has asked her how quick she can make it, and she has

answered in two days, with Marie to help her—that is, today and tomorrow. So I think that the wedding will be on the next day after that. You have two nights and one day to save your Miss Rose."

All this time they were dancing, their feet keeping time to music which they did not hear. Oliver said,

"You've not told me this for nothing, I suppose. How can I save her?"

She lifted her chin and said scornfully,

"You can take her away, my brave Captain."

"As easily as that? I have been told that there is no way out except by leave of the Rennards."

Her eyes were green as she looked at him.

"They have two gates, and they keep them locked. You cannot get out by the gates—that is quite true."

"Is there another way? I have been told there is none."

"Then you must make up your mind whom you will believe."

Oliver said quick and low, "Is there another way—*is there*?"

Her hand pressed his shoulder. She dropped her voice.

"When Philippe was in love with me he would talk about this place and boast about it. You know, some of it is old mines, and some caverns, and some they have made for themselves. The galleries of the old mines run a long way, and they do not use them all. There are some that are dangerous, and some that are fallen in, and some have—what do you call it?—a shaft that has been filled up, and some have perhaps a shaft that has not been quite filled up. I will tell you this, I have seen a star shining overhead when I was there with Philippe in one of those galleries, and when I said to him, 'Now, *mon ami*, I know what I shall do when I am tired of you—I shall climb up to that star.' And Philippe he laughed and said, 'You would have a long way to climb.' "

"What was the place like?" said Oliver.

"Like a big chimney."

"Climbable?"

"For me, no—for you, perhaps. I do not know. It is a long time ago. You would need a rope for your Miss Rose."

"Where is this place?"

"In the old galleries. I cannot tell you more than that. I do not remember the way."

"The way into the old galleries?"

She laughed and shook her head.

"There are twenty ways into the old galleries. All the roads we use run into them if you go far enough. So far they are lighted, but pass the lights and you are in the old galleries, and you may lose yourself and never come back. I have been in them with Philippe, but by myself—*jamais de la vie!*"

"But you suggest that I should take Rose Anne there?"

She shrugged her very white shoulders.

"You might find the star—there is always a chance. Here there is none."

Oliver said suddenly, "I'm going to say just what I think. It seems to be the fashion here."

She looked at him, half smiling, wholly alert.

"Well, M'amselle Violette, I can see that it would suit your book uncommonly well if I were to take Rose Anne into the old galleries and lose her and myself and never come back. That jumps to the eye, doesn't it? What I don't quite see is, what do we get out of it?"

Her eyes flashed green, and were veiled again.

"If you prefer that she marries Philippe—" she said. Then, with a sudden rush of words, "You do not trust me! You suspect—you think that I am not sincere—that I would betray you! Very well then, think what you please—it does not matter to me! I was a fool to be sorry for you, to have the wish to help—and I think that I have danced with you long enough, and perhaps a little too long!"

She twisted away from him and was gone.

Chapter Twenty-Five

OLIVER CROSSED over to Fanny and asked her for a dance. She flushed, looked troubled, and turned her eyes on Ernie.

"Don't you let her dance with anyone else?" said Oliver, smiling. "We're old acquaintances, you know."

Ernie looked troubled too.

"She can dance with you all right, Captain Loddon, but—well, least said soonest mended."

Oliver put his arm round Fanny and steered her into the dance. The pianist struck up a noisy foxtrot, all fireworks and bangs. It made very good cover for a confidential talk. But it was immediately obvious that a confidential talk was the last thing Fanny wanted. Oliver's "I had to speak to you," was met by a nervous giggle.

"Fancy you saying that to Ernie! Why you might have made trouble between us."

"Fanny—"

She rattled on.

"I love dancing. Don't you? And the floor's good—isn't it? They do all this sort of thing awfully well. Have you noticed the lights? They're the very latest idea—natural sunshine. Uncle had them put in because it gave him the pip seeing nothing but a lot of pale faces all the time. To tell you truth and honest, it scared him seeing his own face in the glass without any colour, so he got these lights put in. They make you real brown like being at the seaside. Uncle's ever so pleased with them."

"Fanny—for God's sake—is it true—about Rose Anne—that he means to marry her?"

Fanny was silent. The pianist hit the piano till it screamed. She said at last,

"Who's been telling you that? M'amselle Violette, I suppose."

"Is it true?"

"It's no use your asking me."

"Fanny!"

"It's no use, I tell you. I've Ernie to think about, and my baby, and I'm not going to be drawn in. Ernie and me we've talked it over, and we've got to think about ourselves. It isn't as if there's anything we can do neither. If Philip wants her he'll take her, and she'd better be married to him when all's said and done. There isn't nobody and nothing can stop Philip when he's set on a thing. You shouldn't have come butting in on his affairs, and that's the truth."

Oliver's face hardened.

"It seems to me that it's the other way round. It was Philip who did the butting in, and he's going to pay for it."

"I think we'd better stop dancing."

"And tell the world we are talking so seriously that we've quarrelled? I really shouldn't if I were you, Fanny."

"Well, what about it if you make me cry?"

"You mustn't—that's what about it. You must smile and look as if I was paying you compliments. And if you've got to look scared, look scared at Ernie as if you thought he might be going to cut up jealous."

"Well, and he might too," said Fanny with a shaky giggle. "And I'm scared all right. Get on with what you've got to say and have done. Philip's watching us."

"Let him! He can't hear a word through this din. Fanny, *is* there any way out?"

"Not except through the gates there isn't. Don't you believe anyone who says there is—not on any account. If it's that Violet, you just look out, Captain Loddon. She's as spiteful as a monkey, and she fair hates Miss Rose Anne."

The pianist's fingers raced up seven octaves and down again to a final explosive chord. Fanny disengaged herself with decision.

"*There*—thank goodness that's over!" she said. "And it's no use your asking me again neither, because I'm through."

Oliver smiled.

"Did you ever hear of Jenny Baxter?"

"No. Who's she?" She stared suspiciously.

"She refused the man before he axed her. Thank you for a most enjoyable dance, Mrs Rennard."

Fanny said, "Well, I never!" And then, as Ernie joined her, "I didn't say anything—I didn't really—only about the lights, and the floor, and such-like. But M'amselle's been talking. He knows. Oh mercy, Ernie,—just you look at that! He's asking Miss Rose Anne to dance! Whatever will Philip say?"

"It's what he'll do that matters," said Ernie in a gloomy voice.

What Philip did was to take the floor with Mademoiselle Violette. Their steps went together so perfectly, there seemed a chance that she might retain at least a dancing hold on his erratic affections. No man who fancied himself as a dancer could be insensible to the attraction of such a partner.

Oliver danced with Rose Anne, his hand at her waist, her fingers lightly held in his. He looked down on the bright hair from which she had taken Philip's diamond wreath. His crown had hurt her head. She had uncrowned herself—at Oliver's word? He thought so. He was not sure. He had to be sure.

They moved to the soft melody of a waltz. No fireworks now, worse luck, but a gentle, gliding air, haunting and sweet:

"I was not in love with you
Till you loved me.
I was only in love with love
Till you loved me.
Now the moon and the stars above
All are singing a song of love,
All are singing a song that's new,
For I love you."

The crooner wailed the words. The time slowed and dragged. The air dripped sentiment. Oliver would have liked to take the pianist by one of his flapping ears and the crooner by his second chin, bang their heads together, and chuck them sprawling in amongst the strings of the grand piano. He said in a stiff, hard voice,

"There's been about enough of this."

The lashes lay dark upon her smooth, pale cheeks. She smiled faintly. Without any movement of the lips her voice came to him like a ghost. It carried words just audible, but only just.

"What can we do?"

It was the first response he could be sure about, and it moved him dangerously. His love, his passion, his agony of fear for her had been beating unavailingly against the blank wall of her gentle silence. Now that she answered him at last, he had no words with which to answer her. If they had been alone, no words would have been needed between them, but all those Rennard eyes were watching.

The breath came again. It said,

"We can't talk here. They are watching us."

Oliver said, "Where?"

The question seemed to hang between them. Rose Anne had no answer to it. She said,

"Oliver—go away—you can't help me—better for you to go away—he's using you—to force me."

"How?"

"He'll kill you—if I don't. He says—all the things he'll do—and watches to see—if I am frightened—if I understand. He isn't sure—whether I understand."

"I wasn't sure either."

"Did I really—do it well enough to take you in?"

"Yes, you did. I've been nearly mad."

She said, "My poor, poor darling."

Such a soft, tender breath carried the words. They shook him as nothing had shaken him yet. He said harshly,

"Don't say things like that—I can't stand it."

She said, "It's a bad dream. We'll wake up some day."

"It will have to be soon," said Oliver.

They were at the far end of the dais. Philip and the French girl were on the opposite side. Rose Anne said,

"Try and get away. You must—it's the only way to help me. If you are here, he will *make* me marry him. If you are not here, I can hold him off—I think."

"There isn't any way. If I could get out and bring help I'd risk it, but there isn't any way, only—"

"Only what?"

"That French girl says there's a shaft running up from the old galleries—or there used to be. She swears she saw the sky, and a star shining. She says Philip took her there, and she thinks the shaft is climbable. Fanny swears there's no way out, but Fanny mightn't know—she hasn't been down here so very long."

"I'd trust Fanny. I wouldn't trust Violette."

"You trusted the Garstnets once too often," said Oliver. He felt her wince, and said quickly, "What happened? Tell me what happened that night at the Angel."

Rose Anne said, still in that soundless voice,

"Would anyone know I was talking? Am I moving my lips?"

"No, no one would know. You look half asleep. I've nearly gone mad watching you. Tell me what happened when you went to the Angel."

"Florrie wasn't bad really. I couldn't think why they'd sent for me. Then Nannie said they wanted to drink my health, and would I come into the parlour. So I did, and they had port and I had ginger wine, and when I'd drunk about half I thought it had a funny taste, and the room went round, and I thought I was going to faint. Then I heard Nannie say, 'You've killed her. Oh, Matthew!' And I felt them lift me, and then I didn't feel anything more till I woke up down here with a frightful head. And I thought my best chance was to pretend I hadn't really come round."

"You did it awfully well. You took me in."

"Philip's not sure," said Rose Anne. "He makes love to me, and I have just to keep on smiling, and when he's tired of that he tells me all the things he'll do to you if I don't marry him. It sounds as if he was mad, but he isn't really—at least I don't think he is. He's cruel—he likes to hurt—and nobody has ever crossed him since he was sixteen. He made me write that dreadful letter. Oh, darling, did you find what I wrote between the lines? There was a raw egg Marie was going to beat up for me, and I did it with that, but I hadn't time to finish."

Chapter Twenty-Six

THE MUSIC stopped. It was Philip Rennard who stopped it with a clap of the hands and a word in the pianist's ear. The dancers stood about irresolute. Philip came across with Violette on his arm.

"Well, Rose?" he said. "Have you said good-bye to the old love and told him you're on with the new? You know, you've come here in the nick of time, Loddon. You missed your own wedding, but you won't miss mine. I hope Rose has given you an invitation."

Oliver said nothing. Anything he said would probably gratify Philip. There was nothing to say. Nothing to do either, since if he were to knock Philip down he would most certainly be relegated to a cell and locked in. His present measure of liberty might not be worth very much, but it was better than nothing at all. He thought, "If I kill him, they'll kill me, and God knows what will happen to Rose Anne." No—not until the last desperate moment should he cease to play a waiting, watching game.

"Well, Rose?" said Philip. "You're very silent. Have you nothing to say to Captain Loddon either?"

Rose Anne lifted her eyes.

"What am I to say?"

"Say, 'My dear Oliver.' "

She repeated the words like a child—"My dear Oliver," and stopped there, watching his face.

"Go on, Rose. Say, 'I am going to be married.' "

She echoed this too—"I am going to be married—Am I going to be married, Philip?"

Philip Rennard smiled.

"You are, my dear. Aren't you the lucky girl? Go on—tell Captain Loddon how lucky you are. Say, 'Please come to my wedding.'"

She spoke like a docile child—"Please come to my wedding, Oliver." Her eyes met his sweetly, blankly.

"But you haven't told him that I'm the lucky man. You must do that, you know. He would like to hear it from your own lips, I feel sure. Say, 'I am going to marry Philip Rennard whom I love very much.'"

A small frown drew her brows together.

"But I don't want to be married, Philip."

He dropped a hand on her shoulder and let it lie there carelessly.

"Do what you're told, Rose."

She stood silent.

"Come—I'm waiting."

"Take your hand off her shoulder!" said Oliver.

"Or you'll make me? I don't think I should, you know—not if I were you—not until you've asked, let us say Fanny, to tell you what happened to Gregory Ledowski. He thought he had a grievance. He is dead. Very unpleasant for him. I am none the worse, as you see. I think I am probably stronger than you, and I am almost certainly a better boxer. You had better accept the situation. I don't suppose

Rose would like any unpleasantness over her wedding. You ask someone to tell you about Ledowski."

Mademoiselle Violette laughed.

"Why do you not tell him yourself, Philippe? This Ledowski was a big fool. I told him so, but he would not believe me. He was in love with me, and he tried to kill Philippe—quick. And Philippe killed him—slow—oh, so very, very slow. But he did not make me watch, as he will make your Miss Rose watch when he kills you."

A tremor passed over Rose Anne. She turned on Philip the eyes of a frightened child.

"Please make her stop."

"*Tais-toi, Violette!*" said Philip, smiling. "And now dance again."

He called over his shoulder, "My dance, Jack," and the next moment he had swept Rose Anne into the rhythm of the Rosenkavalier waltz.

Violette turned her eyes on Oliver. She said,

"Do you like to stand there whilst they dance? It does not amuse me at all."

Oliver managed a smile.

"Does that mean that you would take pity on me? I hope it does."

"Pity?" She shrugged her shoulders. "I have none for you, my brave Captain—I need it all for myself. But I will dance with you. You would not be too bad if I were to teach you a little." They were out upon the floor before she added, "I could teach you—how to dance—and perhaps other things too."

Oliver said quite low, "Tell me how to find the shaft, Violette."

She threw back her head and laughed with her lips and eyes, but not with any sound.

"So that you may go away and never see me again—*hein*?"

He said, bending closer, "Do you want to stay here all your life? You are young, you are very pretty, you had Paris at your feet. Do you want to stay down here where Philip neglects and insults you? There are lots of good fish in the sea, you know. You are wasting your time."

He heard her catch in her breath.

"Do you think I stay because I want to, or because I am so much in love with Philippe that I do not care that time passes—that one is not young for ever—that Paris forgets? *Je te dis que non, non, non, non, non*—and no, no, no, no, *no*! I am not one of those who will stay in the empty theatre when the curtain is fallen and the play is over. There are other plays—I ask no better than to find one. With Philippe it is at an end. He has your Miss Rose, and after her there will be someone else. But for me—I ask you who is there for me? If there were—" Her eyes said, "If there were you!"

Oliver looked over the top of her head and saw Philip and Rose Anne go by. He saw Rose Anne's lips move, and wondered what she said. He answered Violette urgently.

"Of course there's no one—down here. But you could have Paris at your feet again. Help me now, and I will help you. Tell me how to get out, and I will get you out of this trap."

She said, "Wait! Don't talk—he is watching you. I must think."

They danced the length of the room and back again before she said,

"It is true what I told you about the chimney, but I went there with Philippe—I do not know the way. And that chimney, I think they will have built it up, but even if it is still there, I do not think it could be climbed."

"You said it could."

She laughed, aloud this time.

"*O mon ami*, I say a great many things that I do not mean—you are not to take notice of everything that I say. But this I know, when Philippe took me into the old galleries we went first down those steps which are over there—near the gate through which you came. There—you see there is an arch a little to the left, and first there are three steps down, and a passage with lights, and then many steps, and after a little no more lights. But Philippe had a torch—"

"Yes—go on."

Her eyebrows went up high.

"But that is all. We turned this way, that way—how do I know what way? I did not think about it—oh, not at all. And then suddenly I look up and I see a star, but I do not say that I have seen it, I hold my tongue, and Philippe he makes his torch flash into my eyes, and he says we have come wrong, this is a very, dangerous place, and we must go back quick. And that is all I know, and it is no use that you ask me to remember more, because there is no more that I can say."

Ernie came up beside them and touched Oliver on the arm.

"Uncle wants you," he said. "What about me for a partner, Miss Violet?"

She looked at him sideways.

"Oh, la, la, la—and what will Fanny say?"

Oliver made his way to the chair that had been set by the Old Fox's throne. He received a hearty greeting.

"Come along, Captain Loddon—come along! I'm your host, you know, and I'd like a bit of a talk with you myself if you're not too busy running after the girls. And look here, you take my advise and don't you do too much running after that Ma'mselle Violet. For one thing, she won't do you any good, and for another you don't need to get Philip any more worked up with you than he is already. She's his property, and he don't like having his property meddled with, so you just sit right down here and talk to me."

The talk was mostly on his side. He was immensely proud of his kingdom, and perfectly willing to impart floods of information about it. Oliver desired nothing better than to listen. The more copious the floods, the more chances of driftwood.

The Old Fox blew out his red cheeks and talked pridefully of his cleverness in securing such an impregnable retreat.

"I'd been thinking about it a long time, you know. I'd seen one or two things happen that made me think a bit. A man I'd dined with regular for ten years and stayed week-ends with in his country place with swimming baths, and tennis-courts, and fisheries, and vineries, and conservatories, and what not—he came crash and got fourteen years. And there was another fellow that I didn't know so well, but I knew him, and one week he was dining with lords and earls and dukes, and the next, so to speak, he was taking poison in the dock, and headlines about him in all the evening papers. Well, it makes a man sit up and think. You can see that—can't you?"

Oliver said, "Yes—very stimulating to thought," and got a sharp look out of the little piggy eyes.

"Well then, there I was. I'd fifteen companies running just then, and it's like a game of musical chairs, if you get my meaning. You've got to keep the money moving and pray the music won't stop in the wrong place. Great times, but a bit on the nervous side. So I thought I'd have a bolt-hole handy. There was a man I met in an air raid—we took shelter together in a tube station and you couldn't get near the trains, so there he was drinking neat whisky out of a flask he'd got on him and telling me the story of his life, and I put him down for the best liar I'd ever run across, but it seemed I was wrong. By the time he was three parts drunk he was telling me about how his family used to smuggle the best French brandy and never pay a penn'orth of duty on it, and lace and silk and anything else they fancied, right back for a couple of hundred years. I wasn't really interested, and I expect that's why he was so set on telling me all about it. He got hold of me by my coat, and every time he had a sip of whisky he told me some more. He told me it all began with the mine-workings, because someone had the bright idea of making a way into the mine and using the mine shaft at night to let the stuff down. The first way through was made between the cellars of a pub called the Angel and the mine behind it. He said the hill rose up steep at the back of the house and they'd only a little way to tunnel before they got into the mine. He said that was at a place called Hillick St Agnes, and there used to be a shaft there, but it was filled up now. Well, his family used the Angel for a long time, and then they found that the mine-workings ran out into a lot of caves. The lode finished there, so the mine was given up. The caves interested his family very much. He said they ran for the best part of ten miles and joined up with another mine which was under a village called Oakham. All that part of the country belonged to his people then—it must have been a long time ago. Oakham Place belonged to them, so all they had to do was to copy the way into the mines they'd got at the Angel, and that's what they did."

"It's ten miles from Hillick St Agnes to Oakham," said Oliver.

Amos Rennard blew out his cheeks.

"Here—who's telling this—you or me? It may be ten miles by road and rail, but it's five the way the water runs."

"Oh, there's water?"

"There wouldn't be caves if there wasn't. It's the water makes the caves. We've covered it in here, but it runs all along that wall. It took a lot of labour, but we paved it over. It made me feel giddy to see it running all the time, so I had it done."

Water... Oliver felt a secret excitement. Water gave you something to follow. Water generally meant a way out sooner or later—*not always...*

"...so I thought he was a liar"—Oliver had missed something there—"and I told him so, and the more I told him the more he told me—how to work the stone and open the secret door, and the whole bag of tricks. He'd finished his flask and he was as drunk as a lord, and I couldn't get away from him, there was such a crowd, and there he stood telling me things I didn't want to hear and shoving his card into my hand. I put it in my pocket and forgot all about it except that I remembered his name, which was Henry Oakham. And there was another raid next day, and I saw in the paper he'd been killed, and then I'd got my hands too full to think of him again. But when I wanted to make sure of having a bolt-hole, something said 'Henry Oakham,' and I thought I'd find out how much of a liar he'd been. Oakham Place was empty, and I got an order to view, and when I got there, every single word that Henry had said came back. I give you my word, Captain Loddon, I could feel him hanging on my coat, and I could smell the whisky, and what's more, I remembered how to open the door, and I opened it same as you must have done— Ernie swears you didn't slip in behind him and Fan."

"No, I opened it."

The Old Fox slapped his knee.

"So did I. And when I saw the steps and all I took off my hat to Henry Oakham and begged his pardon for having called him a liar for the best part of six years. 'And here's my bolt-hole,' I said, and I went back home and bought Oakham Place and the Angel at Hillick St Agnes. Not in my own name of course—that would have been a mug's game. No, I was pretty clever over the deal and covered up my tracks middling well, and when it was all fixed I put my brother-in-law Matthew Garstnet into the Angel, and I told my brother Joseph's widow there was a housekeeper's job waiting for her up at Oakham Place any time she liked, only she'd have to take it under another name. And she said what did she want with housekeeper's jobs when she'd got Ernie to do for? But she took it fast enough, and glad to get it, when Ernie came down under. He's a good boy, Ernie."

Cold through Oliver's mind went the thought, cold as the bleakest north-east wind, "He's giving the whole show away. Why?" And in the same breath the answer, "Dead men tell no tales. I'm as good as dead."

The little piggy eyes looked sharply at him under the red thatch of Amos Rennard's brows.

"You're thinking I talk a lot. Well, young man, and why not? There's not so much else I can do nowadays—I'm too fat. And there's no need for secrets amongst us down under." He planted a coarse hairy hand on either knee and wagged his beard. "Perhaps I like talking, and perhaps I talk too much, and perhaps I'd like you to get it into your head that you're here for keeps. *There isn't any way out.* Would I talk the way I've been talking if there was? You sit back and think that over. And mind you, there's nothing to be down-hearted about. Philip's got your girl—granted. But you're not the first, and you won't be the last by a long chalk that's had to look for another and been all the better off in the end. That French girl's no good to you, but there's Marie—she's a nice girl. And Fanny's got a sister—or if there's anyone you fancied, we'd see what could be done, I'm sure. Young men ought to be married—it steadies them down. I married young myself, and I'm pleased to see Philip setting his mind that way. Mark's married—he's been married for years— but he keeps her on a little place in Devonshire, and all she knows is he has to travel a lot. They've two children I've never seen. That's hard—isn't it? But it was all on account of the children I let Mark marry the way he did. The women down here don't have 'em—or didn't. Fan has brought it off all right. She's the first, and we'll hope she won't be the last. There'll be Mrs Philip now. I want to see Philip's children."

Oliver got to his feet.

"You can't expect me to listen to this!"

"Well, well," said the Old Fox equably. "There's no need for you to listen to what you don't want to hear. There's just one thing I'd like you to bear in mind. You might get ideas in your head about having a smack at Philip and getting him out of the way. Well, he goes armed, Philip does, and pretty well able to look after himself, but—" here the Old Fox leaned forward, his gross weight upon his hands, his ruddy face contorted suddenly into a snarling mask—"if you were to touch him, if you were to lay a finger on him, I'd have you skinned alive, but not till you'd seen what I could do to that girl of yours—what I'd do to anyone who got in Philip's way! *There*— don't say I didn't warn you!" He sat back. His face relaxed. The thick lip came down and hid the ugly yellow teeth. He pulled at his beard and said affably, "Well, that's where we are. You run along and talk to the Doctor. He'll show you round. You shouldn't have made me lose my temper. I'm too fat, and it makes me sweat."

Chapter Twenty-Seven

OLIVER HAD no more chance of talking to Rose Anne. He was carefully shepherded, and so was she. He danced again with Fanny, and thought her nervous and unhappy.

"Whatever did you say to put Uncle out like that?"

"I don't think I said anything. He was warning me what I might expect if, as he put it, I had a smack at Philip."

Fear looked at him out of Fanny's eyes.

"Oh, Captain Loddon, you *wouldn't*!"

"I would if it was going to do any good."

"You mustn't, you *mustn't*! You don't know what they'd do to you, or to Miss Rose Anne—you don't know—"

"Well, he was doing his best to tell me."

Fanny shuddered.

"And it's true—they would. There've been people before—Ernie told me. Oh, you *won't*! If you don't care for yourself, you've got to think about her."

What a nightmare—to dance, and talk of one's chances of escaping torture. He remembered Rose Anne saying, "We'll wake up soon," and wondered whether they would ever wake again...

Fanny was speaking.

"They've fetched your things away from our place. You're to be with the Doctor." She leaned towards him and said quick and low, "Don't trust him—too much."

He said, "Thank you, Fanny," and felt a real regret. He liked her, and he liked Ernie. They were a break in the nightmare. If he ever got out... Amos Rennard's words echoed in his mind—"Do you think I'd talk like this if there was any way out?"

The interminable evening was over at last. Dr Spenlow took him across the hall, and he saw with a quickening of interest that they were heading for the arch to which Violette had pointed. She had gone that way with Philip, and there were three steps down—and a passage with lights, and then many steps—and after a little no more lights—but Philip had a torch...

He tried to recall exactly what she had said. An exact recalling of the inexact—what use—what good?... Her babble came back—"We turned this way, that way—how do I know what way?" And then she had looked up and seen a star. He wondered whether she had not made the whole thing up. Not the arch and the three steps down at any rate. The arch was over them at this moment, and the steps were solid rock beneath his feet.

They passed along the "passage with lights," and came to a cell-like chamber furnished chiefly with books. They covered the rock from the roof to the floor. This was apparently a study, from either side of which there opened a small sleeping-room about the size of a ship's cabin. These had no outlet upon the gallery, but were ventilated through square windows covered by a grating and placed high up in the wall just under the roof.

"I'll show you my laboratory tomorrow," said Dr Spenlow. "There's something to live for! How's the head?"

"I had forgotten about it."

"Have a drink. I can give you some whisky in spite of the old man's temperance talk—medical stores, you know. He expects all his prescriptions to be well laced."

"Are you going to drug me?" said Oliver.

"Not at present—no orders. I do what I'm told, and you'd better too. It's no good trying to fight them, and it's no good trying to escape. Better for you to realise that right away. I know what I'm talking about, because of course I tried."

A spark of interest pierced the heavy fatigue which was settling upon Oliver. He said,

"How?"

Dr Spenlow was pouring himself out a drink.

"Too old a story—too long. Perhaps another time."

Oliver picked up his own drink. The air was hot and heavy down here. He had a parching thirst. He drank, and said urgently,

"Tell me—I'd like to hear."

Dr Spenlow quoted a nursery rhyme:

"Pease pudding hot,
Pease pudding cold,
Pease pudding in the pot,
Nine days old."

"My pease pudding is nine years old, and if that doesn't tell you anything else, it should tell you that there's nothing doing in the escape line."

"You mean you've never tried since?"

"I've never tried since. It's a life sentence, Loddon."

Oliver's face showed nothing. It was tired and expressionless. His mind felt a sharp horror of protest. He said,

"Well, you were going to tell me about it, weren't you?"

Dr Spenlow laughed.

"Was I? I will if you like." He finished his drink and set the glass down among the papers on his writing-table. "Well, it's a moral lesson, only the moral's a topsy-turvy one. 'Stay where you're put. Do what you're bid. If you're in a hole, lie down in it.' "

"Not much of a creed."

"A poor thing but my own. And it had better be yours. Well, nine years ago—" there was a momentary twitch of the muscles round his mouth—"getting on for nine years ago I still had visions of climbing to the top of my own particular tree—by that sin fell the angels and all the rest of it. My head was bloody but unbowed, and I was quite sure I was going to escape. Well, I had a shot at it. I waited a year.

I listened to the Old Fox by the hour. I led him on, and picked up a bit here and a bit there—he liked to boast about his mines and his caves, you know—and I used to get up in the night and explore. We weren't all civilised and electric-lighted then like we are today. The lights run all the way to the Angel now, but in those days we went round with torches and hoped they wouldn't let us down. When I thought I'd got the hang of the place, I put a torch and a couple of refills in my pocket and set out to escape. I won't tell you which way I went, because if you're really set on suicide you'll find one way is as good as another."

Horror took Oliver again like cramp. Would this man be here after nine years if there were any way out? He said,

"What happened?"

Dr Spenlow was pouring himself out another drink.

"I was away a week," he said. "I don't know how much imagination you've got."

Oliver said, "Some." He could have wished he had less.

"Because," said Dr Spenlow, "if you've got any at all, you'll guess what that week was like, and if you haven't, it's no use my describing it. My idea was to follow the water. I expect you've thought of that too—everyone does."

"Everyone?"

"Two out of every three of the men have a shot at getting away at first. The women funk the dark. Women are much more afraid of being alone than men are. But two out of every three of the men have a shot at it. They don't get very far mostly. We pick them up and bring them in—scared to death. And they don't try it on again. We know where to look for them now, but if they get past—well, I won't tell you what—we write them off as a total loss. In my own case I—well, I got past, and they got me back, but, as I think I told you, that was only because the Old Fox had an idea that he'd die if I wasn't handy to dose him."

"Past what?" said Oliver.

"Oh, I'm not telling. If you're looking at the colour of my drink and building on its loosening my tongue, I'm afraid you are going to be disappointed. It takes a great deal to make me drunk, and when I'm drunk, I don't talk, I go to sleep. And I'm not giving anything away."

"All right. Go on."

Dr Spenlow laughed.

"Not enough imagination to fill the week in for yourself? All right, I'll give it something to work on... After twelve hours I knew I was lost. I said, 'If I can't go back, I've got to go on.' I used to wonder for a year or two whether I would have gone on if I had known how to get back. I've doubted it more and more. I had two refills for my torch, and when I was down to one, I didn't dare burn it all the time. The darkness was solid—like rock. It was like being buried alive—in rock. And I lost my sense of direction. I expect you've waked up in the night and not known where you were—where the window was, or the door. It's a bad feeling. I had it all the time. I went on because there was nothing else to do. Sometimes I had to crawl... and I was afraid of going mad... my last refill pegged out... nothing but the dark..."

His voice had dropped very low. He was looking down at his own hand and the glass which held the whisky. The hand was quite steady. He went on speaking.

"There was water in that place—a lot of water... I stopped trying to go on... I thought I would stay by the water... you must have water... and then"—his mouth twitched again and his hand jerked—"I heard something—in the water—"

Oliver said, "What?"

Dr Spenlow put his glass to his lips and drank. Then he said,

"I don't know—I've never known. But I could hear it—swimming. There's a lake—did I tell you there was a lake?—and I could hear it swimming—a sound like paddles, and sometimes a splash. I was there a long time, and I kept hearing it. The last day I lay down by the water—close to it where I could reach it with my lips... I couldn't crawl any more, so I lay down... they found me like that..."

"They found you?"

"Since I am here. They thought I was dead, but they brought the corpse back to satisfy the Old Fox. It was rather badly bitten—"

"*What!*"

Dr Spenlow drank the rest of the whisky and put the glass down again. Then he took off his coat, undid his left cuff-link, and rolled the shirt-sleeve up to the shoulder. From the elbow there was a scar running up and out of sight—an odd puckered scar, or rather a series of scars. It looked as if it might have been made by a large-sized garden rake.

"The teeth of my swimming friend," said Harold Spenlow—"very sharp teeth. I'm sorry no one saw him, but the scar is proof that I didn't evolve him out of my own inner consciousness." He pulled down his shirt-sleeve again. "Probably a prehistoric survival, and I enjoy the distinction of being the first human to be bitten by one of his family for five thousand years or so... Well, there's the tale, and here—" he touched his shoulder—"here is the proof that it's true. I shouldn't try to escape, Loddon, if I were you—I really shouldn't."

Chapter Twenty-Eight

DR SPENLOW showed him round next day. There was a laboratory—obviously a very fine thing in laboratories, but of no interest to Oliver. The little bald-headed man and his wife were working there, also a pale young man whom Oliver had not seen before.

From the laboratory they went to the great hall, and from its farther end into a second cavern almost as large. Here the underground stream ran open to the arc-lights overhead until it came to a low arch in the rock, where they lost it.

"Where does it go?" asked Oliver. He had plenty of interest in the water, but he must be careful not to show it too much.

"Down," said Dr Spenlow. "I'll show you presently. There's a fine fall. It makes a deafening roar. The rock is cutting it out a bit of course, but you can hear it."

Oliver had been wondering at the dull thunder which seemed to come from everywhere at once. There wasn't much chance of following water which plunged to such a roaring fall.

They left the cave by a lighted gallery. Presently it forked.

"Left goes right on to the Angel, or rather to the big steel gate which makes it quite impossible for you to arrive at the Angel.

There's one at the Oakham end too—and, as man to man, Loddon, don't waste your time on them. They're guaranteed burglar-proof, drill-proof, dynamite-proof. They can't be opened by force, and I don't know what the exact mathematical chances of hitting on the right combination are, but I should think they ran into millions or trillions, or something rather daunting of that kind—so I shouldn't waste your time. Come and see our bathing-pool instead."

He led the way into the right-hand fork, which ran quite steeply down hill for some way and then broke into steps. Oliver counted them, and made out that there were round about a hundred.

The thunder of the water was with them again. It grew louder and louder until they came out through a natural rift upon the level shore of a lake. The noise came from their right, the full leaping roar of a most magnificent cataract which fell a hundred feet as white as snow in a cloud of flying spray. Beneath it the lake boiled like milk. A strong white glare made rainbows in the mist, bathed the foaming eddies, and turned every flying drop into a diamond. There were lights high up, lights hooded and concealed, all in the best modern manner. The Old Fox had certainly provided himself with a highly skilled electrician. Oliver remembered suddenly that Amos Rennard had deplored having had to waste the man. There had been a difference of opinion, and Ralston—yes, that was the man's name—Ralston had played the principal part in a funeral. That's what happened to you down under if you set yourself up against the Rennards.

He looked at the water, the foam of the cataract losing itself in the blackness of the lake. Not a very safe bathing-pool. He said so, and got one of Dr Spenlow's laughs for an answer.

"Our Bath Club has only two members—Philip and myself. Neither of us have any passionate affection for safety. Philip finds it dull, and I—well, life isn't so amusing that I mind taking chances."

They walked round the lake.

"It wasn't here you heard your prehistoric friend with the teeth?" said Oliver.

"Oh, no—not here. You have to go a bit farther than this and fare a great deal worse. These passages won't take you anywhere either.

Two of them run back into the main road to the Angel, and the third comes to a dead end. That's why it isn't lighted like the others."

"And where does the water go?" said Oliver.

Was it fancy, or did Dr Spenlow hold back for a moment before he answered? Oliver thought he did, thought he shied and then made up his mind that shying was bad policy. The answer came easily, if late.

"It doesn't—I mean it doesn't go anywhere. It stays here and makes the lake. There wouldn't be nearly so much of it if it went on."

Oliver thought, "He checked. He doesn't want me to think that the water goes on. Water generally does. There *must* be an outlet. All that water coming in—why, the place would flood to the roof in no time. What sort of fool does he take me for? Of course there's an outlet... And if he doesn't want me to know about it?" The answer to that sprang shouting into his mind, "It's the way out—the way out—the way out!"

He began to think, to plan, whilst he talked about anything and everything which would screen his thoughts. If it was a matter of swimming and diving, he would have to make sure of some waterproof covering for his torch and batteries. Well, that could be done. There was oiled silk in the laboratory. He ought to be able to pinch some of it. A little interest in what was doing up there—yes, he thought he could pull it off.

He went on talking until they came to an opening nearly opposite the one by which they had come upon the lake. It ran straight for a while, and then there were steps again—a full hundred of them.

"Know where you are now?" said Dr Spenlow at the top.

Oliver didn't know, but he guessed. Violette had spoken of many steps down, and she had pointed to the arch through which Dr Spenlow had brought him last night. He chanced his answer.

"Your place is along here on the right—"

He was aware of that check again. He had been taken round and about, and the last thing that had been expected was that he should keep his sense of direction. He was rather pleased with himself, and discerned that Dr Spenlow was not so pleased.

They came to the book-lined study, and he was left alone there. Then the consciousness that this was the last day of Rose Anne's reprieve closed about him. The last day, and many hours of it gone. Nothing done, and all yet to do. Tomorrow, with the farce of a marriage rite, she would pass under Philip's yoke. That it would break her, he had no doubt. She would resist and in the end be broken. Better the most desperate throw... If they could not win through to life, they might die together without the last indignities of torture... He sat thinking until Dr Spenlow returned, and then got his chance of going back into the laboratory.

There luck favoured him, and he found it easy to pocket as much of the oiled silk as he wanted. He took also a box of meat tablets. Dr Spenlow had kindled to interest as he explained them. "We could last out quite a long siege if we were put to it. Compressed food is one of the things I am experimenting with. All this importing from outside is risky. It keeps our good Mark awake at night. Now these meat lozenges are about four times as concentrated as the commercial article. Try one. They're best dissolved in water, but you can suck one if you like. You needn't be afraid—it's not drugged."

Oliver slipped the box into his pocket just before they left, and hoped that the loss would not be discovered until a tomorrow which would no longer concern him.

Meanwhile the day dragged on. He was shown an engineering shop, a boot repairing shop, a carpenter's shop. In the last some very fine walnut furniture was being polished by hand.

"Philip's stuff," said Dr Spenlow. "It was all French-polished, but he's had it stripped. They've made a pretty good job of it, don't you think?"

Philip's furniture was being got ready for Philip's bride. Oliver Loddon had been brought here to see it. Why? To amuse Philip? To amuse Harold Spenlow who housed a mocking devil? To give that extra prick of the goad which makes man or animal bolt blindly into danger—or out of it?

"Philip has a very fine house," said Dr Spenlow cheerfully. "You'd like to see it?"

Oliver said, "No."

The black eyebrows went up. "Oh, well, just as you like. It's worth seeing though—artistic—Philip has very good taste. There are some fine pictures—one of them from the Louvre, and a couple from

Venice. Philip takes what he wants, and doesn't care what it costs him or anyone else. Now the Old Man's place is terrific—gilding, you know—pots, and pots, and pots, and pots of it—and masses of crimson plush—and carpets inches deep in expensive pile—all paid for cash down on delivery. Only they weren't delivered here, as you may guess. That's where your friend Ernie comes in—he collects the stuff and brings it along. Want to see the Fox's den?"

"No, thank you."

They saw more caves instead.

When he was alone in his room Oliver tried to make a map of what he had seen. Such as his impressions were, he got them down on a bit of paper, but he had nothing to check them by, and he found it difficult to persuade himself that his map could be of any possible use. With every hour that passed there was a heavier weight upon endeavour, and hope, already dead, became a thing forgotten out of mind.

Chapter Twenty-Nine

IN ANOTHER rock-walled room Rose Anne stood passive whilst Louise and Marie tried on her wedding dress. When she had chosen the dress for her wedding to Oliver she had chosen a soft, filmy stuff, but now for Philip she must wear a silver and white brocade and go as richly as if this were mediæval Venice and she a Doge's bride. The dress was fantastically beautiful. It denied the simplicities of the heart. It flaunted a taste most alien to Rose Anne Carew.

She stood in silence whilst Louise and Marie admired.

"But it is a masterpiece, Madame. And Mademoiselle how she looks in it! Ravishing—like an angel—like a queen!" Marie's dark eyes were wide with admiration and envy.

Madame Louise put her head on one side and stood back for a better view.

"It is true—it is a success! And with only two days to do everything! *Ciel!* How do men think that these things are achieved? If Monsieur Philippe will believe, it is a miracle that we have performed, you and I—a true miracle! And I tell you this, Marie, that if we had had more time, there might have been no miracle, but a dress—very good, very chic. I do not make any dress that is not good, not chic, but not every dress even from Louise is a miracle as this one. Turn then, Mademoiselle—a little more if you please. *O mon Dieu*—the line is perfect!" The curtain over the door was lifted. Philip Rennard stood there smiling. Not one of the three had heard the door open. He stood there and smiled, and repeated Louise's word,

"Perfect."

Rose Anne did not move. She stood as she had been standing all the time, her head a little bent and her eyes cast down. There was a tall mirror against the wall, but she had not looked into it. She refused to see the reflected image of Philip Rennard's bride.

Philip sent the two women away and shut the door. He praised them, and they departed in a flutter of happiness. Philip did not often praise.

When they were gone he stood back as Louise had done, and said in his own words very much what she had said.

"Won't you turn round, Rose, and let me see you?"

She turned with the gentle mechanical movement of a wax-work. She kept her eyes down and her hands folded. Philip watched her for a long minute. Then he said, leaning back against the door,

"It's no good, Rose—the game's up."

Rose Anne's heart knocked against her side. It had been a dumb, desperate game, and she had played it desperately for what it was worth. She had given him nothing—not one look, not one catch of the breath, not one tremor of all the fear which filled her aching heart, not one quiver of her anguish.

He said again, laughing, "The game's up, my darling Rose—my beautiful Rose—*my* Rose."

Rose Anne kept silence, but when he put a hand on her shoulder she drew away.

"I don't like to be touched, Philip."

"Don't you? Well, I'm going to touch you—I'm going to kiss you—I'm going to marry you. This is your wedding dress, you know." He linked his hands behind her shoulders and held her lightly. "I tell you the game is up. You're not drugged, and you're not dumb.

You've kept it up very well, but you gave yourself away last night. I wasn't sure, you know, so I let you sit by Loddon and I let you dance with him, and you gave yourself away. Disappointing—isn't it? Because you nearly pulled it off. You see, you didn't reckon on the fact that I'm in love with you—romantically, enthusiastically, innocently in love with you. And that being the case, I couldn't help picking up the—shall we say, emotional interchange that was going on. You were broadcasting at very high pressure and I got your wave-length. So it's no use shamming dumb any more. Come, Rose—look at me! And let's talk like human beings. I'm sick to death of this wax doll business."

Rose Anne lifted her eyes. Was this bluff? Did he know? Could he be sure?

The moment her eyes met his she knew that he was sure. She met a hard certainty, a challenge, a leaping passion.

"Well," he said, "you see. What next? Let us talk. You're coming to me, you know. From the first time I saw you there's never been any question about that. But I don't want you broken, I want you whole. I want you to come of your own free will. Rose—look at me! You've never been loved as I shall love you—you've never been kissed as I shall kiss you. Look at me! I can make you forget Loddon in a week, in a night, in a single hour. Only come to me of yourself. You haven't any choice—but choose, Rose, choose to come to me! I want you of your own free will—not forced—not drugged."

She looked at him and said in her natural voice,

"Let me go, Philip."

His hands dropped at once and he stood back.

"There—you're free. Now come to me."

She said again, "Let me go, Philip."

"When I'm dead—not before—never before. Don't think it, Rose." He spoke in his quietest tone.

Rose Anne said, "You want me of my own free will, but you'll never have me that way. Any other way would kill me. I really do mean that. You couldn't hold me if I were dead."

She was so pale that it frightened him—the pallor and the faint, steady voice. He took her hand quite gently.

"Rose, don't talk like that. I'm not a brute. I love you. I can make you love me—I know I can. Rose, look at me!"

She looked at him.

"I shall never love you, Philip. I love Oliver."

His hand closed hard on hers—cruelly hard.

"You had better not say that, you know—you had better not think it. If he comes between us, there will be a quick way out for him—or perhaps a way that's not so quick. Rose, I won't touch him if you come to me, but if you set him up between us, what do you expect— that I shall bear it—that I shall stand by and see him look at you as he looked last night? No, no, my dear, wake up. This isn't England, with a policeman round every corner—this is Down Under, and I can do exactly what I like. Loddon—" he paused, changed his voice to a deeper one, and repeated the name—"Loddon—he has exactly as long to live as I choose. If I say he is to die, he will die, and if I say how he is to die, that is how it will be—quickly if I say it is to be quick, or very, very slowly if I say it is to be slow." He turned her hand palm upwards. "It is all in this little hand of yours."

Rose Anne drew her hand away.

"You said, let us talk like human beings, but you are not talking that way at all. Will you listen whilst I talk to you?"

He smiled.

"Oh, yes, I'll listen."

"Philip, you say you love me, and I believe you do. I want you to let me go—I want you to let us both go. It will hurt you, but won't it hurt you if I die?"

He continued to smile his very charming smile.

"Darling Rose, it would hurt me quite unbearably, but you are not going to die. Go on—I didn't mean to interrupt. I love hearing you talk."

A little colour came into her cheeks.

"Please, *please* let us go."

Philip laughed.

"Darling, be practical. With the best will in the world I couldn't very well risk your coming back with the police—could I?"

"Philip, we would give our word of honour—we would promise—"

"Oh, Rose, Rose, Rose!"

His mockery stopped her. Her colour failed. She looked away. There never had been any hope of course, but it is difficult for a woman to believe that she has no power to move the man who loves her.

Philip stopped laughing and put his arms round her.

"Oh, Rose, my darling, don't look like that. Such a beautiful, simple plan, wasn't it? You couldn't expect me not to laugh, could you? You're only a little girl still, and that's one of the things I love about you."

"Let me go, Philip," she said, but this time he held her fast.

"It's no good, my dear—you're mine. Stop fighting me—stop bruising yourself. I won't hurt you—I won't even let you hurt yourself." He looked at her strangely and said the last words again. "I won't let you hurt yourself, you poor frightened child."

"Let me go, Philip." The words came very low, but they were steady.

As she spoke, he released her, but before she had time to step back he stooped and kissed her lightly on the cheek.

"Good-bye, my dear, till tomorrow. Louise has surpassed herself. You'll be a lovely bride."

He went to the door and turned there, looking at her.

"I listened to you, and now, my dear, I want you to listen to me. I'm going to make this easy for you—I'm going to make it as easy as I can. I'm going to give up something I'd set my heart on to make it easy for you. When it's all over and you are my wife I'd like you to give me credit for this. That's some of what I want to say, and here's some more. I don't want you to think that you've got to spend the rest of your life down under—I don't want you to think that. I'm coming and going all the time, and as soon as you love me—and you're going to love me, you know—just as soon as you love me I'll take you with me. I'll show you the world. I'll show you Paris, London, Rome, Vienna. You shall go where you please, and see all the things you have ever dreamt of seeing. We'll have the most marvellous time. Oh, Rose, don't look at me like that! I swear I'll make you happy. I'm going now. You're like a ghost, the ghost of a lovely rose. Rest when I've gone—rest and sleep. You are going to sleep. Sleep well, my dear, and dream if you can about me."

His words came strangely to Rose Anne. There was a bright mist between them, a bright, moving mist. Philip's voice came and went in it. The ground shook and trembled under her feet. She heard the door shut, and the sound jarred the moving mist so that it fell in upon her and she fell with it, down, and down, and down. She knew that she was falling, but she did not know how she fell.

Chapter Thirty

DOWN UNDER, having neither sun nor moon, marked its main divisions of time by the sounding of a great gong. At noon, at midnight, at eight in the morning, and at eight in the evening the gong boomed out its signal from the great hall, and the echoes ran murmuring along the galleries until they lost themselves in the outer silence.

Food was brought to Oliver when the evening gong sounded— soup, and something savoury in a casserole. When he had eaten, a servant brought him coffee, and went out, leaving the tray.

Oliver had poured himself out a cup, when Dr Spenlow came in. He looked at the coffee, looked at Oliver, raised his eyebrows, and turned away with a shrug to rummage amongst the papers on his table. Oliver lifted the cup to his lips, and set it down again.

"Anything the matter with the coffee?" he enquired.

"Very good coffee," said Dr Spenlow with his back turned.

Oliver took up the cup again and smelled it. It smelled of very good coffee and of nothing else. He let a drop of it touch his tongue, and it tasted as good as it smelled. He said bluntly,

"What's the matter with it? Is it drugged?"

Dr Spenlow did not look round.

"When the game's lost and you've thrown in your hand, it's not a bad thing to go to bed and sleep, and the longer the sleep the less likely you are to worry over the lost game when you wake up again."

Oliver stared at the cup in his hand. It was white with a gold rim. The coffee lay black against the gold.

"Does one wake, Spenlow?" he said.

Dr Spenlow glanced over his shoulder fleetingly.

"Oh yes, one wakes. You needn't worry about that—at the moment."

Oliver was tempted. If he drank—if the coffee was drugged, he could drink it and be drugged into a cessation of this intolerable pain.

If he drank... He would see them damned before he let them drug him. But it might be as well that they should think him drugged—it might be as well.

The trouble was that he hadn't the slightest idea of how to get rid of the coffee. He ought to dispose of at least two cups, but how to get rid of even half a cup of coffee in this rock-walled, rock-floored room was a problem.

Dr Spenlow said, "Nobody touches my bottles. There are several on the top of the bookshelf. The big one is half empty... But I think you would be a fool. My own prescription would be sleep, but who am I to come between a fool and his folly?"

Oliver said, "Thank you," and got up.

The bottles were easily reached. The big one had some dark stuff in it—dark, sticky stuff. It smelled like nothing on earth. He poured in two cupfuls of coffee, corked the bottle, and put it back on the shelf. Dr Spenlow rustled among his papers and kept his back to the room. Presently he said,

"If there's any coffee left, you'd better drink it. You can't do anything, you know—she's had some already."

Oliver's hand fell on his shoulder.

"Tell me what you mean—at once!"

Harold Spenlow turned round.

"Oh, my dear Loddon, what's the good of going on like this? Miss Carew has had a cup of coffee. She needs sleep—she needs a little pleasant oblivion. The coffee is really very, very beneficent, and when she wakes up she won't mind what is going to happen tomorrow any more than she would mind a dream about being married. You dream the most extraordinary things, but you don't really mind what happens in a dream, because it doesn't really touch you. Miss Carew won't really mind, because my very humane drug will keep her in a dream until she has had time to adjust herself."

Oliver said in an almost unrecognisable voice,

"You said—he wouldn't—drug her."

Dr Spenlow nodded.

"I know I did. I wasn't lying to you. He didn't want her drugged, but—he's fond of her. I wouldn't have believed it of Philip, but he can't bear to see her unhappy. Also there's this. He was afraid of the drug because he thought it had done something to her—he thought she couldn't shake it off. But when he found out that she was shamming, well, he made up his mind not to risk a scene, so she's had her cup of coffee, and when it comes to the ceremony tomorrow she'll say her piece without a tremor, and our Reverend Luke won't have to risk one of his rather tiresome attacks of conscience. There you are—everything for the best in our best of all possible worlds."

Oliver was silent. Then suddenly, urgently, he said,

"Spenlow—help us to get away. You could if you wanted to."

Dr Spenlow smiled his bitter smile.

"Oh, my dear Loddon, do you think so? Wake up and face the facts! Suppose I helped you to what you term get away. You would get, perhaps, as far as I got, perhaps not so far, and there you would die miserably, as I very nearly died. You would have the added torture of seeing Miss Carew die too. As far as she is concerned, I take leave to think that it would be very much better for her to marry Philip, who worships her in his own erratic way. As for yourself, if you want to commit suicide, I can give you something that will do the job painlessly. There remains my own point of view. I don't particularly enjoy my life, but I should rather like to finish the experiments on which I am at present engaged, and I shouldn't fancy the lingering end which Philip might consider appropriate. In fact there's nothing doing. I really advise you to finish the coffee."

"No," said Oliver.

Dr Spenlow shrugged his shoulders.

"Have it your own way. And now it's my duty as your guardian to lock you up for the night, so if you don't mind—" He waved towards the open door of the room in which Oliver had slept.

"Why am I to be locked up? They've never done that before."

"Just a precautionary measure. I don't think Philip would place any obstacle in the way of your committing suicide alone, but it's natural that he shouldn't want Miss Carew to be involved."

Oliver looked at the door, at Harold Spenlow, and at the key in Harold Spenlow's hand. And then he was looking at something else—the small automatic pistol which Harold Spenlow had taken out of his pocket.

"No, no, Loddon, you can't rush me. Pistol practice is one of my recreations. In with you, or there'll be trouble!"

Oliver walked into the small, bare room. He heard the door slam and the key turn in the lock.

Chapter Thirty-One

THE BOOMING of the midnight gong had died away an hour before. In the galleries of Down Under the lights burned all night long, a light to every twenty yards. Rose Anne opened the door of her room from the inside, withdrew the key, closed the door, locked it again, and after a moment's hesitation slipped the key into her pocket. She wore the blue jumper suit in which she had run across to the Angel to see little Florrie Garstnet on that other wedding eve which seemed so long ago. She stood looking up and down the gallery for a moment, and then ran along it till she came to a left-hand turn, which she followed. There were three turns, but she knew her way.

She came to Dr Spenlow's door without meeting anyone at all. She stood fingering the handle, afraid to turn it, afraid not to turn it, waiting for her heart-beats to grow quieter so that she could listen for a possible sound from within. There was no sound. She turned the knob, the catch moved back, and the door swung gently in. Rose Anne followed it, shut it behind her, and looked around her with wide, seeking eyes.

There was a light in the room which showed everything plainly— the littered writing-table, the book-lined walls; two doors, one open, one shut; the table in the middle of the room, across which Dr Spenlow sprawled, his head on his folded arms.

Rose Anne stood looking at him. A tray had been pushed from the table. The metal coffee-pot lay on its side, spreading a dark stain upon the carpet. The sugar-basin had spilled its lumps. The cup was broken. In the place where the tray had stood were two whisky bottles, both empty. The room reeked.

She went to the open door and looked in—Dr Spenlow's empty bedroom.

She went to the other door, and found it fast. This was expected. Her hand went to her pocket for the key of her own room. There was so little hope that it would fit, but there was so little hope in any direction. You had to do what you could, and nurse your hope, and pray to be kept from Philip.

She put the key in the lock with a steady hand, but it wouldn't turn. She went on trying, but it wouldn't, wouldn't turn. She put it away again and looked about her. If Dr Spenlow had locked the door, then Dr Spenlow must have the key.

She crossed to the door which gave upon the gallery and bolted it. Then she came back to Harold Spenlow.

Where would he have put the key? In a pocket? Men had such a confusing number of pockets. She was afraid of touching him, but she had to do it—she had to have the key. She felt in the two pockets she could reach, but it wasn't there. How was she to move the heavy, inert body? She did put a hand on his arm, and under its light touch he made a sound between a groan and a snore, and stretched so that his right hand hung over the table edge. Something fell from it out of her sight. She had to go round the table before she could see what it was.

And it was the key.

When she had it in her hand, when it turned in the lock, when the door opened, she was saying over and over in her heart, "That's the second good thing. I got away, and now Oliver can get away. Oh, *please* let the good things go on."

The room was very empty and bare. There was a light in it, not very bright. It showed her Oliver asleep on the narrow bed. He had not taken off any of his clothes. He lay with one arm over his head as if he had thrown it up to shield his eyes. The other lay stretched out upon the blanket. Rose Anne sat down on the edge of the bed and took the hand which lay beside him. It comforted her just to stay like that for a moment, quietly, with Oliver's hand to hold. Then she said in her gentle voice,

"Wake up, darling."

The words came into Oliver's dream of despair and broke it. He had not thought that he would sleep—he had not meant to sleep—but sleep had taken him and cast him into an evil dream full of the torment of a never-ending search for Rose Anne whom he had lost and would not find again. He woke and found her with her hand in his.

They forgot everything for a time. If the world must end, let it end now. If time must cease, let it cease now. If there were no more of life, this was enough—to meet, to hold one another, to be at rest.

Rose Anne stirred first.

"We must go."

Oliver put her away a little, looked in her face, and said,

"They all say it's certain death."

"I know—they talk like that. But then, you see, they're drugged—most of them."

"Spenlow isn't drugged. He says it's suicide. He tried, you know."

She nodded.

"I don't trust him. He drinks, and he's lost his nerve. I think he could get away if he really wanted to. But I don't think he wants to. He wants to finish his experiments. If he got out he wouldn't have any money or anywhere to go. I don't think he really wants to get out."

Oliver put her hand to his lips.

"Rose Anne, I don't think there's very much hope. It's a very desperate chance. I don't think I ought to take you."

She pulled her hand away.

"Do you want me to go alone? If you went without me, I should follow. Oh, don't you see that we must be together? Don't you see that I can't, can't bear to marry Philip?"

Oliver's hand pressed her shoulder for a moment, hard. She shuddered and turned pale.

He sprang up.

"Very well then, come!"

He went to and fro, getting his torch, his spare batteries, wrapping them in the oiled silk. Then he passed through into the other room. Rose Anne followed him. She felt calm and happy now. She had an implicit trust in Oliver, and was quite sure that everything would be all right. She ran to open the door, and as she reached it, Dr Spenlow lifted his head and stared at them with the portentous gravity of a drunken man. The hand from which the key had fallen now held his pistol. It steadied itself upon the table and took aim at Rose Anne.

"My dear Miss Carew—sounds like a letter—but—my dear Miss Carew—if you open that door—I'm going to shoot—"

Rose Anne stopped with her hand on the bolt and said,

"Why?"

He shook his head mournfully.

"You ought to be in bed—asleep—that's what you ought to be—have some more coffee."

"What's all this nonsense, Spenlow?" said Oliver. "Put down that pistol!"

Harold Spenlow laughed.

"Nice little pistol," he said, the words running one into the other. "Very nice little pistol indeed—very humane death—nice and swift—and I'm a very good shot."

"Then I should suggest your shooting Philip."

Harold Spenlow laughed again.

"Philip's my—very dear friend. You don't shoot your—very dear friends."

Rose Anne pulled back the bolt, and instantly the pistol cracked. The noise was horrid in the little room. The bullet flattened itself against the rock a couple of inches beyond her shoulder. Oliver caught the table by its front edge and drove back with it. The pistol went off again and Dr Spenlow came down with a crash. The table, the chair, and the whisky bottles were all involved.

Oliver got the pistol, and felt better,

"We'll have to tie him up," he said, frowning. "Get me a sheet, darling."

They tied his hands and feet with strips of linen, and he lay passive, staring up at them with a dazed expression.

When they had laid him on the bed and Oliver was tearing off another bit of the sheet to make a gag, he said suddenly,

"You won't pull it off, you know. Not—one—earthly—chance."

Rose Anne went down on her knees beside him.

"Oh, Dr Spenlow, tell us the way!"

He wagged his head on the pillow.

"No way—my dear Miss Carew—suicide—my dear Miss Carew—"

"Tell me," said Rose Anne.

He laughed.

"Like asking a policeman the way—in Piccadilly Circus—none of us—will—ever—see Piccadilly Circus—again."

"Tell me," said Rose Anne. "Please, please tell me."

"First to the right—second to the left—and straight on—until you come to Tottenham Court Road. Oh, my hat—Tottenham Court Road! But this is—a one-way street—and—no thoroughfare. My dear Miss Carew—how can I tell you the way—if he puts a gag in my mouth?"

"Oh, *please*," said Rose Anne in a despairing voice.

He turned his head and looked at her as a man looks who has been suddenly awakened.

"You're leaving me to Philip. He'll kill me."

"Then your best chance is for us to get away and come back in time to save you," said Oliver.

"Touching interest in my welfare," said Harold Spenlow. "Most kind I'm sure, Loddon. Well, it makes no odds, because we're all as good as dead—so I'll tell you. Come a bit closer."

Oliver stooped. The mocking voice dropped to a whisper.

"Behind the waterfall—there's a crack—I don't know if you can—get through—one doesn't put on flesh down here—and so—you may—very bad going—more caves—I don't know how many—I don't know—if there's any way out—"

Oliver stood looking down at him for a moment.

"Is that true?"

Dr Spenlow's lips drew sideways in a twisting smile.

"*In vino veritas*—I don't know the Latin—for whisky. It's true enough—as far as it goes—I meant to have—a shot myself—when I'd finished—the job I'm on. That's why I pinched—Philip's pistol. You didn't really think—he'd trust me with one—did you?"

Oliver said, frowning, "Do you want to come with us—now?" He was thinking, "Philip will kill him if we leave him here."

"Well, well," said Harold Spenlow—"very sporting offer—but—the answer is in—the negative. The whisky is willing—but the legs are weak. That's always been the trouble—my dear Miss Carew. When I'm sober I haven't got the nerve—and when I'm drunk I haven't got the legs. Very good legs—absolutely necessary. I say—I'd rather you didn't gag me—"

"Better for you," said Oliver, and gagged him as thoroughly as he knew how.

They locked him in and took the key—anything to delay discovery. And then they were out in the gallery and making for the pool.

Chapter Thirty-Two

THEY WENT quickly and in silence. The lights watched them. If anyone heard, if anyone came, their adventure would be over before it had begun. They came down the steps which Oliver had climbed that morning with Harold Spenlow and out into the cave where the cataract fell roaring to the black lake which was Philip's swimming-pool. Harold Spenlow had said, "Behind the fall." Perhaps he had spoken the truth, and perhaps he had lied.

They approached the fall by a path which was sometimes wide enough for two, and sometimes offered only a bare foothold. The spray made it slippery and blinded them. The roar of the water was so loud that their senses shook with it and the very rock itself seemed shaken.

"Behind the fall..." Oliver, going ahead, perceived with a lift of the heart that this, at least, was possible, and not a mere mockery of Harold Spenlow's mocking tongue. The fall dropped clear of the rock, and the path went on behind it. There was a blackness of overhanging cliff, and a brightness that shone through the descending flood, the brightness of the great arc-lights in the cave beyond. They burned green through the veil of the water and painted strange rainbows on the shuddering air.

Rose Anne slipped once, and the voice with which she cried out was beaten back between her parted lips. Horrible to be voiceless, to go down into the boiling pool without a cry. Oliver's hand caught her, held her for a dizzy moment, and brought her back to safety.

There was no safety of course, but it felt like safety to be in the narrow cave which the water had cut for itself a long, long time ago. The shimmer and the roar of the fall hung like a curtain between them and the world of Down Under.

The cave ran back a couple of yards and no more. The stone was smooth and water-worn. There was no crack in it anywhere. Oliver got out his torch and sent the beam travelling. It showed the drip of the spray from the roof, and the trickle of the spray on the walls, and the wet black floor under their feet, but it showed no way of escape.

"There isn't any crack," said Rose Anne. "He wasn't telling the truth." And then, with a quick remorse, "We must go on looking. Perhaps it's farther on."

"I'll go and have a look. You'd better stay here."

"No—*please*, Oliver."

"You'd be in the way. I'll be as quick as I can."

Rose Anne leaned against the wet wall and watched him go out of the cave and out of sight. He was quite right, people who slip are no use when it comes to a climb over slimy rocks—only she wondered whether Oliver had any idea of how dreadful it was to be left here alone. Suppose he didn't come back. Suppose she never saw him again. Suppose Philip came. She put one hand over the other and held fast. There was something in her that could endure. She called upon it, and endured.

It seemed like a long time before Oliver came back. He pulled her close and shouted with his lips at her ear, "There's another cave higher up—a very rough climb—I'll have to rope you." Even so the roar of the water made it difficult to hear.

He was pulling strips of linen from his pocket and knotting them. They had torn up a sheet for Harold Spenlow, and here was what was left of it.

"He said, 'bad going,' " shouted Oliver, "so I brought it along. There's quite a good path for a bit."

They went out again into that bewildering roar and glare. The path ran on for two or three yards and then began to narrow to a cleft. Rose Anne followed the path, and followed Oliver because she must. She tried to look at the dark rock and not at the fall of the water, but whatever she looked at seemed to dazzle and shake before her eyes.

Where the cleft broke the rock, Oliver stopped and began to climb. He had to shout to her to tell her what to do. Sometimes the words reached her, and sometimes they were lost. She slipped again, lost her hand-hold, and swung against the slimy rock like a spider on its thread. In an anguish of terror she thought of Oliver, because how could he bear her weight. She would drag him down. She prayed for the sheet to break quickly—but it held. Oliver's voice came to her with hard insistence.

"Lift your left foot a little. Feel against the rock. Reach up your right hand to me."

Her foot found a crevice, and her hand found Oliver's hand. He pulled her up, and they were on a ledge not more than a yard wide. They moved along the ledge. It followed the cliff and pierced it. There was a wall on either side of them, and a low roof overhead. The walls closed in and the roof came down. Oliver stopped and spoke over his shoulder.

"This might be the place. There's a crack all right. I don't know if we can get through."

She could hear him better now that the rock screened them from the full roar of the fall. She said,

"Let me look. Is there room?"

Oliver said, "Just," and she came up beside him and looked over his shoulder, and along his arm, and along the beam of the torch. What she saw was really the crack that Dr Spenlow had called it. If it had been just a straight crack, there would have been no chance for them, but at the bottom end it gaped as if the sides had been pushed apart. This gap made it barely possible that they might squeeze through. Rose Anne's spine crept at the thought, the palms of her hands tingled, and her throat went dry. Where they were now they could kneel in an upright position, but the gap would give them no more than two foot to crawl in. She drew in her breath and said,

"I can't!"

Oliver said, "Nonsense!" And then, in his most practical voice, "You'll have to go first. I'll give you the torch. You see, if you stick I can pull you back, but if I got stuck you wouldn't be able to do anything about it."

Rose Anne achieved a terror-stricken obedience. She would really much rather have died, but you can't just die quietly when you want to—you have to go on. She took the torch and crawled into the crack. Then it wasn't possible to crawl any more. She lay flat and wriggled forward an inch at a time. Oliver's hand was on her ankle, and the torch showed her the darkness.

It showed her something else. She felt a new agony of despair, and slowly, inch by inch, she began to worm her way back again.

"What is it?" said Oliver when she was clear of the crack.

She kneeled up and faced him. There was a smear of green slime on her cheek and another on her chin. She said in a forced, exhausted voice,

"There's a grating—we can't get through."

"*What!*"

"We can't get through. There's a grating."

"Give me the torch."

She saw the light disappear into the crack. She saw Oliver disappear. She waited.

She waited. Oliver came back. The light came back. Oliver said, "It's all right."

She stared at him.

"I saw it—"

"Yes, it's there, but it's been cut through."

"What do you mean?"

"Someone's cut it through. I wonder if it was Spenlow. Look!"

He dragged the grating clear of the crack. The mark of a file showed bright against the rust with which it was encrusted.

Rose Anne crawled into the dark again.

Chapter Thirty-Three

THEY WERE through—bruised and breathless, coated with slime, their clothes half torn off them, but through. And then Oliver went back, because if Philip followed he would find the grating. He took off what remained of his clothes, and managed to reach it, drag it into the crack, and leave it more or less in its old position.

He put on his torn garments, and they sat for a while and rested. The torch showed them a long, low cave winding away into unknown darkness. There was a small sound of water flowing. The roar of the fall was gone. It was pleasant to hear the little sound again.

They were silent for a time. Then Oliver said,

"I thought they had drugged you. Spenlow said they had."

Rose Anne said, "No." And then, "Philip came and talked to me. It was rather dreadful, and it was very stupid of me, but after he had gone away I fainted. Marie and Louise came back and found me. They had been making me try on the dress—I was to wear—to marry Philip—and when they were getting it off me I began to come round and I heard them talking, and Marie said it was a shame, and Louise said no, I was lucky, and I ought to be only too pleased to have such a handsome man as Philip for a lover. She said he was as beautiful as an angel—'*beau comme un ange.*' But I can't think why Philip should remind anyone of an angel—can you?"

Oliver said things about Philip.

"Yes," said Rose Anne. "But I think he must have been badly brought up. He's been so frightfully spoilt. If we have children, we won't spoil them—will we?"

Oliver said "No." The word choked him a little. Life with Rose Anne—a home—children—they were things hoped for but not yet seen... He held her close and thought bitter thoughts.

But Rose Anne was happy. She had hated the water, and she had hated climbing up a horrible dripping cleft, with that roar in her ears, and a death trap of a pool just waiting for her to slip and go down and be pounded to a jelly on the stones. But that was all over now. When horrid things were actually happening she could be as frightened as anyone, but when they were over she found it very easy to be hopeful, and to feel sure that everything was going to come right. It was lovely to be with Oliver again, to feel his arm round her, and to put her head down on his shoulder.

She went on telling him about how she had got away.

"Where was I?... I know—I was telling you about Louise saying how lucky I was. It made me so angry that I very nearly sat up and told her what I thought about it, only fortunately I didn't. I went on swooning, and Marie said, 'It is such a pity she must have the drug. She would be—oh, much more beautiful without it.' Marie admires me very much, you know. And then Louise said it was much better that I should be drugged than that I should spoil my face with weeping. And Marie said, 'That is true. I will put it in the coffee—she drinks two cups always—and then she will sleep, and forget that she is unhappy, my poor m'amselle."

"They put the stuff in my coffee too, but I didn't drink it."

"Nor did I. But I made them think I had. I sent Marie for a handkerchief, and whilst she was out of the room I tipped the coffee back into the jug, so when she came in, there was her full cup and my empty one. She always has a cup with me, and I thought, 'There won't be any drug in her cup,' so I poured out my second one, and I managed to change it for hers. She was going to and fro, you know, putting that horrid silver dress away and talking about Philip. She didn't notice, so I drank hers and she drank mine, and then I said I was tired and I went to bed. Marie soon got sleepy. The stuff must have been very strong. She got out the key and locked us in—we're always locked in at night—but she was too sleepy to get to her own room. She sat down on the couch and went to sleep there with the key in her hand, and I dressed myself again and waited till I thought it was as safe as it was ever going to be, and then I took the key and locked her in, and came to find you. Oh, darling, isn't it lovely to think we've got away?"

Oliver said, "We've got to go on. We're not away yet, Rose Anne."

She sighed.

"I suppose we must. I do hope there aren't any more waterfalls."

The cave was low. Their voices echoed. It narrowed, widened out, and then narrowed again. A stream ran through it, and they followed the water. Presently the roof came down and met the floor.

The water went on under an arch which stood a bare handsbreadth above the flow. Rose Anne looked at it, and looked at Oliver.

Oliver got on to his knees and sounded the stream. His arm went down into it to an inch or two over the elbow. He shone the torch into the gap, lying on the bank and getting his head level with the water. Then he scrambled up again.

"Look here, darling, I'm going to see if I can get through. It's a tight squeeze, but I don't think there's more than about a yard of it. I think there's another cave."

Rose Anne said, "You *think*—"

"Well, I'm practically sure."

She looked at the low arch and sickened. Six inches above the surface—eight inches—and the rock to keep your head down so that you couldn't reach the little air there was. She said in a muffled voice,

"Oliver—*don't*! Let's try and find—some other way."

"Darling, there isn't any other way—I've been looking all along. And we must stick to the water—water's bound to come out somewhere. But if we lose it we might just wander round in circles and never get anywhere at all. You'll see it'll be quite all right. I'll go first and prospect." He spoke in an assured and cheerful tone.

Rose Anne tried to keep her mind on that, but when she saw him go down into the water and disappear, terror came on her again. Suppose there wasn't a cave beyond the arch at all. Suppose the stream went on, and on, and on, with just its own channel to run in and no more. Suppose it fell sharply into some dreadful chasm in the darkness. Suppose—her mind stopped.

She had the torch in her hand. Oliver had put it there, and what she had to do was to hold it low down over the water so that the beam might follow him and show him the way back. She watched the arch and the water, but she did not think. Her mind had stopped.

And then something round and dark came into the beam, and it was the back of Oliver's head. He put up a hand to feel whether he had head-room and lifted his face clear of the water, blinking, and gasping, and drawing long, deep breaths. Then he pulled himself up beside her and sat there dripping.

"It's all right—about six feet of passage and a fairly tight fit—plenty of head-room on the other side—the feel of a biggish place. Come along, we'd better get on before you get cold feet."

"They can't be any colder than they are."

Oliver said, "Nonsense!" And then, "I'm afraid you'll just have to get wet. Fortunately it's warm down here. Now look here, darling—it's quite easy, but you'll have to do exactly what I say. You see, we've got to make it in the dark. We can't afford to let the torch get wet. It will be all right done up in the oiled silk, and I think I'd better have it and go first. I want you to get down into the stream behind me, follow me right up to the arch, and then wait there until you can see the light shining through from the other side—you'll be able to see it all right. And as soon as you see it you can take a long breath and start pushing yourself through the arch. I'll be there to pull you out at the other side. Now come along."

The torch changed hands, the torch went out. They were both in the water. Rose Anne was about six or seven feet from the arch, because she had to leave room for Oliver to get down on his hands and knees and then straighten out before he began to worm his way along the channel. She moved up behind him, the stream knee-high and running fast. It was very cold. Her teeth chattered.

Oliver was down under the water now. She took a few more steps and touched the rock with her outstretched hands. Then she knelt down in the water and stared at the arch which she could not see. If Oliver got through, there would be a light. She couldn't see anything now, but if Oliver got through, there would be a light and she would see the arch.

She began to count to herself, "One, two, three, four, five..." She got up to fifty, and there was no light, so she made herself go on counting. There was no light at a hundred, or at a hundred and fifty, or at two hundred. It was very difficult to go on counting. It was like rolling heavy stones up a very steep hill. She had the feeling that she mustn't stop, that something dreadful would happen if she were to stop.

She got to three hundred, and then all in a moment there was the arch—a bright arch painted on the darkness, and the stream flickering with little points of light. She thought Oliver called to her, but she couldn't be sure, the water made such a noise in its narrow bed. She filled her lungs with air, ducked down where the arch spanned the stream, and pushed herself forward, thrusting with her feet against the rock, reaching out with her hands to feel for any projection which would help her.

It was not as bad as the waiting had been, but it was bad enough. She was a good swimmer, but she did not like diving and had never learned to swim under water. She just shut her eyes and fought her way through. Oliver's hand touched hers and she was clear.

He pulled her up, and when she had got the water out of her eyes she saw the torch jammed in a crevice, and its ray very faint and small in the great dark cave to which they had come. They sat and dripped, and turned the torch here and there.

The cave was very large. The stream ran down into a lake. On this side there was a wide rocky shore, but on the farther side the water lay against the wall, and both were as black as ink. It came to Oliver that this was the place which Harold Spenlow had reached, and as soon as he thought of it he wished he hadn't. Marks on a bare arm—marks that looked as if they had been made by the teeth of a rake... Much better not think about Spenlow and what he had heard in the dark. He said, suddenly and aloud,

"If Spenlow got as far as this, how did they get him back? By his own account he was more dead than alive."

"I expect there's another way," said Rose Anne comfortably. She didn't care in the least how they had got Dr Spenlow back. As long as she wasn't expected to crawl through any more tunnels, she didn't really care much about anything. Her teeth still chattered, but only from cold, and that hardly seemed to matter.

They wrung the worst of the wet out of their clothes and went on. Very bad going, as Harold Spenlow had said. Close down by the edge of the lake was easiest, because there the rock was smooth with the endless lapping of the water. The cave receded before them—black walls, black roof, black water, black rock beneath their feet. If they stood still they could hear the stream flowing in from under the arch. There was no other sound. When they spoke their voices made strange echoes.

The cave went on, and on, and on. And then, just when it seemed as if it would go on for ever, it came to an end. The black rock barred their way.

Oliver sent the beam of his torch to and fro, but this time there was no arch, no movement of the water to show whether it flowed on through some channel which they could not see. He thought, "If there were no outlet, the cave would fill. There must be an outlet." He thought again, "There must be an outlet, but if it were of any size, we should see the current setting that way."

He had a box of matches in his pocket. He went back fifty yards, tossed half a dozen of them out into the lake, and kept the beam on them. They clustered together and moved slowly away from the shore. They moved very slowly indeed. Sometimes they hardly seemed to move at all. Yet in the end it was clear that they were setting for the opposite side, where the rock rose sheer from the water's edge. He thought, "There's a current, but there's no strength in it. That means that there is an outlet, but not a big one. Anything big enough for us to get through would set up a much stronger current than that."

He turned from the lake with an overwhelming sense of relief. If this were indeed Spenlow's cave, there must certainly be another and an easier way out of it. Spenlow, bitten to the bone and in the last stages of exhaustion, could never have been brought back by the way that he and Rose Anne had come. Besides, who would have taken such a way to find him? No, they must look for an exit somewhere above water level, amongst these piled and tumbled rocks. If they had more light—The ray seemed only to make the darkness visible. They slipped and scrambled, climbed, and fell back again, and all the time were hampered by the drag of their wet clothes.

They came back to where they had started. Rose Anne looked at the arch. Would they have to crawl through that dreadful place again with the water against them? She supposed they would if Oliver said so, and if there were no other way. She turned with a shudder. The torch was in her hand, and as she turned, the beam turned too and ran slanting to the roof. Rose Anne cried out,

"Oliver, look—there's a hole!"

They both looked with all their eyes. The hole was half way up the wall, like a window with a blunted corner. If it had been anywhere else, they might have seen it before, but they had come up from the water blind and dripping, and when they could see again their eyes were all for the lake and its rocky shore. The opening was in the wall of the cave, but so close into the corner that it had been behind them and the beam had never touched it at all. The rock fell from it ledge by ledge to where they stood.

They climbed, and found a passage running on the level—a passage, not a cave. The sides were rough, but they had been shaped by men. For the first time hope really entered Oliver's heart.

The passage went on a long way. Twice it forked. Each time they took the right-hand fork, because it was in Oliver's mind to get back to the water. If they could strike it again they would have something to follow, and they would at least not have to be afraid of thirst.

Rose Anne walked wearily. She was very tired. The immediate excitement of the escape had died down. She thought the black passage would never end.

Chapter Thirty-Four

IT WAS HOURS later that they heard faintly the sound of flowing water. It was the most blessed sound in the world. They had been wandering, with all sense of direction lost, from passage to cave and from cave to passage again. Sometimes the roof came down and they had to crawl, sometimes it rose in gloomy arches far above their heads. There was a cave that was full of stalactites, shining white in the beam of the torch like pillars of salt. Rose Anne thought dimly about Lot's wife. There was a cave that was full of strange echoes. Their very breathing came whispering back from its dark hollow sides. There was a cave where the air was so heavy that it was hard to breathe at all. There was a place where they were hemmed between narrow walls and the torch failed.

Oliver replaced the battery, but that interval of darkness was most dreadful to Rose Anne. She tried very hard not to think of what would happen when they had used this battery—and the next.

Now they stood in a cleft, and heard water lapping. It was below them. Oliver thrust the torch forward, swinging it this way and that. The beam showed them a tumbled, rocky shore, black water lapping it and stretching away to a black wall beyond. His heart went cold in him. He turned his head and said in a dry, steady voice,

"We've come back."

Rose Anne looked over his shoulder. It was true. The sound in their ears was the sound of the stream flowing out from under the arch through which they had crawled. Their cleft was the window with the blunted corner. She was too tired to care very much.

They climbed down the ledges to the lake and drank.

It was whilst she was filling her cupped hands for the second time that she heard the sound. It came to her through the sound of the running water. She lifted her head and said in a surprised voice,

"There's something in the lake—something swimming."

Oliver lifted his head too. The torch was behind them on a shelf in the rock. There was a sound. It might be the sound of something swimming—it might be... He reached for the torch and sent the beam across the lake. The surface was unbroken, but there was a place where it heaved as if it had been broken, or as if it were very near to breaking. A swell moved upon it, a long, dark ripple that set towards the shore.

"Drink what you want and come," he said, and for all that he had just been drinking, his mouth was dry.

Rose Anne, kneeling by the stream, looked up at him bewildered and said,

"What is it?"

"I don't know. Be quick!"

She drank, and they climbed back into the passage, moved wearily along it, and sat down. Oliver put out the torch. They leaned against one another and against the rocky wall, and slept a dim, uneasy sleep in which they wandered endlessly and lost one another, and met again only to part and wander on, and on, and on.

In Oliver's dream he was straining to lift a weight of stone which was crushing him. He knew that he could not lift it, because it was the roof that had fallen in with the weight of Oakham Hill behind it. But he had to go on trying, because you have to go on trying even when it isn't any good.

In Rose Anne's dream she had come into a place which was full of pillars of salt, and every pillar a woman who had tried to escape. She stared at them, and they said with one wailing voice, "You'll never get out." Then she looked down, and she was wearing the silver dress which Louise had made for her wedding with Philip. It was so heavy that she couldn't run, and it got heavier every minute, heavy and hard, and she knew that she too was turning into a pillar of salt.

And Philip said, "Journeys end in lovers' meetings."

She opened her eyes in a glare of light. Philip Rennard stood above them. He held an electric lamp high up so that the light fell on her, and on Oliver, and on himself. In his other hand he had an automatic pistol. He said,

"Wake up, Rose—I've come for you. I hope you're pleased to see me."

Rose Anne stared at him. If this was part of the dream, she hoped she was going to wake up. When a dream got too bad you generally did wake up. She was very stiff. She felt Oliver move, and saw that his eyes were open. He was looking at Philip's pistol, and Philip was pointing it at him.

Oliver said, "You've found us. What are you going to do about it?"

Philip Rennard laughed.

"I'm going to take Rose back. I have a very forgiving nature."

Rose Anne got up.

"What are you going to do with Oliver?"

Philip laughed again.

"Well, I didn't think of taking him back. I'm not quite so forgiving as that."

A confusion of thoughts rushed into Rose Anne's mind. "He's going to shoot—Oliver will be shot—I can't bear it—if he moves, he'll shoot."

She made a snatch at the pistol, and at the same time Oliver flung himself forward on the ground and caught Philip by the ankle.

It was a desperate clutch, but there was no strength in it. His right arm was numb and the hand without feeling.

Philip kicked out and swung Rose Anne aside. Something broke in her, and she ran screaming down the passage to the cleft. There was a moment when Philip's will swung between his enemy and the woman he wanted. If she went down over the rocks in the dark, there was hardly a chance in a hundred that she would not crash. There were other chances too. He kicked out to free himself and, lamp in hand, ran down the passage after Rose Anne.

Rose Anne saw the light coming up behind, throwing her shadow before her—the black shadow of her own terror that ran as she ran, and would presently go down over the ledges into the lake as she must go, because she couldn't stop herself now, and Philip was behind her—Philip, and the light, and Philip's shadow. It came up dark and menacing—the shadow that had killed Oliver and would kill her too.

"Rose—Rose—Rose!" She heard him calling her with entreaty, with passion, with despair.

And then the light showed her the fall, the ledges, and the lake beyond. She could not stop, but she would not have stopped if she could. The extremity of fear drove her on—and down. Her foot touched the first ledge. She would have slipped if her flight had been less headlong. There was no time for slipping. The descent was a fall checked as her foot just touched one ledge after another, and the impetus carried her across the narrow belt of shore and into the lake. She went down into it and came up gasping for breath in about three feet of water. There was light all round her. Philip's lamp was shining into her eyes as she blinked the blinding drops away, and Philip was on the bottom ledge, quite near, quite dreadfully near. She looked past him and saw Oliver in the cleft. If he came down, Philip would shoot him. She saw the pistol in his hand and shuddered and backed away from the shore. The lake water was cold. It came up about her waist in an icy ring. It came up under her breast, under her armpits, very cold—like death.

Philip called to her in a striving voice.

"Rose—come back! I won't hurt you—I swear it. Rose—for God's sake—it's not safe!"

Safe—when they were all come here to their death! She went a step deeper, and felt the water touch her chin.

Philip turned, saw Oliver behind him, and fired. It vexed him to waste an enemy. Oliver should have died at leisure—by and by. But he must get him out of the way before he went into the lake after Rose Anne. He fired and Oliver fell. Rose Anne cried out, and the cave was full of echoes—dreadful echoes of violence, and pain, and the mockery of Philip's laughter.

He set the lamp on the last ledge and the pistol beside it, and came wading out into the lake.

"Rose—my darling Rose—why do you fight me like this? It's no good, you know—it's no good at all. Loddon's dead, and you're mine. You've always been mine, and there's nothing in the world that can come between us now."

Rose Anne went back, and felt the water at her lips, and back again, and the rock rose under her feet so that she stood with her head and shoulders clear of the surface.

Philip came on. His coming sent ripples towards her. She felt behind her with her foot, and the rock went down again—down, down, and deep. When he came too near she must go down and drown there. She looked at Philip, and he at her, with the length of a few yards between them. He stood still, imploring her, with the water at his shoulders. Neither of them saw Oliver drop from the cleft and crawl along the ledge below.

"Rose—come quickly!" He stretched out his arms and took the next step. It carried him under. Rose Anne saw the black water close over his head. Then it broke again. There was a threshing and a struggling and he was up out of the hole into which he had fallen and breast-high in the water clearing his eyes.

He would have heard the sound if his own breath had not choked him. Rose Anne heard it where she stood, the sound of something that beat the water and moved through it, and made a wash which broke against her breast.

Oliver heard it, on the last ledge as he stooped to snatch the pistol. He had it and he was on his feet again. But Philip Rennard was gone. The lake heaved and boiled, and the wash came up against the shore. And Rose Anne came too, wading, stumbling, shuddering as she came, to fall into his arms and weep there, clinging to him and saying his name over and over again,

"Oliver—Oliver—*Oliver*!"

Chapter Thirty-Five

HE GOT HER away and into the passage again. They had the lamp, and whatever it might cost them later, they kept it burning its precious current now. They held each other fast and talked in whispers.

"I thought you were dead." Comforting to say it with her lips against his ear.

"I beat the pistol. I saw he was going to fire and dropped. My right arm was asleep. I wanted time. I hadn't the grip of a baby."

"Oliver—did you see it—did you see what happened?"

"No, I didn't. I was picking up the pistol. It was all over so quickly. I heard the noise, and when I straightened up he had gone. I didn't see anything except the wash."

Rose Anne trembled against him.

"I heard it coming and I shut my eyes—so as not to see—and he gave a sort of gasp—and I heard the water—and I heard him go— and I opened my eyes and saw you. Oliver, I thought—I thought— we were both—dead."

Oliver said nothing. He kissed her as a man may kiss the woman whom he has lost, and found again, and found on the edge of death. They held each other close.

He said at last, "We must go on, you know."

"I don't want to."

"We've got to, darling. We've really got a chance now, and we mustn't throw it away. We know what isn't the right way, and we've got this much better light."

She gave a tired sigh.

"I don't think we've got a chance. I think we're going to die. I'd rather die here—I would truly."

"Darling!"

She lifted her head, and said with a catch in her voice,

"It's no good—I can't—I can't really. I can't, because I don't want to. I'd much, much rather sit here and die quietly. Even if I knew we were going to get out alive, I think I'd rather die here than go through those awful caves again."

Oliver said, "All right." He kept his arm round her and let the silence fall.

After a little time he said, "We might as well talk. Let's talk about pigeons."

"Why?" said Rose Anne with her head on his shoulder.

"Well, I'd like to. They're very interesting. There was an old chap in our village who was a big bug in the pigeon-fancying world—bred them, and flew them, and went in for competitions, and won prizes—lots of prizes. I used to hang around and talk to him in the holidays, and he used to tell me things. Did you know that a pigeon will fly five or six hundred miles in a day?"

Rose Anne shivered.

"No, I didn't. How far do you think we have walked?"

Oliver laughed and shook her a little.

"Not five or six hundred miles. Now you listen to what old Harding told me. They take the pigeons away, you know—two, three, four hundred miles away—and they have to find their way home across country. No one quite knows how they do it. The experts quarrel over it. This is what old Harding said—he used to wag his finger at me and call me sir. He said, 'A pigeon won't home unless it's got pluck. Some say it's instink takes them home, and some say they fly high and view the landscape over, but I say, whether or no, it's pluck that does it, sir, and if a pigeon hasn't got pluck he don't home. What brings him home is that everything in him is just set on that one thing. Hunger, and thirst, and hardship, and being dead beat—they're just nothing to him against the need he's got to get home. If he loses his way he tries again—"

Rose Anne pushed him away.

"You're making it up because you want me to go on!"

"I'm not. I swear he said it. Are you going to let a pigeon beat you?"

"A pigeon hasn't wet clothes on," said Rose Anne, but she got to her feet.

Oliver picked up the lamp.

"They'll dry much sooner if we keep moving," he said.

It was at about this time that Mr Benbow Collingwood Horatio Smith stood looking down upon the wet street outside his study window. It had been raining all the morning, and judging from the look of the sky, it meant to go on raining all the afternoon. Mr Smith was not, however, thinking about the rain. He was thinking about Oliver Loddon. Behind him, on his perch, Ananias picked delicately at a peanut. He did not really like peanuts, and presently, having sampled the flavour of this one, he spat it out and emitted a rasping Spanish oath. To his disappointment, Mr Smith took no notice. He therefore proceeded still farther in the exercise of a forbidden vocabulary. Mr Smith continued to look down upon the grey and rainy street.

The telephone bell rang, and Ananias stopped swearing in order to imitate it.

With a perfunctory "No, Ananias!" Mr Smith turned from the window and took up the receiver. A voice said, "Who is there?" and he answered in his gentle, cultured tones, whereupon the voice said, "Just a minute if you please," and was almost immediately replaced by a different voice—a superior voice, a voice of authority.

"Look here, my dear fellow, I've had your note—"

"Er—yes," said Mr Smith. "Miller delivered it an hour ago."

The voice took on a shade of apology.

"Yes, yes—I've been busy. But, my dear fellow, I really don't think—"

"But you should," said Mr Smith. "It is—er—extremely desirable that you should think."

The voice showed a trace of annoyance.

"I don't think there is anything that I can do in the matter. You say Captain Loddon has disappeared. I really don't think there is sufficient proof of this, and in any case—"

"I know," said Mr Smith—"I know—it's not your affair—we have an efficient police force. If I am uneasy, I have only to approach the proper department through—er—the proper channel, and when Captain Loddon's body has been recovered, I shall be able to attend the funeral with the—er—consciousness that there has been no departure from the correct official procedure."

There was a pause. Then the voice said,

"Are you serious?"

"I am always serious," said Mr Benbow Smith in a tired voice.

There was another pause.

"What do you *want*?" said the voice.

"I want to have the old mine-shaft at Hillick St Anne's opened up and investigated. I want a considerable body of police. I want them to be armed. I want the Angel inn at Hillick St Agnes placed under observation. I want—"

"Look here, Ben, we'll be the laughing-stock of England."

"I do not—er—think so."

"Anyhow the police aren't my pigeon."

"Er—no."

"You're asking me to butt in."

Mr Benbow Smith smiled faintly, but did not speak. The voice came louder.

"You want me to butt in and make a show of myself. You either haven't got any evidence, or you're too damned superior to pass it on."

"My dear James—"

"Well, have you any evidence?"

"Not a great deal that would appeal to the—er—official mind."

"That means you haven't any. I suppose it's one of your hunches."

"I should not—er—so describe it myself, but—"

"That's what it amounts to. The bother is, you do have hunches, and they do come off. Truth and honest, Ben, how sure are you?"

Mr Smith's voice took on its suavest note.

"Sufficiently sure to—er—risk your reputation, my dear James."

The eminent Cabinet Minister at the other end of the line used a highly regrettable expression and capitulated.

"All right. But remember, if it doesn't come off, I'll make it my business to see that you're thrown to the Press—photographs and snappy pars—the whole bag of tricks. Now you'd better tell me all over again just what you want done. What about coming round to see me?"

Mr Smith glanced at the clock on the mantelpiece.

"Er—yes—I shall have time."

"*Time?*"

"I am—er—catching the two-fifteen to Malling."

"*Malling?*"

"Malling is the station for Hillick St Anne's," said Mr Benbow Collingwood Horatio Smith.

Chapter Thirty-Six

A LONG TIME had passed. They didn't know how long. Rose Anne's clothes had dried on her again. They had found water once or twice. They had rested a good many times. They had sucked Harold Spenlow's concentrated meat tablets. Sometimes they had dropped asleep quite suddenly whilst they were resting, but always when Oliver said, "We must go on," Rose Anne got to her feet and went on. There were no more protests. She would go on as long as she could, and when she could go on no longer she would just drop down and die—there wasn't any more to be said about it. Oliver talked sometimes, but for the most part they walked in silence, because Rose Anne had no words left, and it is hard to talk alone.

They took the first of the left-hand turnings and followed it a long way only to find themselves at a dead end. The second left-hand turning ran some way and then forked. They kept to the left, and came back again to where they had last rested. Rose Anne had missed a handkerchief and they found it there.

They tried another passage. They were now completely lost, and must keep on without any sense of direction. They went on, because to stop was to despair, and despair meant death. Fatigue weighted their limbs and deadened feeling. Philip's lamp held out, so they had light to walk by.

Oliver thought, "We must go on—we must—we must. If we go on long enough we shall get somewhere. We must go on."

Rose Anne thought, "I can go to the next turn," and when they got there she thought the same again, and so on, and on, and on—endlessly. It was getting more difficult. To the next turn—more difficult still. The next turn—difficult—the next—

Oliver was shaking her by the shoulders.

"Darling, look! Look where we are! That's one of the gates."

That last turn had brought them out upon an open space which narrowed to an arch—not the low arch which the water had cut and through which they had painfully crawled, but a gateway nine feet high with a steel door closing it like the door of a safe. The door rose solid to somewhere between six and seven feet, and the space between it and the top of the arch was barred with inch-thick bars of steel.

Rose Anne looked at the door with dazed eyes. If it opened, she would have to go on, but if it wouldn't open, she could lie down on the rock and go to sleep. She leaned against the wall and saw Oliver try the door and go on trying it. She let herself down into a sitting position. The wall held her up. She shut her eyes.

Oliver said, "Like a safe, you know. It opens with a word—a six letter word. If we knew what it was, we could open the door and get away." His voice sounded as if it came from a long way off. She heard her own voice say,

"I know—Philip told me."

It was funny that Oliver's voice should sound so far away, because he had his arm round her. He shook her a little. His far-away voice said,

"What did he tell you? Darling, wake up! It's terribly important."

Rose Anne had pictures in her mind, some of them vague and misty, some of them small and bright. In one of the little bright ones Philip was telling her about the door. "It opens to you and me." That was what he had said. And in one of the large, vague pictures he was boasting about the door, and how clever it was, and how no one could open it if they hadn't the word. She opened her eyes and saw Oliver's face close to her own. She said,

"No one can open it if they haven't got the right word. He said only his father and Mark had the word. He said—" She stopped.

Something came to her. She said, "Oliver, he used to talk to me a lot—when he thought—I was drugged. He said—things—"

"About the door? Think, darling, *think!*"

She nodded slowly.

"Yes—about the door—he said it would open for us—he said he had made a new word for it—out of our two names—that's what he said."

"Six letters... Phil—let's try that. And your name—he always called you Rose... Philro—that might be it. It's worth trying."

He went over to the door. Rose Anne shut her eyes again. He came back. She had to open them.

"That's no good. Darling, think if he said anything else. Think—think!"

Her eyelids fell. She looked at the pictures again—Philip saying, "Rose Anne's *his* name. I'll never call you by it. I'll call you Rose, or I'll call you Anne. I love you Rose—I love you Anne." And then Philip laughing and repeating over and over, "Love Anne—love Anne—love Anne. That will do to open our door, or to shut it and shut you in with me."

She said the words stumblingly.

"That's what he said. Oliver—I'm—so tired—"

"Love Anne—lovean—that's six letters, but it hasn't got his name in it." He gave a sudden shout which sent the echoes shouting back at him. "Philan! Phil means love, and it's his name too! Wait—wait whilst I try it!"

She leaned back against the wall. If he had the right word he would leave her alone. That was all it meant to her now.

She wished he wouldn't make so much noise... She couldn't go to sleep while he made so much noise... He wasn't leaving her alone... He was talking—shouting—coming back to her and shouting...

"It's open! I've got it open! Philan—that was the word! Darling, darling—*darling!*"

She opened her eyes and saw him through a dancing mist. He pulled her up, kissed her, hugged her, and went on saying, "Darling—darling—*darling!*"

The mist cleared a little. She saw the door standing wide, the archway open, the way clear before them. They went through together. The door shut with a clang. She heard Oliver say,

"It opens from either side. It's all quite easy once you know the word."

And then the mist closed down. She thought, "We're safe." She felt herself slipping. She felt Oliver's arms. And then she let thought and feeling go.

Chapter Thirty-Seven

Rose Anne opened her eyes. The sun was shining into the room. It was her own room. She was in bed in her own room, and the sun was shining in. That meant it was somewhere between ten and eleven in the morning, because the sun was off that window by eleven at this time of the year. She didn't think this in words. She knew it without having to think about it at all, as she had known it for twenty years out of the twenty-two that she had slept and wakened in this room. She stretched herself a little and wondered why she was so stiff, and turned a little in bed and remembered Down Under, and Philip, and the escape, and the black passages, the cave, the lake, the terror of the darkness. She made some sound, some sobbing catch of the breath, and Elfreda was beside her in a moment.

Rose Anne put out her arms, and the two girls clung together, Elfreda blinking away the silly hot tears which would keep running down her cheeks, and Rose Anne not crying but trembling from head to foot. She said,

"Where's Oliver?"

"He's just got in," said Elfreda gulping. It was really too idiotic to cry when everything had come right and she was going to be bridesmaid after all.

"He's just got in. He had to show them the way. They've been out for hours, and hours, and hours. You know they brought you in in the middle of the night—dozens of policemen. And I thought you were dead, and I believe Oliver did too, only the largest policeman kept on saying you weren't—he was the one that was carrying you—and that's why I'm making such a fool of myself now."

"Oh!" said Rose Anne rather faintly.

Elfreda got up and made a dart at the bell.

"You were to have hot milk the very instant you woke up," she explained. "You had some last night, but you never woke up, not even when we gave you a hot bath—darling, you were simply all over green slime, and you'll never be able to wear any of those clothes again."

"I don't want to," said Rose Anne with a shudder.

"It was such a pretty jumper suit," said Elfreda regretfully, "but it's quite, quite ruined."

"I want to see Oliver," said Rose Anne. "I want to know what's happened. Fetch Oliver."

"I think he's having a bath, but I can go and see. Aunt Hortensia said you oughtn't to see anyone for a week."

A little colour came into Rose Anne's pale cheeks.

"Don't tell her. Fetch Oliver."

Elfreda ran out of the room.

Rose Anne moved her pillows and sat up a little. She looked at the sunshine, and she thought about Oliver. Everything in her sang a tremulous song of joy. It was all over—the dark, and the cold, and the fear, and the time when she thought she would never see the sun again, and the time when all she wanted was to lie down and die and Oliver wouldn't let her. Now they would be married, and have their little house, and unpack their wedding presents together, and love each other very much. Her heart was quite, quite full of loving Oliver. She hoped he would know how full it was, because she didn't think she would ever be able to tell him.

Elfreda burst in with hot milk in a cup.

"You're to drink this first, and then you can have some tea and a lightly boiled egg and three bits of toast and some butter—and Oliver's just coming, so you'd better hurry up with the milk."

Rose Anne hurried, and Oliver came—in a dressing-gown. Which would have shocked Aunt Hortensia very much if she had been there to see. He had bathed and shaved, and had so eager a look that it was not until after their long embrace, when he sat back on the edge of the bed and gazed at her, that Rose Anne saw how pale he was and how tired.

"I've been sleeping, and you haven't. Oh, Oliver!"

"Don't you worry, darling. I'm going to do about eighteen hours, and then your father's going to marry us, and we're going away like we planned."

She kept tight hold of his hand.

"I want to know what happened. It was stupid of me to faint, but when we got through that door and I heard it shut, I thought, 'We're safe,' and then I couldn't go on."

"I know—I didn't know what to do. You—you frightened me. I stood still, and then—I thought I'd gone queer in the head, because I thought I heard voices—all confused and a long way off. I went that way, and when I'd gone about fifty yards I felt the wind blowing down on the top of my head, and someone gave a shout, and someone sang out, 'Who's there?' and I looked up—and I saw a star—"

"Oh, Oliver—where were you?"

"At the bottom of the old shaft at Hillick St Anne's."

"Hillick St Anne's?"

Oliver nodded.

"That's why they killed that poor fellow John Smith. He was investigating the shaft, and the shaft runs down into the passage between the steel gate and the Angel."

"Who shouted? Who was there?"

"That old trump Benbow Smith with the Chief Constable and a posse of police. I gather he had moved heaven and earth and the Cabinet to get them there in time. They brought you along by way of the Angel, and when I was sure you weren't dead I went back with them."

Rose Anne looked at him with piteous eyes.

"Nannie?" she said in a whisper.

Oliver put her hand to his lips.

"Don't mind too much, darling. They're under arrest—all three of the Garstnets. She might have killed you—I can't forget that. It's a beastly business. She broke down and confessed everything.

She says they threatened Florrie, and she didn't dare to go against them—it's her own expression."

"Poor Nannie!"

"Garstnet went to pieces too. He'll turn King's evidence. He showed us the way back."

"What happened—tell me."

"The Old Fox is dead. There was the most frightful shemozzle when Philip found out that we were gone—"

"Marie—he didn't hurt Marie? I felt dreadful about her afterwards."

"No—he hadn't time. He was going to all right. She very nearly kissed me, poor girl. She and Spenlow were both for it, but the old man dug in his toes about Spenlow. He was firmly convinced he would die if Spenlow wasn't there to keep him alive. So he and Philip had a blazing row, and it finished with Amos falling down in a fit. Mark chipped in then, and fetched Spenlow to his father. Philip flung away to hunt us down. We found the Old Fox just about gone when we got there, with Spenlow looking after him, quite sober and uncommon lucky to be alive."

"And the others?"

Oliver frowned.

"Horribly pathetic. Poor drugged creatures—quite a lot of them didn't want to come away, but Spenlow says they'll be all right. The French girl had hysterics, but she had come round enough to roll the glad eye at us before we got back."

"Us?" said Rose Anne.

"The Chief Constable, Benbow Smith, all the policemen, and me," said Oliver firmly. "Ernie and Fanny got away with their baby, and so did Mark Rennard."

"Oh, I'm glad," said Rose Anne.

"So am I—at least I'm glad about Fanny and Ernie. I thought I'd make a bit of time for them, so I didn't say anything about the Oakham Place entrance until right at the last, just as we were coming away. That door opened to the same word as the other. Ernie wouldn't know it, but Mark would, and he must have let them through. Anyhow they were gone, and Oakham Place was empty. I don't think they'll look very hard for Ernie. I don't know about Mark."

"Mark hated it," said Rose Anne, "He's got a wife and children somewhere in the country, I don't know where. They run a road house—at least I think they do. I'd like Mark to get away."

Miss Hortensia came in with a highly disapproving air.

"Good morning, Rose Anne. I am glad to see that you are better. You slept long enough, I am sure. Oliver, on the other hand, has had no sleep at all, and he ought to be in bed instead of lounging about in here. If you really insist on getting married tomorrow, he had better go to his room and get some rest. Anything less like a bridegroom than he looks at present—"

Oliver turned round laughing. Even Aunt Hortensia couldn't make him angry on this blessed day of release.

"I'm going—I'm really going. Eighteen hours' beauty sleep and I shall be the admiration of all beholders."

He kissed Rose Anne's hand again and got up to go. A striped pyjama leg showed beneath the dressing-gown.

"Modesty is evidently out of fashion," said Miss Hortensia in her most acid tones.

Oliver fled.

THE END

Printed in Great Britain
by Amazon

39685763R00126